BADLAND
BLUES

BADLAND BLUES

Jason Kessler

NEW PULP PRESS

"Small town dreams often face a fate worse than death. We run to them and from them our whole lives, strung along, grasping at the straws of love and meaning. If we lose faith in our purpose, out here in the badlands, the atmosphere develops a certain edge to it that twists our minds. This madness can be felt in the heat, or in the silence, or in our inebriated brains praying for checks that never quite seem to arrive on time. And it's in the waiting; waiting for some kind of magical moment to save us; appearing just beyond the prairies and valleys, reflected in the shine of a crucifix, or climbing to life out of some dormant and dusty gulch. But it never does appear and we pass on the watch to our children."

- Anonymous (Boroughtown, North Dakota, 1921)

BADLAND BLUES

ACT ONE

1

"You've got me, boys. Just watch the eyes!" First he had to stop struggling, acquiesce to the punishment. It was a metaphor for how he lived his life.

Jean was held against his will by two teenage boys, while a third pelted him with rocks. He wanted to make a stand. He wanted to break loose. But Jean is 4' 1" tall with a drunkard's belly & no arm strength to overcome their grip. That doesn't mean he didn't try but when he tried and he failed he knew he had to take it. Rocks stung his stomach, stung his legs, stung his arms and yes, a few stung him right in his face. *Close your eyes. These goddamn boys want me blind.*

His saving grace was that he had a friend taking a leak across the tracks. When he heard the yelling Bobby Two-Shanks came storming in their direction. His British accent was gravellier than a quarry, "Oi! Ye little weasels get the 'ell out a' here. Leave the man alone." Shanks smashed his bottle of Irish Rose cross the convenience store wall and waved a jagged shard at the two boys.

They backed off slowly; screaming, "Fuck you man!" Realizing they faced a man without a fuck to give the boys turned tail and ran.

"That's right. Get lost! I know who yer parents are ya

1

twats!"

Jean rolled over onto the grass, lifting up his shirt to check for bruising. It was mostly just redness round the torso but his skin broke open here and there. Crimson blood seeped out onto his filthy white t-shirt.

"Thanks Bobby. I owe you."

"Anytime mate."

"Did you have to waste a perfectly good bottle of Irish Rose?" Jean forced a facetious smile.

Two-Shanks laughed, "They didn't bruise yer 'umor at least."

~ ~ ~

With the whiskey river run dry and the men out of money, Jean headed back to the center of town in search of scratch. There was a usual routine in the downtown park begging there between the boutiques and the banks, "Spare some change, please." As the old Greek philosopher Diogenes had once done he begged like a dog for their scraps. Businessmen flush with cash would pass through or shoppers cradling newly purchased necklaces and hats. So he'd hang out, start conversations and hope the God of Fortune gave him a nibble. Every once in a while someone would gift him a "donation" of a few dollars or more. He looked every bit the character folks would pity: unkempt, in hobo wear head to toe, eyebrows thick like an inbred Eastern European villager, and widely spaced eyes below a tall forehead. That sympathy money was practically *his*.

That afternoon, an itinerant musician was stealing Jean's spotlight, camped out by an old oak tree singing ballads. He wore a patchwork jacket on his back and a dusty derby hat with feather to one side atop his head. He sang a lude song, strumming his banjo. Jean grew jealous because the bard was hogging all the cash flow. In six weeks since the balladeer had arrived, Jean's profit quotient had seen a steady decline.

He's not even any good, Jean thought, *It's all in the novelty. On that ground I can't compete. My public's no longer impressed. I should learn to play. If he can do it so can I.* But he couldn't. His hands were too small. Besides he was just too goddamned lazy to do that kind of thing. So he'd mostly just sit there in the grass watching people carry goods from place to place, drive away vehicles, or kiss lovers under shade of tree. He watched the musician collect ten, twenty, *thirty* dollars over the course of an hour while he couldn't even mustered a, "Hang in there, champ."

But then something grand happened. An attractive redhead strolled into the park. He cast up his best puppy dog eyes. She spotted poor Jean at once, sitting under the shade of a tree, like a little homeless Buddha. Her lip quivered a bit. Jean knew he'd *FINALLY* found his mark. The gorgeous redhead had truly selfless humanitarian eyes. She unsnapped the button of a pocket book in her purse, reached inside, and handed him a five dollar bill. What luck! "You're as kind as you are beautiful, ma'am," he thanked her with genuine gratitude. But damn his heart! He also felt a pang of sorrow. Why'd he been born so ugly he'd never be loved by such a desirable woman? She was so pretty it made his head swirl. He wanted most in the world for a great beauty to glance his way, not with pity or disgust but with unquenchable, immutable, unstoppable *desire.*

Jean fell into desperate melancholy dreaming these impossible dreams. Reality was endless rejection, a loathsome scene. He wanted love more than blankets and hot soup on the coldest winter night. For this reason Jean kept coming on, despite the odds. *I must be a fool to keep setting myself up for these failures,* he'd lament. What would be the scapegoat when he lashed himself tonight? Would he curse his height or his belly, as he often had, or his madness, or his poverty? Sometimes women put it to him bluntly so that he'd know his own failures. The streetwise women told him, the ones with temerity. The things Jean knew a goodhearted woman would never want to say. Still, he loved to look at all the women; at their shapely legs beneath summer dresses in the springtime and their breasts squeezed tight behind knit sweaters in the wintertime. For Jean, heaven didn't exist behind clouds, but up a short dress. Both places remained decidedly out of his reach.

But to hell with it, that redhead had been good to him. No sense in looking down on a few free dollars. Money was too hard to come by these days and prospects were slim. The recession had hit Boroughtown hard like the fist of an angry god smashing down from the heavens. Outsiders like Jean struggled in unemployment for years. Folks outside the gas stations, county fairs and diners said things had gone south. It'd been like that so long that no one actually remembered true north. Only the most optimistic of folks had arm strength required for treading water.

By the end of the day Jean had approximately matched what the musician made in only his first hour. But it'd been a good hour. Jean counted himself an impressive haul of eighteen dollars and seventy-five cents. After a month's drought he was tempted to panhandle a little longer, but dusk was fast approaching. He thought better of it, stuffing what he had into his pants' side pocket and flipping the bard the bird.

If you wanted to survive in Boroughtown in those days you had to recognize the rules. Most of the good folk left the streets after sundown. They headed home to the safety of their families and TV dinners. Then, out into the night, came the scoundrels. The nighttime crowd was a different breed, desperate and more than a little dangerous. Most were looking for distraction with the universal pleasures of a buzz or late night rendezvous. Here in the badlands the boredom of small town living could turn terminally contagious. There were plenty of raging animals with more savage appetites too. Men hung out to dry by recession, chips on their shoulders, howling at the moon. These savages needed fixes to whatever strange addictions loom out here in the badlands. They'd become mockeries of civilization, hunting on the fringes, on the weak. These men would stab you for five dollars if it meant a fix for an hour or two.

Depending on his take for the day, after eating a meal at the local soup kitchen, Jean would buy either one beer, a lottery ticket, or drop a few quarters in the slots of the town's antique porno theater. That night he had the rare privilege to purchase both a beer and a theatre ticket. Brown-bagging a 24 oz. beer from the Lucky Horseshoe convenience store, he tucked it beneath his jacket and strolled to the old porn dispensary. It was a $3 ticket distributed by a bored-looking cashier behind a stand. The fellow was forty pounds overweight, red-eyed, sleep deprived, an anachronistic mullet squatting atop his neck. His eyes were glazed over like a cow.

"Enjoy the show sir," he entreated in listless dry monotone. *Gods the way this world eats men alive,* Jean thought with pity in his heart. He knew how the man must have felt: worn the fuck out with a life of constant failure and lowered expectations.

Jean walked through the double doors into the darkened theatre and sat down. The theatre was empty except for a man and woman in the back left corner. The man's face was planted directly in her lap practicing his best cunnilingus. She was moaning to beat the band, mouth agape. On screen flickered a retro stag film. There was a chiseled, hairy chested man and a busty, brickhouse California blonde going at it in a garden.

Retro films are probably the only kind the theatre can afford, Jean thought, taking a swig of his beer. Honestly,

5

Jean couldn't think of a reason the joint was still in business except for the rumors. Supposedly the Gambini Brothers' retail chain bought the place up for less than a dollar by disreputable means. The bartender at Dew Drop Inn once told Jean it was all a laundering scheme.

Meanwhile in the stag picture, the Venice Beach bodybuilder had mounted the blonde on a bench overlooking a cherubic water fountain. He was pulling her hair like she was a naughty schoolgirl. "That's right. Pull it, you ape. Treat me like your bitch."

"Oh you've been a baaad girl," he scolded her.

Jean pulled out his hard cock and started to jerk. In the back of the theatre, the man was really going to town on his girlfriend, recklessly slurping between her nether regions. The woman moaned. It wouldn't take much more before she'd cum all over his lips.

"Ooooohhhh ..." she moaned in ecstasy.

The sounds of their love making turned Jean on even more than the film. He finished shortly thereafter whispering to himself, "Oh you've been a bad girl. You fucking bitch," before releasing himself onto the red linoleum floor. His business concluded, he pulled up his pants and headed up the aisle towards the exit. He glanced over at the couple on his way out. The woman had her head rested on her lover's chest. His arm was wrapped tight around her waist and they were passing a cigarette back and forth. When they looked at Jean, he noticed his zipper was down and felt a flush of embarrassment. He zipped up.

From the theatre it was a short walk to the train tracks. He sat down in an abandoned boxcar to drink the rest of his beer. When he finished the last swallow he wanted to buy more. But being a tired and lazy sort, went to sleep instead.

2

The next day Jean decided to check out one of his favorite haunts, Savoy's Diner off Rte. 23. There were many times the day's heat was too hot or the panhandling bore no fruit, so Jean would find a table and sit there through the entire day and, sometimes, into the night. The holy rollers who owned the joint would often supply him free coffee with a cream cheese bagel.

Breakfast, lunch and dinner Savoy's filled up with large, hard solitary men with powder kegs for hearts or thin, jittery men on too much caffeine and too little sleep. Fresh faced students from the local college crammed into corner booths, pleased with their fortunate youth, dreaming of love and money: "the American Dream".

A fat waitress named Dolores often interrupted the jukebox honky-tonk ambiance with boisterous conversation and a smile. Most of the local women who came in knew her; gossips with leathery faces and dyed hair or cagey with tight muscles and searching eyes.

These latter women, wives of angry men, reminded Jean of a stray bitch that used to hang outside Outlaw's Bar. She'd hang around the dumpster scavenging whatever scraps she could find. One night a local sadist kicked her when she was with pups. The next time Jean saw her slinking around the alley, he tried to offer her a bit of steak as apology on behalf of the human race. But she bared her teeth and jumped back into the shadows.

After breakfast, Jean would swipe a newspaper left behind by patrons, standing on his tippy toes to see that it was a local paper. Then he'd have Dolores pour him a fresh cup of Joe while he looked over the weather, lottery numbers, entertainment news and comic strips; usually in that order. Jean knew the odds against winning the lotto but he'd still buy the ticket because he wanted to take the ride. He'd tuck it safely into his wallet and pull it out in the morning with bated breath. Every time he'd summon hope just long enough to be stung by how the blasted numbers failed to match up. He'd curse under his breath and bury his head in his hands like he'd only *just* missed his big chance.

The eye-popper of the joint was a short, slender brunette beauty named Marissa. A college drop-out in her early thirties, word had it that she'd picked up a bad habit years ago that had forced her to give up on higher education. So she settled for waitressing to save up a few bucks and focus on staying clean. In that capacity, Jean never heard anyone say she'd been doing anything less than wonderful. Plus, she still had all her teeth, straight and white, which placed her one smooth-skinned, freckle-faced head above most of the women in Boroughtown. Marissa was also kind, responsible and fun, with a round booty that, under her tight white waitress uniform, would jiggle to devastate men's hearts.

And that she did. Many suitors came away empty handed. She had two types: a tall, skinny and dapper college boy and the muscled workingman with a five o'clock shadow and a sly tongue. Sometimes the fortunate men who'd bedded her would revisit the diner, exuding the absolute confidence that the world was made for them- to be their playground. The little signs were there though Jean tried to ignore them: a flirtatious joke, a kiss, a handful of ass cheek for her to resist and then one day, surrender to.

It was always like a dagger shanked into Jean's heart. How could he ever hope to see a woman surrender to his affections in those ways, much less a beauty like Marissa? Jean was a realist about his ugliness to the opposite sex. His large forehead, widely spaced eyes and unkempt dirty-brown hair might not have hurt him so bad if he was as tall as Marissa's beaus instead of the smallish imp he was born to be. Despite all these things, no matter how hard he tried, Jean couldn't resist looking. He was still a man.

"Take a picture. It'll last longer," she'd tease him.

"Maybe I will."

One time he'd made a little pocket money helping with a construction cleanup around the new prison. With the day's take he'd gotten drunk and stoned with some of the old roustabouts by the railroad tracks. The good times and laughs rolled down the tracks all day into the twilight.

"Got any jokes ta make us laugh, Jean?" leathery old Bobby Two-Shank asked him, "Give us a good laugh and I'll let you 'it me good weed."

"Ok, I'll take you up on that. Just let me remember a moment ... Ok, I've got one. So there's this strict religious family: father, mother, a son and a daughter. They've just arrived at a hotel and they're going to check in. While the wife and kids are taking their suitcases up to the room, the father approaches the front desk clerk and says, 'I hope the porn is disabled.' The front desk clerk's face crinkles with disgust and he replies angrily, 'No, the porn is regular, you sick fuck!'"

Bobby Two shanks exploded with laughter, "Har! Har! Jean Genie, you're the sick fuck here!" He pulled out an old corncob pipe and sprinkled some marijuana inside, "I'd say you've earned this."

It wasn't long before the winds changed to cool and strong, maybe sweeping down from Canada. It was apparently time for them to move along, out of the elements. Normally Jean wouldn't have gone to any respectable establishment in that state of inebriation, but the weed had him starving for his regular bagel at Savoy's. Clearly his reasoning faculties had devolved Protozoan.

When Jean got to Savoy's he sat down in Marissa's section (trying to convince himself it was on accident). She was playfully teasing a talkative and flirtatious old man sitting with his wife. The tip-getting reflex was strong in her. She loved people and she loved the money-making game. After the couple handed her a few bills she sauntered over to his table, fantastic in her form-fitting outfit and wearing a smile befitting a queen. It was a happiness Jean couldn't remember ever knowing himself.

"Howdy, Jean Genie. How are you, hon?"

"Hello, beautiful."

With mild annoyance she went professional on him, "What can I get for you?"

He looked her in the eyes, "I already see what I came here for."

"Uhm, ok Jean. Are you ok? It seems like something is wrong with you."

A wave of shame washed over him but he'd already begun speaking from the heart. It was too late to turn back now, it was either double down or just sit there wishing to disappear.

"If you were my woman I'd dote on you like none of these other clowns would," Jean swung his arm in a wild circular motion, "I'd clean my act all up if I had a woman like you."

"That's sweet. I'm very flattered." She nervously checked around to see if anyone else had noticed their conversation. She was embarrassed. "I bet you'll make some woman very happy one day".

Jean's eye twitched and he crinkled the brow of his large forehead. It was the classic blow-off and Jean felt it writhing in his gut the way a slug must feel covered in salt. But the more inebriated a man becomes the more he gets in touch with his loins and soul while losing touchstone with his grey matter.

"I'm not kidding," he begged, "Give me a chance."

"I'm sorry Jean. I'm tired, it's been a long day and, to be honest, you're creeping me out right now." Marissa turned her back and walked into the kitchen. When the waitress returned with his bagel it was Dolores and she just shook her head at him disapprovingly.

Some days Barbara Savoy, the owners' daughter, would sit in a corner booth of the diner listening to teen fantasy books on tape: *Harry Potter*, *Twilight*, etc. She was a grown woman but she'd giggle and rock back and forth in glee with the innocence of a child. Barbara was born with Down syndrome and her parents didn't trust her to be alone at home. So on the days when her nurse needed a holiday this is where she'd end up.

To Barbara, Jean looked like a brave and magical dwarf from one of her fantasy stories and she was taken with him. She carried around a pink My Little Pony backpack containing colored construction paper, safety scissors and magic markers which she'd use to cut asymmetrical little paper hearts and scribble Barbara + Jean on the front. Her parents thought it was the most adorable thing in the world although they occasionally scolded her for being too aggressive. She had few qualms about letting Jean know exactly how she felt.

"Jean, you're reeeaal hand-some", she'd slur with a big grin on her face. She'd give him a big hug and run her hands along his back.

For his part, Jean felt a bit uncomfortable, not wishing to appear to be taking advantage of her, or stigmatizing himself in front of Marissa. He politely accepted the valentines she brought him while simultaneously trying to communicate a bored indifference. But sometimes this dog and pony show strained credibility. His loneliness, his ostracism, his horniness, and his affection for outcasts made him just a little curious. But a terse, "Thank you," and a tortured smile was, he felt, enough to portray an appropriately polite gratitude. In truth, Jean always cursed his bitter heart that *this* was the woman who loved him.

On that particular day, Barbara was at home waiting for her mother, Mrs. Mary Sue Savoy, to arrive so they could spend the afternoon together. But business was unexpectedly heavy, there were payroll issues, a late bread delivery and so on that kept her from making it home on time.

Mary Sue Savoy wiped some cow's blood from her hands onto her apron and retrieved a package from the office desk containing her daughter's medication. Having a mentally challenged daughter was a gift from God, she reminded herself, like a mantra. She hated herself for thinking about any foregone new-model automobiles or trips to St. Bart's but in moments like these she had to say a little prayer in her mind, "Lord Jesus forgive me for my selfish and base thoughts."

The upside of caring for the Lord's vulnerable creatures is that sometimes they could be trained to do the handiwork of the righteous, or even take care of one another. Like two negatives multiplied into a positive. Give poor Jean a bagel and some coffee and he'd be a willing little soldier, delivering medications to her infirm progeny when business was too heavy for her to do it herself.

"Jean, you be a good young man and get her the medication before 5. I'm giving you a few dollars for helping me out this time. Don't be late".

She set a plastic bag on the table in front of him containing Barbara's epileptic medicine and a Styrofoam doggie bag smelling of freshly cooked steak hoagie with seasoned French fries.

~ ~ ~

Jean stopped by the corner market for a beer and took it to the train tracks. Sometimes there were friends there but mostly he just went there to be alone. It was a brilliant vantage point where you could stare past the tracks onto the lake and fields beyond. The beer felt good washing down the French fries and the bread from the hoagie. Combined, they expanded his gut until it felt like it was near to burst. He was blissful feeling full of food and drink.

From there Jean went station to station into all the bars on the way to the bus stop: Outlaw's, The Dew Drop Inn and The Last Call. When he finally made it onto the public bus with a little change left in his pocket he was good and ripped. Rain clouds had formed overhead and a light mist streamed down. He got off in the uptown suburbs, walking through the quiet streets until he reached a large wood and brownstone house behind impeccably trimmed rectangular hedges. Stumbling drunk, every stair was a challenge to climb. Jean grabbed a stick lodged into the hedge so that he could poke up at the doorbell. It was a challenge to hit it at just the right angle to depress the button. When it finally chimed Jean gratefully rested himself against the wide stone railing, lighting a cigarette.

After only a few drags the door swung open. Barbara rushed onto the porch with her ringlets of shiny blonde hair flowing behind her. She hugged him with such enthusiasm that he nearly fell from the bannister onto some thorny rose bushes along the base of the house. Digging her forehead into the crook of his armpit with a little squeal, Barbara couldn't help inhaling the smoke shrouding Jean like a low-flying rain cloud. She started coughing.

"Jean, put dat out! Why you want to do something bad for you?"

"Well it's better than the alternative I guess ... something to occupy my idle hands."

"I dull? You aren't dull Jean. You are reeeaaalll smaaart," she tried to reassure him.

"Thank you. Uh, please don't mention this to your

parents, sweetheart."

Her father, John Savoy, was a lung cancer survivor who'd grown extremely protective of his family and property being exposed to cigarettes. One time, Jean left a cigarette butt near the base of the hedge. When John found it he yelled at and embarrassed Jean in front of the entire diner. Jean spit into the palm of his hand, rubbing it between the thumb and index finger, then squeezed the cigarette cherry until it became moist and extinguished. Jean stuck it into his breast pocket for safe-keeping.

Barbara ran down the steps to the rose garden, picking a flower, the sky finally opened up into torrents of rain falling on them both. Barbara squealed as she ran to give Jean the flower.

"This is lovely dear. Thank you so much", he said although he thought, *your parent's will probably blame ME for defacing their garden.* "Now let's get out of the rain."

Barbara held his hand in hers. "Come inside, Jeanie. I've got a surprise for to show you".

They shook off some excess water in the foyer, standing over the welcome mat so as not to dribble too much water all over the wooden floor. Still, they were so thoroughly soaked it was an evident losing effort. Jean tried mopping it up to no avail with a handkerchief he'd kept in his pocket.

"Don't worry that. Follow me, Jeanie." Barbara pulled him along.

"Sure sweetheart. Show me."

Just beyond the foyer was a large staircase backlit by stained glass windows, unusual in a civilian brownstone. It gave the place a feeling of austere antiquity. Pictures hung on the walls of the hallway depicting the extended Savoy family in awkward, unnatural poses with oddly shaped hairstyles and slightly confused expressions. For some reason they reminded Jean of some kooky characters from the hit 1980's comedy, *The Burbs*. They wore the same things people always did in these photographs: Christmas sweaters, graduation caps and gowns, tuxedos, wedding dresses, officer's uniforms.

"Bambino! Bambinnnnoooo!" Barbara called.

Arf! Arf! Arf! A little brown and black patchwork puppy came running into the hallway to its master.

"Puppy!" Barbara cried with joy, bending down to pet the little dog. Maybe it was the romantic rhythm of the rain tapping the roof, his drunkenness, or the desperate loneliness within his heart, but he began to long for her. With her bent over, stroking that puppy, Jean noticed she had an incredible ass. He tried in vain to curse himself for the thought but the words sounded hollow in his mind.

Barbara gave the dog a big hug and held him down for Jean to reach him, "He's my baby. All miiine".

Jean stroked the long, soft fur on the pup's head. The little dog's eyes glowed with joy. Bambino enthusiastically sniffed Jean's hand then licked his palm until it was covered in saliva.

"Hi Bambino", Jean purred, "Aren't you a sweet doggy?" He wiped the saliva onto the dogs fur coat.

Barbara carried Bambino into her bedroom and laid him down onto the bed with her. She had the pinkest bedroom Jean had ever seen. Her walls were decorated with posters of boy bands, puppies and angels. Though a grown woman of twenty-three it was her nature to always keep a vestige of the childlike innocence so many in Boroughtown would never know. In that sense, she was nothing short of a little miracle.

Her bed was a bit high off the ground. Jean used a blue plastic stool from the corner to climb onto the bed's soft white comforter. Some paper crinkled beneath his back when he laid down. It was a few of Barb's paper hearts. He brushed his arm against them and they fell to the ground.

Barbara laughed at the puppy who was trying to catch his own tail. She rolled over to hug Jean and Jean kissed her. Through her wet clothing he could see her nipples poking through the white t-shirt she was wearing. There were regal elephants from the Serengeti on the front. Jean felt a stiffening of the member in his pants and he reached to unbutton Barbara's pants. She cooed.

4

Jean spent the next two weeks avoiding Savoy's Diner. He just couldn't face up to the guilt of what he'd done, couldn't understand whether it was right, wrong, or somewhere in between. To pass the lonely hours, he'd had picked up a gig advertising outside Outlaw's bar. Every afternoon he'd hold up a sign reading "Everything's bigger at Outlaw's. (Well almost everything.)" Humiliating, but at least it paid for his drinks.

Sometimes he got so drunk he'd fall over and prop himself against the wall, but he simply couldn't allow himself to think about what he'd done with Barbara. It still seemed so wrong. Tonight he was feeling mellow. A cigarette between his lips, the sign in his hands, as the blood orange sun sank behind purple clouds. A bass-y slab of rock & roll music pounded inside the bar. Patrons were beginning to stream inside for Friday night's exorcism of the work week blues.

A tall, fat trucker with a grizzled beard wearing a leather vest over plaid shirt, boots and a baseball cap walked across the parking lot from the truck stop. He had his arm around a local girl, maybe Jolene or Maybelline. A party girl in her late 30's skinny, but looking a little worn. When they approached, Jean could smell the weed and pussy on them.

"Bwahaha! Looket the midget, willya? Bet I could toss 'im like a football!" the trucker hollered to his girl.

"Naw ... He's so cute baby. Don't mess with 'im".

"You know I can hear you right?" Jean interjected, "And you might be able to throw me but you'll get some nasty cigarette burns along the way," he threatened, shaking the lit cigarette in his fingers for effect.

The woman wrapped her arms around the trucker's ample gut, "Baby, I want to see him dance like the little men from the candy factory".

"Bwaha! Like an Oompa Loompa you mean? Haha! How 'bout it little fella? Will you dance for the lady?" he slurred.

Jean groaned and stretched out his hand, "Pay first."

The trucker grinned, extracting a crumpled ball of cash from his jean pocket. He separated a twenty and placed it, with great emphasis, in the palm of Jean's hand.

"How about a bit more for the little man?" Jean coaxed hopefully.

"Don't push your luck buddy."

Jean sighed and pocketed the cash. "Fine. Twenty it is."

Jean couldn't remember if the Ooompa Loompas even danced in that damn movie. So he wiggled his hips a little bit and raised the roof. The bass boomed through the darkening twilight. The couple clapped their hands in time with the both music and Jean's prodigiously rhythmic dance moves. "Hey! Ho!" The couple hooted, dancing with Jean.

They were all having a good time. Some other patrons came up to dance along with them. One brunette woman with perky tits and a bare midriff stuffed a few dollars in his waistband. Jean playfully humped her leg a bit. The woman guffawed and pulled out a joint. She lit it and blew smoke into Jean's face as he leaned in for suction. It tasted funny. Not like anything he was used to. Laced. Things started to get hazy from there ...

~ ~ ~

When Jean awoke, he was outside of Outlaw's, but the trucker and his girlfriend were gone. So were all the other people for that matter. And everything in town looked as if hued through a mellow orange prism. An otherworldly presence seemed to hang in the air. For Jean, the experience of it was fear.

A thunderclap roared and a flash of lightning exploded across the sky. The hands of an enormous entity parted the clouds in the sky overhead. This figure had a mane of snow white hair, flames burned in the pits of his eyes and a beard of snakes writhed from his cheeks. Jaw agape, Jean mouthed the name he hoped he'd never utter again: "The Great Ulysses".

The Great Ulysses was, more or less the boogeyman of Grandmother Scaputo's bedtime stories*. Ulysses the omnipotent. Ulysses the cruel. Ulysses the unforgiving. He who delivered the wicked of the world into his damnable domain of eternal suffering. That Ulysses.

~ ~ ~

*Nevermind that the old bird was a little mad and an alcoholic to boot. She had a knack for telling a haunting tale.

He descended to Earth on a golden chariot drawn by six white-winged stallions. Jean was completely mesmerized, to the point where he found himself unable to move a single muscle. It felt like he was living in some badland waster's fanciful yarn. The kind about being caught in the thrall of an "alien tractor beam". Yet, clear as day, Ulysses himself exited the chariot, motioning his palm with a regal gesticulation towards some unseen allies. From just outside Jean's periphery marched two contingents of fearsome monsters: from the left there were what Grandma Scaputo had called the Laestrygonians: one-eyed, man-eating giants. And from the right there came the Lotus Eaters: a breed of clawed hunchbacks, skilled in the arts of witchcraft. Together they formed a terrifying contingent, cornering Jean into the killing square. A wooden gallows formed behind him, plank by plank, out of the ether. Ulysses clenched Jean by the nape of his neck and drug him up the steps of the gallows.

Then, incongruously materializing out of some much sweeter dream, Barbara appeared, rushing forward to comfort him. But before she could reach his side, a stringy-haired, hunchbacked Lotus Eater obstructed her path, grasping her in its thin, clammy claws. She cried out for Jean. He tried to run towards her but was forced to take cover from a lumbering Laestrygonian at the edge of the platform, gnashing its bladelike teeth with feral animosity. The Great Ulysses stroked his serpentine beard for a moment, as if contemplating how to most perfectly execute his latest atrocity. By telepathy alone he commanded a particularly stenchful Laestrygonian. Flies buzzing round its rank crown, the beast brought forth the poor bitch Jean once saw beaten in an alleyway outside Outlaw's. Jean wept to see the poor dog forced once again into cruel hands. Ulysses snapped off one sharp talon from a Lotus Eater's finger and used it to cut an incision into the poor dog's womb. Out spilled a pile of ash. The dog evaporated, leaving behind only a single flower atop the ashes. The Great Ulysses plucked it, strode back up the platform and placed it mockingly behind Jean's ear.

Ulysses snapped his fingers. A hooded executioner floated up on a wooden platform held below the gallows. The executioner held a length of rope with which he fitted Jean for a noose. He swung the other end tight against a tall hanging post, then lumbered over to grip his fist around the killing switch. Ulysses gave Jean a Judas' kiss smack on the lips. The executioner took this cue to pull his lever and swing open the trap door. Jean dropped, instantly burning with pain around his neck. The pain spread upwards until his entire head felt like it was on fire. It continued, longer than any dream should, until he felt like he was on the precipice of death. Then, mercifully, the rope snapped and he fell to the ground gasping for air. Jean looked up at just the right moment to see the look of astonishment on Ulysses' face.

Ulysses the almighty hadn't expected the rope to snap.

~ ~ ~

Jean had the mother of all hangovers. *"What was laced in that weed?"* he wondered, *"and why am I face down in an alley?"* He was covered in a damp body sweat too. To his right he noticed several cardboard cups and wrappers emblazoned with Savoy's Diner branding. *At least I know where I am.* But before he had time to get to his feet a fierce blow rocked his head. Blood streamed down his face. Through the crimson mask he could only discern a blurry, amoeba-shaped figure standing over his crumpled body. Wiping clear his eyes, this mysterious figure sharpened into focus: It was John Savoy. John reared his leg back and, with unbridled hatred, drove his greasy tennis shoe painfully into Jean's head. Jean's vision blurred again. John Savoy might've been only a violent stain on a petri dish. But there was no microscope. This motherfucker was huge.

"You little bastard. She's a child!" *il a accusé.*

"She's a grown woman. 23 years old last I checked."

John Savoy went for another kick but this time Jean caught him by the ankle, clinging on for dear life with desperately clenched muscles. John shook furiously at the little man on his leg.

"She ... made ... her own ... de ... cis ... sion, motherfucker." Jean lifted John Savoy's khaki pants leg and clamped his canines down into hairy leg flesh until the bitter taste of blood flowed out onto his tongue. A chunk of flesh came with it. Jean spat it out.

John howled in pain. The sight of a man biting into his flesh was too much for his stomach to bear. He retreated behind the dumpster, vomiting half-digested burger meat onto the pavement. Jean took this as his cue to limp away from the fight and lick his wounds elsewhere.

"She's a sweet girl," Jean yelled back in retreat, "You can't cloister her way from being a woman forever."

5

Pieced together from the civil deposition of Marissa Stotgard as well as numerous interviews with the concerned parties ...

Marissa's thoughts went everywhere and nowhere during her droll job as a waitress at Savoy's. At the moment she was wiping off a customer's table and thinking about some words her NA sponsor had given her. What had she said? "You're doing a great job now, baby. You've been clean for two years. I know you're not satisfied with that. I know you don't have *everything* you want but a *good* man takes time to find." *Sure. It's easy to find a man if you like them short and broke*, she thought glancing over at Jean's table. He'd been staring at her longingly but quickly averted his eyes back to a newspaper.

Her customer was still at the table- a debonair man, about fifteen years older, classically fashionable, dapper and hygienic. He reached out and grabbed her arm, stopping her from her task, "Excuse me. My name is Dan Holsham. I-I've been mesmerized by your beauty all night and dying to introduce myself."

"Thank you, Dan," Marissa replied curtly.

"I know how to treat a woman," he squinted to read her nametag, "... Marissa. Believe me you'll never have it better. Do you like assertive, successful men like me?" Dan smiled confidently.

The answer was yes, although the successful part seemed to be in theory only. There's been a few lowdown hustlers who'd stolen her heart and made their way into her bed by exuding a false confidence borne of arrogance rather than reality. But this man, Dan- his type she'd been falling for all too often lately: wealthy, confident ... and unavailable. He had a light tan on his skin, enough for Marissa to notice a thin pale circle around his ring finger, where a wedding band usually went.

"Sorry. I'm flattered but I'm not looking for anything right now." She started to pull away from him but he increased his grip.

"Neither was I. Neither was I," Dan pleaded, "But the moment I saw you my plans had to change. My heart started to pound to beat the band and I just became overcome with this, this grand spontaneity."

Marissa was growing tired of this game. She momentarily saw in Dan all the married men who'd broken her heart before. A flash of anger came over her and she lost it, "I know you're married, asshole. LEAVE ME ALONE!"

She tore her arm from his grasp and looked around. She'd yelled so loudly that everyone in the diner heard her. Some of the crowd was awkwardly trying to mind their own business but most had turned around to gawk at her. Jean had stopped reading his newspaper. Dolores looked up from the act of refilling a coffee mug. Hot joe overflowed all over the countertop. Marissa could see the concern in Dolores' eyes but she wanted no part of it. She'd been on her own taking care of herself since she was a child of fifteen and wasn't about to start crying for help now. She walked briskly over to Dolores, embarrassed, keeping her head down to avoid noticing the stares.

"I'm going to need a fifteen minute break."

"Take as long as you need, hon. I got you covered," Dolores responded.

There was a little "break nook" in the back of the restaurant. It was basically just a chair next to a supply shelf in a space smaller than your average public restroom.

Marissa sat down there, plugged a pair of headphones into her ears and lit a cigarette. She fingered through her smartphone's music collection. There was a lot of music to choose from on her phone but she was sick of half of it. Specifically, the love songs neither appealed to her nor made much sense anymore. Their sickly sweet romanticism was a poke in the eye- a taunting reminder of almost twenty years of bad decisions.

These days she preferred to listen to hip hop, particularly the kind that made her feel degraded and objectified. The sexuality of the body was all that remained real to her anymore. At least when a man complimented her body and told her how he wanted to fuck her she could believe he was telling the truth.

From the front counter she heard a loud, angry voice, "I've never been so humiliated in all my life. That waitress was completely unprofessional and... she isn't fit to work here, frankly."

Marissa leaned forward so that she could see around the corner to the front of the house. There was Dan, red-faced mad and complaining about her to Dolores.

"I'm only one of the shift managers," Dolores replied, "but I'll have one of the owners give you a call at home."

"No, that won't do. I'm a very busy man and I'm rarely at home."

"That's fine. Is it okay for them to leave a message for *your wife*?"

That seemed to knock some sense back into Dan. "Ehrm ... no that won't be necessary. Just tell them that they've lost my business for good."

"Okay sir. Have a good night."

Dolores looked back at Marissa and stuck her finger into her throat. Marissa smiled. She could hear the shop keeper's bell above the door tinkle on his way out. Then after a few more seconds she heard it tinkle again with an even more pleasing result. Two tall, musclebound hunks walked in. One was white with a crew cut and the other was black with a shiny bald head. Marissa fantasized that they'd have six pack abs and chiseled pecs under the muscle tees they wore.

She stamped out her cigarette and rushed back out onto the floor. Dolores was already en route to intercept them at their table when Marissa caught up to place an insistent hand on her shoulder, "I've got this."

"I'm sure you do, baby," Dolores responded with a knowing grin and a wink of her eye, I'm sure you do."

These two men were not nearly as debonair as Dan but they had a certain macho charisma all the same. When she got to their table they were so rapt in conversation they didn't notice her at first. She lingered there a moment eavesdropping on their conversation.

"Damn, you always horndoggin' it, bro. When you ever goin' make time for bidness?"

"Fuck you, man. You saw the phat ass on that broad."

"Ahem," Marissa coughed to get their attention. They both looked up and then looked her over. The black guy looked like his eyes might pop right out of his skull.

"Speaking of phat asses ... What's your name, mommy?" asked the white one.

"Marissaaa," she drew out the pronunciation flirtatiously.

"What you got goin' on tonight woman? Cause I'm about to blow this joint witchu," said the black one.

"What have I got going on? Unfortunately you're lookin' at the extent of it. How about yourselves? You just got here and you're already looking to leave with me."

"You know we're just those bad boys your daddy warned you about; them boys know how to show a woman a good time. You like to have a good time, shawty?"

For some reason she glanced over at Jean. He was

trying to pretend that he wasn't checking her out, lovelorn tears welling in his eyes.

"I actually *love* a good time," she answered.

The black one opened the fold of his leather jacket and pulled out an envelope from an inside pocket. He flipped it open and fingered the contents- a stack of one hundred dollar bills.

"Will something in here cover it?" he asked. The two men exchanged a glance and laughed.

"Daaamn, boys. That's a lot of cash." Marissa bit her lip. She knew these guys were bad news but she was *so bored*. "Can't say I'm not interested but you'll just have to wait until my shift is over. I gots to pay my billllls."

"Well ... Marissa," the white one responded, reading her nametag, "I'm Bobby and this here's Jerome."

"Wassup, girl?"

"Okay Jerome, Bobby ... if you think I'm worth waiting for, and trust me I am, meet me outside in twenty minutes when my shift ends."

"Aight," they replied in unison.

Twenty two minutes later Marissa threw her smock into the dirty clothes hamper and rushed outside to meet them. She looked around the parking lot. Her attention was almost immediately drawn to their shiny, black Cadillac by the insistent rumbling of the bass blasting from a subwoofer in the trunk. Jerome rolled down the tinted passenger side window. A plume of marijuana smoke wafted out into the night air. It looked positively otherworldly accented by the blue vanity lights mounted inside the vehicle. Marissa heard the unlocking mechanism.

"Hop in," Bobby ordered.

She did and they took off together. Jerome offered her a hit off the marijuana blunt they'd been smoking.

"No thanks."

She was afraid the marijuana high would make her

paranoid around these strangers.

"Alright. Alright," Jerome ran his hand along her naked leg up onto her thigh.

"Is this your vice? Cause it's mine."

"Not now. Maybe later," she responded frankly, removing Jerome's hand from her thigh.

"So what *is* your poison?" Bobby asked.

"I dunno."

"You must have one or you wouldn't be out here with us. We ain't game playin' niggas, Marissa."

Jerome snapped his fingers, "I know what you'd like. A pick me up!"

Bobby looked askew at Jerome and they simultaneously busted their guts laughing. Jerome pulled out a small metal pipe and a whitish-yellow chunk of crack rock. He'd guessed correctly. Marissa silently nodded her head. Jerome packed the pipe and handed it over to her. She reached for it with trembling fingers, set the rock on fire and inhaled the diseased smoke.

"That's more like it, baby. Damn you look sexy hitting that pipe."

She laid out on the plush leather seat. A wave of guilt washed over her but she just took another hit to forget about it. The car came to a stop and Bobby shifted it into park. They'd arrived behind an abandon factory off Tulane Boulevard. She heard Bobby and Jerome unzipping their pants. Jerome came around to his side of the door, pulled down her panties and mounted her. Bobby came in from the other side. When he pulled out his penis she took him into her mouth and lathered the head with the tip of her tongue like a lollipop. It was going to be a very long night.

Jean felt like a broken man. He slept on a train car filled with coals. The veiled will to live was slipping through his little fingers and all his dreams involved fire and death, if not the wrath of The Great Ulysses himself.

But he had thirty-seven dollars in his pocket and so a spark of hope, however temporary, remained. He stumbled through the doorway of the Lucky Horseshoe corner store with a gauze bandage wrapped around his bleeding cranium. He bought a pack of smokes, a bottle of whiskey and two lottery tickets from the Indian clerk. He transported this booty to the tracks where he shared an all-nighter with Bobby Two-Shanks and a piss-soaked military veteran named Griff who, for his part, contributed a jug of cheap wine to the bacchanal.

Late into the early morning, when the full moon hung over the Earth, the winds blew down from the mountains and the compadres bellies were filled with drink, their eyelids finally grew heavy. Jean crawled into a dilapidated boxcar where he'd stored a couple soft, old blankets and a pillow scavenged from the Salvation Army dumpster. Friends were just what he'd needed in these times of trouble. His heart felt a bit lighter for having shared their company. By contrast, that night was filled with dreams of freedom, detached from consequence, flying over canyons, bedding beauties and laying down in grasses by the ocean with rays of sunshine warming his pale skin.

~ ~ ~

Chirping birds and sunshine are the hobo's alarm clock. Jean opened his eyes to blinding light. *Curse the damn bluebirds right now!* he thought. Head aching he rolled over, pulled the covers up over his eyes, and went back to sleep.

~ ~ ~

How many hours later was it? Who cared? But the afternoon heat had soaked his clothes through with an uncomfortable sweat. Jean rolled out from the under the blankets and lowered himself down onto an old school desk he used as a makeshift stepstool. He walked around the corner to the convenience store.

On the window sill of the Lucky Horseshoe Market rested a quarter cup of cold coffee. Jean retrieved it along with a copy of the Boroughtown Standard fished from the wastebasket. He opened the paper. The front page story was about preparations for the Black Gold Festival: celebrating 200 years since the town's founder, Bill Borough struck oil in the fields behind his farmhouse, bringing jobs, industrialization and prosperity to the hole in the wall outpost then known as Dade City.

As the story goes, everyone thought the man was crazy. He'd claimed to have had a dream in which his long dead grand pappy told him about oil located somewhere on the family farm. So Borough tore up his fields looking for black gold. First, he ruined the property around the house, digging holes everywhere. The property value plummeted. His wife left him and took the kids with her. That's when he took to drinking: rye, gin and peppermint schnapps. Next, he tore up the fields behind the house until the grasses began to die. Borough sold off the cows because there wasn't enough fertile grazing land anymore.

Then it was just him and the bottle. He worked himself day and night, only resting when he'd blacked out from drinking. The town doctor lobbied for his commitment to a new sanitarium in Carson City but the Wild West penchant for libertarianism ultimately prevailed and folks left

Borough alone with his obsession. At that point, the poor bastard even took to masturbating in the field, believing that he could "seed the ground" for oil.

But when all hope had seemed lost several times over and the scorching heat of the midday sun baked his toes through the cracked roofs of his shoes, he felt it. They were like drops of rain on a cloudless day. Borough stared down through the shoe's exterior onto his naked digits sprinkled with thick, black droplets. As he stood there in a state of shock, a stream bubbled out of the dirt, soaking his entire foot in oil. He fell to his knees and wept.

Bill Borough became a millionaire many times over and the town was renamed in his honor. Prosperity reigned for years, love grew in everyone's hearts, puppies and chocolate chip cookies were had by all, blah, blah, blah. But the oil dried up about one hundred years before Jean was even born so it never felt real to a lot of folks in his generation. He thought it a cruel irony that Boroughtown folks would celebrate a fortune as old as dirt while the present citizenry were mired in prolonged economic recession.

Yet, be that as it may, the newspaper article stated the city planners were already preparing the festivities for late August. They'd arranged a barbeque cook-off and commissioned the building of a large open-air event stage in the town square. The city planners were particularly excited because they'd managed to hire a man named Claude James from South Texas as artistic coordinator. He'd be designing the festival logos, banners and so forth that would be hanging all over town. Claude's great claim to fame was that he once illustrated the cover of an Louis L'Amour novel. L'Amour had a lot of fans in North Dakota.

Jean settled down onto a dirt and gravel patch along the south-facing wall of the Horseshoe. He folded his legs Indian style and flipped the newspaper to the weather on page four. It looked like a pretty nice week of weather, if a tad on the hot side: a light shower on Wednesday; sunny and breezy the rest of the week.

Finally, he turned to the bottom of page five for the winning lottery numbers. He retrieved the two lotto tickets folded inside his billfold, unfolding them onto his lap. The winning numbers were 5, 17, 11, 22, 18, and 26. He'd only matched the five on the first ticket but since it was the first number it sent his heart aflutter momentarily. Shaking his head, he slid it under the second ticket. When he saw what was printed on the next ticket he involuntarily gasped and wept for joy in one bodily convulsion.

7

ream too big and the disappointment sets in. Better to just be happy with what you can get in the moment and let the booze handle the rest. That's always been my rule. At least since I grew old enough to know dreams don't always come true, Jean thought, *This, this is a freak accident. I have no skills, talents, or prospects and I'm physically incapable of employment in most careers.*

I was born to make peace with my disappointment; to die penniless and alone. My journey was to settle accounts with Mr. Death in the quiet moments, throw the shit hand I'd been dealt in his face and laugh at the cruelty of it all. But now it all changes. I can't just feel sorry for myself. I'll need a whole new act.

Jean had been skipping stones over the surface of Bison Lake, just across the railroad tracks, for the better part of an hour. He ran his hand along the rocky beach until his fingertips brushed over a small, smooth stone. He picked it up and rubbed it in the palm of his hand for a moment. Then he extended his arm adjacent to his chest and threw the rock in a sidewinder fashion with all his strength. It jetted through the air and, with beautiful physics, skimmed the surface a whopping twelve times before submerging into the water. Concentric circles trailed its descent for a few blissful moments.

I have a fortune now and I didn't earn it. So fucking what? Maybe a few drinks will get me over this lame-assed guilt. Just a few drinks in me and afterwards I'll be able to start my big, hedonistic fantasy without this nagging guilt weighing me down.

From the lake it was a short walk to the Dew Drop Inn, where he pulled himself up onto a stool at the bar. The bartender at Dew Drop is Lazy Pete, so called because he has one glass eye that just hangs there lifelessly, no matter which direction the good eye is looking. He's also a pot-bellied cunt with a golden-brown tan, greasy black hair and an omnipresent aroma of cheap cologne. But despite all that he was a good bloke: about as even-tempered and understanding as anyone in Boroughtown.

"How's it hangin', Jean Genie?"

"Good actually, Lazy P. But I need a favor."

"Oh yeeeaaah? I wonder what that could be," Pete rolled the one good eye.

"I'm all out of money right now ...."

"Oh no...the surprise. It's too much," Pete clenched his chest with one hand like he was having a heart attack and reached towards the heavens with the other, "This is the big one! Elizabeth, I'm comin' to join you honey."

Jean gave him a sarcastic clap. "Har. Fucking. Har. You know I love your Red Foxx impressions as much as the next guy but give me a break. I have a big take coming down the pipe. Like nothing you've ever seen."

"Sheeeiiit," Pete teased.

"...And I just need a line of credit for the night."

Lazy Pete closed a lid over his glass eye and squinted at him with the good one, "Okee, but just this one time. But make good *this time* or there is no *next time* for you and me buddy. Capiche?"

"Sure. Capiche. I'm going to be golden from now on Pony Boy. You'll see. So how about starting me off with a fine brew, good sir?"

Pete uncapped a bottle of Blue Ribbon and set it down on a napkin in front of Jean. As Jean was making quick work of the beer an attractive blonde walked up to the bar from one of the back booths where she'd been sitting alone.

She had on a comely black skirt with a matching black and white checkered blouse. Her sparkling blue eyes were accented by the gold necklace lying curved against her generous breasts. In short, she had the appearance of a class broad. Jean wondered why a woman like that would have been sitting by herself in dive like Dew Drop.

The blonde ordered an island drink with rum and juice while Jean downed another beer. She sipped on her drink then fingered the salt around the rim of the glass. After finishing that beer, Jean determined it was time for a change of pace.

"Hey, Pete. How about some wine?"

"You got a preference mate: white or red?"

"Well, what's the difference?"

The blonde suddenly laughed, so loud they both turned to look at her. She yelled across the bar in disbelief, "Are you serious? A man that puts beer away like you've been doing tonight doesn't know the difference between red and white wine?"

"That's a good point, Genie," Lazy Pete ribbed him.

The blonde picked up her island drink and moved down to the stool next to Jean, gold necklace jangling all the way. "Basically the white is the light and fruity one. Most people prefer it for the spring or summertime. The red is dark and bitter. People tend to prefer it in the wintertime."

"Hmm ... dark and bitter, that sounds like my drink. A merlot for me."

"You got it boss," Pete said with a wink.

"Jennifer," the blonde held out her hand.

"Jean," he introduced himself, shaking it.

"Pardon me for getting involved in your business but I overheard you mention a big score and I was a little bored over there. Care to fill me in on what that's about?"

"This, I'd like to hear myself," Lazy Pete added, pouring the glass of wine.

"Wow. You have really good hearing. I thought you were all the way back there in the booth when I talked about that," Jean scutinized the blonde. He took a sip of merlot and thought about his choice of words, "I've just come into a little money is all."

Lazy Pete gave him a wry smile, "How little exactly? You gonna buy the Borough family estate on Jacenta Boulevard? You know Maddie Borough put it up for sale last week so she could run away to Greece with her Puerto Rican lover. If you got the scratch it's all yours."

"You know what? I just might now that you mention it."

"Ha! Ha!" Pete laughed, "Now I know that you're pulling my leg. That or you've had one too many already."

"Sure. Sure. Laugh it up Lazy Pete but you'll see."

With that, Pete left them to check on a middle-aged couple who'd just sat down at the opposite end of the bar. It was then that Jean made the outline of a miniature pistol just above Jennifer's ankle.

"Are you police, FBI? Private detective, maybe? "Jean asked motioning towards the heat.

She giggled playfully, "This? No. A girl can't be too careful when she spends time in dives like this, now can she?"

Lazy Pete overheard and took exception, "Hey! What're you callin' a dive?"

"But seriously," she ran her hand, red fingernails and all, along the inside of Jean's crotch, "tell me about this BIG score."

~ ~ ~

He'd never gotten this far with a beautiful woman so he got nervous, started putting them away like mad. Soon voices and images blurred into a drunken phantasmagoria of disconnected moments: broken and beautiful. Stumbling, lurching, stumbling- by the time they decided to head back to her motel room he'd long since crossed the line passed "one too many".

"Congrats pal. Are you sure you're alright though?" Lazy Pete asked.

Then he was hanging out the car window, then shifting to his feet again in a blur that became a shifting kaleidoscope. Ascending an Escher staircase, fumbling with keys she gave him and catching them one by one as they fell in slow motion towards the steel walkway; using them to open a hundred doors to a hundred locations across time and space- exposing breasts that could have beaten the armies of both Sparta and Vlad the Impaler dead in their tracks.

"Shit! It wasn't supposed to be that big. Just go ahead and put it in already."

Screaming, echoing through a limitless canyon and an atomic bomb ejected into the moon, blowing it up into a constellation of stars. Then, after the Big Bang exploded across the universe: a return to darkness.

~ ~ ~

Jean opened his eyes in a haze, sprawled out on the bed with vomit on his chest. "Jennifer", or whatever her name is, was standing next to the dresser in only her panties. She was searching the pockets of his clothing looking for the lottery ticket.

Initially, he was surprised she hadn't bothered to tie him down. But he figured she probably assumed she could easily overpower him if it came down to that. And in that she was probably right. Standing there in her panties, Jean could see the miniature pistol fully exposed above her ankle. He rolled out of the bed, slopping a bit of vomit onto the carpet in the process. Thanks to his diminutive stature, he didn't even have to squat to be completely hidden behind the mattress. He cautiously craned his neck around the corner of the bed. She hadn't noticed him yet but she *had* discovered his billfold in the back pocket of his trousers.

And she began, at that very moment, removing the lotto ticket hidden inside. The time for action was now or never.

With a rebel yell, he rushed at her from across the room. She caught him, palm smashed into his face, holding him just out of reach of the gun. He juked to her right for an inch or two but she reached around and twisted his ear. Jean howled out in pain like a wounded animal. They became a tangle of limbs, sweaty bodies, adrenaline pumped brains and heads that butted against one another until blood dripped from their wounded craniums onto the caramel colored carpet at their feet. But Jean needed only a couple of extra inches in that position. He extended his little fingers, with his shoulder nearly popping out of its socket, until they could *just* unhook her holster. The piece slid out and fell onto the carpet with a thud. "Jennifer" scrambled for it but Jean was closer to the ground. He dove on top of it like it was a pigskin fumbled by the Monday Night Football quarterback. "Jennifer" tried to wrangle the pistol from his fist but he stuck it into her abdomen before she got any traction.

"Shit," she groaned.

"The ticket please," he demanded, feeling very Bond-like, with a come hither motion of his fingers.

He left her tied to the bedpost, informing the cleaning staff on his way out to tidy up the room before noon. Although he smelled of sweat and vomit, Jean marched directly to the Lucky Horseshoe to confirm his winning ticket.

Even after a month, Jean still couldn't believe he'd gone from sleeping on coals in the bed of a train to living in the Borough family mansion, the most valuable estate in Boroughtown. The jackpot ended up clearing about 32 million dollars, in one lump sum, after taxes. The estate had gone for a cool $5.6 million, a steal at that price really, but undervalued due to either the lack of millionaires wanting to live in Boroughtown or Maddie Borough's haste to liquidate her assets and purchase a palatial home in the Greek Isles with her lover.

Ranchero, the secluded, wrought iron gated home nestled into the side of the Barbarosa Mountains was surrounded by imported palm trees. The white stucco exterior with faded red ceramic shingles on top had a distinctly Spanish flavor to it. Who knows why? It didn't fit with any other architecture in the area but seemed to serve only as an example of the former owners' aesthetic eccentricity. The rear of the home featured a second story balcony overlooking an Olympic size swimming pool on a deck which itself overlooked a picturesque valley. Beyond that lush valley was the town of Boroughtown itself.

The interior of the home contained numerous priceless works of art: a Picasso, a Rembrandt, the authentic Maltese Falcon prop and, cased pristinely in glass on a marble stand, the manuscript of an unreleased Mark Twain novel. There were seven bedrooms, eight bathrooms, a music room with a grand piano once owned by Burt Bacharach, an entertainment room with an HD film projector and a closet full of 35 mm prints including Citizen Kane, Back to the

Future, The Road Warrior, Blue Velvet and innumerable other classics. The library had signed Bukowskis and Nathaniel Wests, the bed frames were plated in silver and gold, the wine cellar contained casks from the 1800's and every bathroom featured European-style marble bidets for washing one's regal genitals.

"So," Jean wondered, "why aren't I satisfied?"

What a world of dumb luck; luck that the universe would explode into being from an area the size of a pinhead; bad luck to be born a dwarf but, then again, good luck to win the lottery. And there were many other dwarves in the world with the bad luck to never win the lottery and there were some people doubly lucky who were born both normal-sized and had also won the lottery. Everything happening and not happening chaotically like the violent collisions of subatomic particles or the asteroid that killed the dinosaurs. It made his head hurt.

Shaking off the weight of his existential quandary, Jean swallowed a gulp of sour mash whiskey straight from the bottle and drove a golf ball off a hooker's ass with his *L'Homme Mini Signature* driver.

"Ow, bay-bee", the hooker groaned. The club had nicked the racing saddle planted on her ass.

Yet even without a clean hit, the ball sailed over the many trees of the valley, into Boroughtown, where it landed with a splash into the coffee cup of an itinerant priest.

"A hole in one!" Jean exclaimed, looking through a pair of binoculars.

"Yaaaay!" seconded the whore.

~ ~ ~

It had taken two weeks' time since the media got wind of a dwarf millionaire lottery winner until he actually stood on the stage with the hot lights and invasive cameras on him, capturing all his discomfort. A man wearing a plaid checkered suit with a comb over handed him a big cardboard check. They both produced Pan-Am smiles so the multitudinous flash bulbs could light like jellyfish: stinging, drowning them in a sea of cameras. The cardboard check was just a pretense, contractually obligated by the state lottery commission. Shortly after media day, the real money was transferred into his freshly formed account at the New Valley Community and Trust Bank of North America. Until then he'd avoided the media circus as best he could by continuing to sleep at the train tracks in his boxcar, under ratty old blankets, on a pillow found in the Salvation Army dumpster.

That's not to say everything was completely normal. Bobby Two-Shanks treated him like a celebrity, bringing him an offering of booze and marijuana every night. "Just remember me, ole pal. We been true blue since the beginnin' and I 'ope ya won't forget yer friends now that you've made it," he'd implored that first night after the big announcement, pouring a Pissweiser into Jean's Styrofoam cup. And Jean didn't forget him. In fact, Two-Shanks ended up moving into in one of the mansion's seven guest bedrooms.

Besides Two-Shanks, he had unusual visits from Lazy Pete with a celebratory cake and sweet, fat Dolores who brought him an egg and toast sandwich out of the goodness of her heart. John Savoy even showed up to apologize for his violent outburst. One night, Jean had to promptly dismiss Action News Team 6 when they intruded on his 3 a.m. boxcar slumber looking for "the true Jean Genie: dwarf with the magic touch".

Marissa showed up briefly to congratulate him but Jean was disappointed that she hadn't come alone. She was flanked by a couple of boorish, muscle-bound men named Bobby and Jerome. Jean hated seeing her with those thugs. Wasn't she better than that? Because they looked like real bruisers, Jean nicknamed them The Bash Brothers in his mind. The Bash Brothers weren't the brightest bulbs. Their conversation lingered on knowledge of some pretty awful pop songs and they told some limp, humorless jokes about gays and Mexicans. *Fuck political correctness up the ass with a broomstick,* Jean thought, *but these lame, old jokes were better when I heard them in high school.* Jean struggled to smile out of the politeness in his heart but longed for them to get the hell off of the tracks so he could go to sleep. Either that or for Marissa to finally confess her love for him, but he tried not to linger his mind very long on that remote possibility. They finally left his company long after wearing out their welcome and Jean wondered which, if not both, had bedded Marissa for the night.

Jean woke up feeling especially cynical the next morning. A woman like Marissa would never respect him, even with all his money. Entertaining idiots had taken the wind out of his sails. *Besides,* he thought, *if those two mongoloids were any indication, I couldn't possibly be any farther from her type.*

He considered leaving Boroughtown behind, purchasing a sailboat. Hire a salty, experienced crew to sail with him to the Seven Wonders of the World. His troubles would surely disappear somewhere out at sea. But ultimately, he'd been a hometown boy for too long to take that plunge so suddenly. And, if you want the truth of it, he was just a little bit scared of what he'd find out there.

He noticed a seashell among the rocks around the railroad tracks. Where could it have come from? The nearest seashore was over 2500 miles away. He picked it up, held it to his ear and listened to the winds blow down through the vacuum of centuries.

Apparently there was a downside to moving from a cozy little boxcar to a vast estate; how creepy a big silent mansion could become. This was especially true of someone with Jean's paranoid imagination. He couldn't help but wonder if such a wealthy family might've paid to cover up a murder here. It was so isolated no one would've ever known. What was that creaking noise? Could it be the killer returning to hide some forgotten piece of evidence? And a big empty house makes its share of strange noises here and there. The mind can form a dark fantasy out of any errant noise. A mundane problem with the plumbing could be ascribed to any number of sinister origins.

But aside from that, Jean really enjoyed spending time alone in the big house. He could take a few deep breaths there, forget worrying about daily survival. It was relaxing for the mind. He could play a Zeppelin or Zevon record on the mansion-wide sound system, smoke a joint in privacy, or dive into the clear blue water of the swimming pool on a sunny day. The warm breezes would sweep down through the valley to dry his wet, hairy dwarven body during the day.

He took a lot of joy in reading up on the wonders in the library while sitting by the pool with a cold drink in hand. These were the first occasions he'd ever read the works of Nietzche, Voltaire, Laclos or H.P. Lovecraft. Time passed. He moved on to the books of Palahniuk, Fante and William Gibson.

And he wasn't completely alone in the house either since Two-Shanks stayed upstairs. He was the same old true blue friend he always had been to Jean. Only now, Shanks had a limitless supply of booze. Unfortunately, Shanks occasionally took this abundance to excess- tripping over ottomans, spilling vodka in the pool and returning home with regrettable new tattoos.

As for sexual companionship, there was a steady procession of astoundingly beautiful hookers flown in to keep Jean company. There were voluptuous Latinas from South America, classically gorgeous Euros from Holland, tiny entrepreneurial spitfires from Thailand and good old American working girls from Los Angeles and Vegas- definitely the most entitled of the bunch but confident and daring too.

At night he'd watch the "giallo" thrillers from Italy in his personal theatre room. He especially loved the works of the great masters of the genre: Bava and Argento. Then, at the end of the night, he'd smoke a joint in the garden and stare up at the lazy, golden moon.

He enjoyed that serene period where he could just exist as this rich, eccentric hermit. But, unfortunately, it wasn't long before the wolves came knocking at his door. The first time the buzzer went off he was quite alarmed. He had been passed out naked in bed, with his face resting on the tit of a Peruvian whore named Ana.

"Eeeeennnnnhhhhh!" the buzzer screeched.

He covered himself in a silk kimono embroidered with blue and gold dragons. There was a rapier from the French Civil War displayed in the hallway. He decided to bring it along for protection. Upon unhooking it from the wall, a shower of dust rained down on his head. It really was passed time to hire a maid.

"Eeeeennnnnhhhhh!"

He tracked the location of the demon machine to a panel on the wall by the front door. But couldn't reach it on account of his height. Whoever built the place obviously didn't have dwarves in mind. There was a prominent grey button on the panel, most likely the intercom switch. He managed to poke it in with the tip of the rapier.

"Yes, hold on just a second. I'll be right back."

He retrieved a metal stepstool from the kitchen, placed it flush with the wall and climbed up to the intercom.

"Yes? What can I do for you?"

"Mr.Scaputo! Good to speak with you again. This is John Savoy. You know? From the diner?"

"Hi, John. I'd never forget a man who once treated my face like a soccer ball. What is it? I was just taking a nap."

"Well ... uh, Mr.Scaputo, I think we need to talk. It's about Barbara."

He released the voice control button for a second, "Shit!" He pushed the button back in, "Sure. I'll buzz you in." He figured out the control to unlock the gate and then banged his head against the wall a few times.

Stupid, stupid dwarf! Your drinking and libido has really done the trick. Taking advantage of a poor, lonely girl like that! What kind of animal would do such a thing? And why would her father come back here now unless.... She couldn't be! Could she? You really are a fucking asshole. My god. Please don't let her be pregnant!

Jean swung open the front door and John was standing there ready to knock.

"Come in please."

John stepped inside. "Wow. This really is a magnificent home you have here. The good Lord has bestowed some real blessings upon you," John exclaimed looking around the foyer, "For what reason, I don't understand."

"What can I do for you John? I thought we'd already worked out our issues related to the ... uh, incident."

"So did I, Mr. Scaputo. So did I. Mind if I have a seat?"

"Go ahead. And you can call me Jean."

He took a seat on a striped green and white La-Z-Boy in the living room.

"I thought we had too ... um, Mr. Scaputo. But you see the thing is I've had second thoughts. You see you've broken my daughter's gentle heart. A father doesn't take kindly to that kind of thing."

Jean flushed red with shame.

"She started crying nights when she realized you wouldn't be coming back. Barbara doesn't understand. She thinks that maybe she did something wrong."

Jean poured himself a shot of gin and swallowed it down. Never had he felt like such a shit heel.

John continued, "You know Barbara, she doesn't care about this whole *millionaire* thing. She just wants her little dwarf back. She doesn't care about the money."

"She's a really special girl," Jean admitted.

Savoy leaned in, "She doesn't care about money. But *I* do."

"Yeah. Maybe I deserve that. If I could make her feel better I'd give it in a second," Jean also admitted.

"Yeah? What's more some might see a man who takes advantage of retards as a rapist. You wouldn't want the media to get ahold of that tidbit. Trust me."

"Retard huh? How can you talk about your own daughter like that?"

"Oh give it a rest. I may not be the most sensitive man in town but I am a servant of the Lord. You on the other hand must be Satan's favorite son for him to reward you so. The Lord has instructed me to reclaim what is rightfully his."

Jean sat down cross-legged with the sword on his lap. "You mean His or yours?"

"The Lord rewards his most righteous servants. This is His word, not mine. *You*, however, are to be punished for your ... *perversions*."

John Savoy was wagging his finger at Jean like he was an impudent child. The fire in his voice was typical of the fiery Baptist preachers you'd hear in Boroughtown churches on Sunday mornings.

"Maybe this is hard for you to understand from your position but she did seduce *me*, in a manner of speaking."

"Not another word!" John became red-faced with anger. He took a moment to calm himself down before continuing, "The child is under my protection."

"Forget all your platitudes. If you promise to use the money mostly for Barbara's good I'll give it to you."

John shook his head in agreement, "I will."

"Do you promise?"

This doubt made John angry, "A promise from a servant of the Lord is worth more than every penny you own."

"So how much does this cost me?"

"I'd say we could settle this for...a million dollars?"

Jean almost fainted, "Gods! Why not two?"

"You said it," John grinned.

"Fine, but I can't give it to you all at once or it'll be suspicious. Someone would figure it out and come around asking questions. I've had enough media jackals after my hide already."

"Then what do you suggest?"

"I'll have my lawyer draw up some kind of installment plan."

Savoy stood up with a gleam in his eye, "That ... sounds like a reasonable start. And I know I can trust you to follow through, Jean. I have it on a higher authority," Savoy smiled big, like the wolf about to eat a lamb.

"Yes. And please call me, Mr. Scaputo. Now that that's settled I'm sure you have places to be. Sadly, I'm not in the most sociable mood."

They both stood up. Jean motioned John Savoy towards the door and he left. Jean pulled back the curtain and watched him pass through the gate, close it behind him, and drive away in his yellow Range Rover. He had to be sure the man was really gone. *You can never be too careful when someone is out to get you*, Jean assured himself. As soon as he turned his head John Savoy could have given him the slip, then lurked somewhere on the property for days, sniffing women's panties and peeing in the swimming pool. In the immortal words of Curt Cobain, "Just because you're paranoid/ don't mean they're not after you".

With that settled, Jean walked into the sun room overlooking the pool. There was a large, brass antique rotary phone by the furniture. It was almost as tall as he was. He dialed his lawyer.

"Hello. McCutcheon, McCutcheon, McCutcheon, McCutcheon & Schroderberg. How may I direct your call?" asked the soft, feminine voice of the secretary.

"Mitch Schroderberg, please."

"May I tell him whose calling?"

Jean hoped to conceal his identity from her to avoid any awkward conversation. "Just tell him it's the dwarf. He'll know who it is."

But the secretary recognized him immediately. It was becoming an annoying habit now that he was famous. Thankfully, she was every bit the professional, "Ah. Hello, Mr. Scaputo. One moment please."

While on hold, he heard a few notes of low bit-rate calliope music. Then it stopped abruptly and there was a rustling against the phone receiver, "Good afternoon, Mr. Scaputo! What can I do for you?" It really did take only a moment. Being filthy rich did wonders for how much dignity you're treated with. The old rule was true: the poor have to wait but don't make the rich irate.

"Hey Mitch, I'm going to need some legal advice. I need to make some money transfers and I'm not sure how to go about it."

"Sure. I'll make an appointment for you and we can

draw up any necessary papers. What else you got?"

"Um...I know this isn't your purview exactly but can you help me find a maid?"

"Sure. There's a fantastic maid that cleans my own house twice a week. I'll ask her to visit you next time I see her."

"Thanks Mitch."

When he got off the phone Jean realized his stomach was growling. He hadn't, in fact, eaten since yesterday afternoon. He felt hungry enough to win the famous 2 lb. steak challenge at the Steer Shack by the interstate.* The food issue was becoming a predicament. There was a dearth of food in the house, he'd never learned to cook, nor even stocked a kitchen before. The prospect of being hounded by folks looking to meet the local celebrity furthered his reluctance to venture out to the grocery store.

Fortunately, he'd sent Two-Shanks to the store a couple days ago for a few essentials. Shanks had returned with the two most important ingredients in Jean's unique culinary oeuvre. Actually there was only a single meal he knew how to prepare himself: scrambled eggs and Cheetos. He found a partially eaten bag of Cheetos Shanks had left for him in one of the lower cabinets. From the next cabinet up he took out a shot glass. It read, 'Up All Night at the FULL MOON PARTY. Ko Pha Ngan, Thailand'. Maggi Borough had left it behind in her haste. *I bet the beaches of Thailand are beautiful this time of year. Maybe one day I'll go there myself and find Maggie Boroughs doing the limbo*, he thought.

Next, Jean poured a layer of Cheetos onto a dinner plate, covered them with a napkin and crushed the pieces with pressure from the bottom of the shot glass. He pulled a Styrofoam crate of eggs from the fridge, cracked four in a mixing bowl, stirred them and poured in the Cheetos bits. He started heating up a pan on the stove and poured in the concoction. As Jean watched the heating coils burn cherry red he thought about the personal significance this strange goddamn meal held for him.

His mother never used to cook for the family (such as it was). Instead, he'd learned the recipe from her last husband: a hard, cruel man named Ambrose Jones. Jean particularly remembered the man's bald, phallus-shaped head. Ambrose called scrambled eggs

~ ~ ~

*Finish in under 8 minutes and your meal is free.

and Cheetos "prison food"; said he'd learned it from his brother who did twenty years in San Quentin for racketeering.

Ambrose himself had been a middleweight prize fighter of minor repute out of Duluth. He claimed to have once knocked out Boom Boom Mancini in an alley outside a bar in Chicago. But there were allegations of fight fixing and running protection for the mob which ultimately cost him his boxing license. Strangely, his next move was into middle management for the Gambini Brothers chain of retail stores. He'd had no previous experience or qualifications for the job but got hired over many more qualified candidates. His employees saw him as an absentee boss, the kind that doesn't show up for weeks on end. And when he did reappear he'd often have cuts and bruises on his knuckles or bruises around his face.

After about 15 years of loyal service to the company, he was allowed a transfer to the new Gambini Brothers branch opening in Boroughtown. It was a virtual retirement in all but name only. He mostly just sat around in the store's back office smoking cigarettes and playing cards with his buddies. Other than that he did some minor consultation and collected checks. It was during this period that Ambrose met Jean's mother and the rest was history.

The ironic thing about Ambrose teaching Jean to cook

his only meal was that Jean despised the man. He was hateful, irritable and violent. And that was on a good day. Ambrose had no compunctions about bullying someone with an age and size disadvantage. It hadn't prevented him from pouring a pot of boiling grease on Jean's back. It hadn't stopped him from tackling J through the sliding glass door of the shower. Nor think twice about beating Jean when the microwave timer went off, or strangling him when a floorboard creaked. Ambrose eventually forced Jean out of the house, onto the street before he'd even finished his public education. Jean's mother had consented of course, "It was his fault, Ambrose. You were right. You were. No use getting worked up when you're right." Thereafter he lost contact with both his mother and Ambrose. A small miracle that. Six years later, while reading The Boroughtown Standard, he would discover Ambrose had killed his mother in a murder suicide. Jean brooded on it all every time he cooked the goddamn meal. He turned the eggs over with a spatula, sprinkling a little salt on top.

The phone in the sunroom started ringing. It had a weird ringtone like the classic analog ringer echoing inside an empty metal can. The fact that it was ringing at all struck Jean as pretty odd. He'd purposely neglected giving out the number to all but a few close associates. Reluctantly, he left the food on the stove, ran into the sun room and picked up the telephone receiver. "Hello? Who is this?" he answered.

It was a cool, feminine voice, "Guess who, silly."

He recognized the voice. It got him grinning ear to ear. "Hmm ... is this the ghost of Margaret Thatcher?"

"Hahaha ... hunh? It's Marissa. How you doing way up there on the mountain, little man?"

"I feel good... still adjusting. Frankly, I'm not quite living in my own present. I was just brooding on some of my old demons."

"Oh wow. That's sounds heavy," she brushed it off, "Maybe if you show me around your new digs and I can help shake Lucifer off your back for a while."

The dark innuendo was turning him on. Yet he decided to exercise a little caution, "I'm not sure what you have in mind but I like the way you say it. Listen, I haven't been giving my phone number out to anyone. How did you get ahold of it?"

"I called up your lawyer and got it off him, of course. He said he was the only one who had it."

Jean wrote on the back of a drink coaster: *Tell off that fucking lawyer for giving out my number* and underlined it twice, "Well almost. I didn't even know *he* had it."

"Caller ID."

"Ah. That makes sense ... I guess you must have been pretty persuasive to turn my own lawyer against me."

"You know I was," she giggled.

Jean hopped up on the couch and lit a cigarette. He blew out the smoke. "Sure you can come over. Just wait until five o' clock so I have time to finish up what I'm doing. You know how to get here?"

"I'll GPS it. What's the address?"

"22573 Jacenta Boulevard: you can't miss it."

"Ohhh ... by the way, do you mind if I bring Bobby and Jerome along? You know the guys you met with me on the tracks the other night? They've never been in a mansion before and they're real curious to check it out."

Jean's smile faded, "No, I don't think that's a very good idea. Better leave them at home this time."

"Oh, alright. Then I'll see you at 5."

"See you then," he replied, hanging up the receiver. Jean felt extraordinarily proud of himself. In the past, he'd have been very nervous nailing down plans with a woman for a specific time. Whenever he'd done that before they'd stood him up. So he tried to see them right away before they thought better of going through with it. It was shamefully embarrassing to always be stood up in public like that, shuffling his feet for 20 minutes, staring down at his shoes, loathing the smiling, laughing couples walking by arm in arm. He blamed it partly on the specter of the Great Ulysses hanging over him. Maybe it was only a convenient excuse to save face but Jean really was convinced that The Great Ulysses haunted his every chance for happiness. Things in his love life went wrong so damn often in so damn many ways. Statistical probability should've dictated he'd come out ahead every once in a while. How could the failure of statistical inevitability be explained if not for the dark influence of some malicious entity?

But in this case he was confident; carefree even. Maybe it was all the strange pussy he'd been paying for lately. There was no doubt that getting laid had relieved some pressure from behind his eyeballs. No doubt being rich meant he never had to walk around with a full sac. Balls or eyeballs the pressure was gone. *And maybe, just maybe*, he thought, *Ulysses is all in my mind*. Or perhaps the dark entity had found some even more vulnerable target and moved on.

Jean smelt a burning from the kitchen, "Shit!" He ran back to check on his eggs and Cheetos. Smoke was roiling up from the bottom of the pan. He dumped the semi-charred meal out onto a dinner plate as soon as possible. "Eh. It's not too bad," he assured himself, grabbing a fork from the drawer. He shoveled a fork-full into his mouth and chomped down on the crunchy entrée.

He thought about Marissa and how sharply different she'd spoken to him now that he was filthy, stinking rich. It wasn't so long ago that she'd recoiled from his every advance. She'd called him a creep then. He certainly wasn't any handsomer or more charming now than before. Something unsettled in his stomach. Something other than the abomination he was eating: doubt about her intentions. But he reminded himself that he was living his dream one way or the other. *Put those thoughts out of your mind.* It wasn't the path he'd envisioned to get there, but the destination was everything he'd ever hoped for. A beautiful horizon awaited.

After breakfast Jean dismissed Ana, the Peruvian working girl who'd been sleeping upstairs in his bedroom and called up a taxi to take her to the airport. When it arrived he put some cash in her pocket for the plane ticket back to Peru. Ana was one Mitch Schroderberg had set him up with; not a very enthusiastic lay, but unbelievably beautiful: soft black hair, smooth light-brown skin, a big South American booty, with an omnipresent scent of lovely lilac perfume.

Ana's English was broken at best. Still, he'd managed to gather why her head hadn't been in her work. They'd had a long conversation late at night drinking cocktails in the Jacuzzi. Ever since last winter she'd been in love with some Egyptian businessman who'd always frequent her services during his company functions in South America. She'd even showed Jean pictures of her beau stored on a cell phone. He was older, with a gut and a grotesquely bushy black moustache. She'd recount with wistful enthusiasm how the Egyptian would take her out shopping for the most expensive purses, shoes and jewelry; dine her at the most exclusive restaurants. She beamed about how much she 'felt like a princess' around him.

Recently the Egyptian had to return home for a few months business in Africa. The night before they parted, still sweaty from lovemaking, wrapped in each other's arms, she promised to give up sex work for him. In return, he promised that next time they met he'd stay with her forever and make her his wife. But as the months dragged on she got lonely waiting for him. The bills for the dresses and the hotels and the wine had left her starved for cash. When the escort agency came calling, she jumped at the opportunity to visit the U.S. and part a nouveau riche millionaire with some of his fortune. Long story short, since then Jean had been balls deep in her for the better part of a week. Anyways, despite her broken promise she was genuinely anxious to go home and await the return of her beau.

Just before she headed out the door for the taxi, Jean noticed the mess he'd made out of his new home. There were beer cans, dirty clothes, condom wrappers, pizza boxes and old books, read and discarded, all around. "Hold on, Ana! Un minute, por favor."

She turned around, "Yes, señor pequeño?"

"Just señor is fine really. Ana, I was only wondering ... if maybe you'd like to stay a little longer and be my maid ... until the real one arrives."

She squinted, "Uh, no entiendo."

"Ok, you don't understand," he made a sweeping motion with his hand and pointed to the living room, "Clean, please. Por favor. Mucho dinero...for you."

Her eyes lit with understanding, "Oh. Thank...you, mister. No. I am Latina woman, yes. But that no mean I am maid. I need go now mis-ter."

"Ok. Ok. Adios. Uh, muchas gracias muchacha." Jean closed the door behind her and groaned. His longtime crush was coming over in a matter of hours and he was living in a worse pigsty than he'd had in the boxcar.

Ok, that might be overstating it, he thought. But at that very moment a sparrow flew in through the open patio door and started pecking at a pepperoni in an open box of pizza. While Jean stood there in disbelief, a white-haired stray cat with a black ring around one eye sauntered in and killed the bird. Then with a warrior's swagger, the feline carried its prey up the staircase and disappeared.

~ ~ ~

By 3:45 he'd managed to chase the cat out of the house

and wipe up the pool of blood under the guestroom bed where the tabby had been gorging on his supper. He'd just found the trash bags when the buzzer went off. It was 4 O'clock.

"Eeeeennnnnhhhhh!"

What in the world is she doing here this early? he wondered, pushing the big grey intercom button.

"Ey mate! It's Two-Shanks 'ere. I'm 'ere with a few friends."

He surveyed the remaining mess again and at the antique clock in the hall. It'd just recently struck four. He buzzed them in. When the door opened Jean saw that Two-Shanks had brought along Lazy Pete and Griff. Griff looked two sheets to the wind. His arms were hoisted between the shoulders of the other two men, who managed the brunt of his weight like he was a wounded soldier carried from the battlefield. His face was a seaweed shade of green. Perhaps the whole "male maids" idea wouldn't pan out so well after all.

"Get him out of here. He looks like he's about to hurl and I have company coming over in an hour."

They ignored Jean, laying Griff out on the couch. The pupil of Lazy Pete's good eye rotated left to right, surveying the opulent splendor of the home. The glass eye sat languidly in its socket, surreally inert. After taking it all in, Lazy Pete's mind returned to self-awareness and both eyes floated back into synchronicity.

"Hooooold on, pal. He may not look it right now but this man here," he drunkenly gesticulated in poor Griff's direction, "this man is an hero." Two young women Jean recognized as Jolene and Maybelline walked in through the front door. They wore tight spandex tank tops and tattered Daisy Duke jean shorts. This man," Pete continued, "bet these fine young women their company for the night that he could drink *A WHOLE GALLON OF BUTTA!*" Pete slapped

Griff on the chest. Griff simultaneously pissed and vomited on himself and the couch.

~ ~ ~

Jean marshalled their labor like a budding entrepreneur, offering each of them one hundred dollars to clean up the mess before five. With five people cleaning, they made quick work of the mess: Griff was carried into a spare bedroom, the bodily fluids mopped up and the trash bagged. Meanwhile upstairs, Jean washed himself and put on a clean pair of clothes. Just as his merry maids had found and bagged the last bird's head the buzzer went off.

"Eeeeennnnnhhhhh!"

Jean came down the staircase wearing a freshly washed t-shirt and sweatpants. He shooed his guests into the pool house for the evening. He cleared his throat and answered in a slightly deeper, manlier tone, "Yes. May I help you?"

"It's me," responded the familiar voice.

He buzzed her in and waited there a while, listening to the insistent, drum-like palpitations of his heart. Then he finally heard the long awaited rapping on his front door. Jean took a breath, exhaled slowly, and then opened the door with a queasy stomach and weak knees.

There *she* stood: Marissa. The visionary beauty, who'd taunted, teased, beckoned, tormented and tantalized his dreams since he was just a young man. She did not disappoint in any sense of the word. Her perfume smelled like a fragrance of intoxicating wildflowers. Her long, auburn hair shined a bit, falling smoothly down over the tantalizing curve of her bountiful breasts.

She wore new-ish dark blue jeans, tight enough that she must have been teleported inside to make the fit. For a top she wore a sleeveless dark purple blouse. Jeans eyes momentarily flitted to the golden, lightly sun-browned arms her outfit revealed. There were the lightest little blond hairs on them, illuminated by the porch light. He loved even those about her.

"Hey Marissa."

"Hey yourself, little man," she greeted him with a shit-eating grin, "Can I come in?" She peaked around through the empty space in the doorway with curiosity.

"Sure. Come ooonnn in," Jean motioned inwards, with an open palm like an amiable butler. He was always had a servile disposition with the opposite sex.

Her eyes had grown wide as diamonds. The corners of her mouth uplifted into little arches with their own even tinier arches. She looked around the sun room, at the lavish furniture and large screen television. She cooed looking out the glass at the swimming pool, with its picturesque view of the valley below. Lazy Pete and Two-Shanks were in the pool making out with Maybelline and Jolene, splashing water; having a good time.

"What kind of drink would you like?" Jean asked.

"A margarita, I guess," she answered, "Know how to make that?"

"We'll see. I think I know the gist," Jean answered not wanting to have to call on Lazy Pete, for his drink-mixing expertise.

Jean approached the bar near the dining room. It was better stocked with liquor than the kitchen was with food... by a long shot. Every type of expensive liquor and mixer was found there. Liquor were bottles backlit gorgeously in front of a mirrored wall. There was a fridge with lemons, limes and a freezer with crushed and cubed ice. He grabbed a bottle of tequila, a bottle of triple sec, tabasco sauce, a lime for garnish and some ice. It wasn't the ingredients that confused him so much as the amounts of each to use. Nevertheless, he took a good guess and mixed them all together, even adding some salt around the rim of the glass for panache.

He heard Marissa laughing over in the sunroom. He

fixed himself a vodka and water then walked back to see what the commotion was about. Marissa held a hand over her mouth to stifle her laughter. Outside in the pool, his esteemed guests were naked and copulating. Maybelline was riding Lazy Pete on the stairs and Two-Shanks was thrusting into Jolene against a wall in the shallow end.

"Looks like they're having one hell of a party out there," she said.

"Looks like," he agreed.

"They're lucky to have you."

She turned around to look at him. Jean handed her the margarita. "How is it?" he inquired, hoping the blend was alright. Marissa took a sip. Her face contorted a bit though she tried to hide it. *Too much tequila*, he realized.

"Tastes good," she lied. Then a flush of excitement came over her, "Ooh, can you show me around the house now?"

"Sure," he replied dutifully, downing a swallow of vodka. Tours of the house were so tedious... although everyone was inevitably impressed.

He powered on the stereo and tuned it to a romantic mix of piano concertos to set the mood. They walked together past several of the regal guest bedrooms. Marissa liked them so much she jumped on one of the large designer mattresses with goose down pillows. It was so soft she bounced around on it for a while, shooting Jean a flirtatious smile.

Even the marble bathrooms were a revelation to her. "*What* exactly do you do with this thing?" she asked, coming upon the bidet. When Jean explained it was for cleaning off genitals she busted out in a laugh so contagious, Jean joined right along. The entertainment room was next. He opened the closet to show her the collection of 35mm film prints. While he was explaining which films were kept on the shelves, she reached down and began rubbing his shoulders affectionately. It was like a massage from an angel, one you could melt right into. Then, when he turned around to face her, she got down on her knees and gave him a light kiss on the lips. When she swaggered out of the room, chasing her next curiosity, Jean followed like a loyal servant to its master. Marissa's magical ways had captivated him completely.

And when his other guests had crashed out for the night in the pool house, they both stepped out back to enjoy the romantic panorama of the valley below. The night was clear of clouds or pollution. Constellations of stars sparkled throughout the sky. Jean pointed up at them. "What do you see when you look up there?" he asked.

"I see...a universe so much larger than anything I was ever *supposed* to have. I see the difference between being another forgotten nobody in another small town and being a shining star that reaches out and achieves her dreams," She turned around, "I don't want to be forgotten so easily, Jean."

Jean reached out and held her hand in his own. "You're somebody to me, Marissa; someone *very* special."

Marissa took the last gulp of her margarita, leaned in close and kissed Jean again. This time her lips lingered longer on his, more forcefully, more enthusiastically. Marissa moved inside onto one of the couches and sprawled out onto her back. Under the coffee table there was a round metal tin. Inside were several joints. Jean took one out and replaced the tin. The joint burned marvelously against his flame. They each took puffs, passing it back and forth, inhaling deeply.

Jean furrowed his large brow with angst, "So, let me get real with you for a second. Why the sudden change of heart about me? Last time we talked I was a 'creeper'."

She started to laugh. The lies just didn't seem to wanna come out. Giving up on an excuse, she raised her hands in defeat, "You got me. I'll admit it's the money. I can have my pick of the hottest studs in town. Some of them have real sweet hearts or real big dicks," she let out a giggle, "but it's real apparent they're *going nowhere* Jean. You are."

"What?"

"The world is laid out in front of your feet, dude. You can go anywhere, be anything and do anything you want."

"I guess you're right about that but none of this is really me. You saw the *real me* and it disgusted you."

"Maybe you're different now. Anyway I'm tired of talking now, babe? How about we take this upstairs?"

Jean wasn't quite satisfied with that answer. He tried to muster up the courage to tell her no. But she looked too fine with her body stretched out across his couch like that. Her eyes pierced right through his heart with a confidence and a wanton lust that stiffened his manhood on sight alone. His self-respect had fought valiantly but lost in a rout to libido. "Uh huh," he nodded. She stood up, kissed him again and they moved into his bedroom upstairs.

First, she undressed and then she helped Jean remove his shirt and pants. Her naked body was so artistic, so much like fireworks on the Fourth of July that his head grew a little light. She bent over onto the bed, purring like a lioness. Jean wrapped his arms around her taught stomach and ran his hands along her warm, radiant body. Then they run up until they were cupping her soft round breasts, hanging there, wild and free.

He rubbed one finger against her clit until she got wet. Once he'd really worked at it, till her pussy was dripping like a faucet, he stuck that finger inside her.

"More," she moaned. Jean put in another. "Mooore," she moaned again insistently. So this time he put in another and another. Her cries of pleasure grew louder and louder so he just kept going until all four were reaching inside. "Mmmm hmmmm," she encouraged him. So he gently pushed his entire fist inside her and pumped. *Not so extreme,* he thought, *I do have a smaller than average fist.*

Marissa's rear end pounded against his hips with animalistic fury. Ample breasts jangled wildly from side to side, cries of ecstasy growing to a crescendo. Her moment of orgasm arrived; taut stomach tremoring with ecstatic convulsions. Now was the time. He peeled off his underwear, laid his fat belly on top of her big ass and entered her with his manhood. Jean reached around to rub the clit and thrusted inside her with all his limited energy.

"Oh. Fuuuuuck!!" she screamed, releasing herself onto his prick once again.

Within seconds, Jean had released himself as well, *Thank the gods for foreplay,* he thought, falling backwards onto the pillow.

11

Afterwards, Marissa fell right asleep. But Jean dragged himself out of bed to check that all the doors had been closed up so that no more stray animals could wander inside. He shambled down the stairs. The morning sun was already shining through the sliding glass door. It was open. Jean strolled through to check on his friends in the pool house.

There they were. Sprawled out in each other's arms like beasts, as if they'd never heard of shame or the corruption of civilization; completely lacking self-awareness like stray dogs humping or two desperate lovers kissing in an alley during a rainstorm. They were the rainbow that shined through a prison cell window: beautiful trash.

He walked back inside and slid the door shut. A check of the big, old antique clock in the hall revealed it was just a little after 9 a.m. Jean heard his soft bed calling, promising peaceful oblivion or dreams to come, yet he had one more very important task on his mind. He called Mitch Schroderberg, Attorney at Law. Mitch got on the line quick as anything.

"Good morning, Mr.Scaputo. How are you today?"

"Fine, Mitch. I have a favor to ask of you and it's an unusual one ... But I'm willing to pay top dollar."

"Ok. I'm all ears."

"There's this brown, female dog that sometimes hangs around downtown by the dumpsters at Outlaw's Bar: really shaggy hair, lice jumping off her left and right. I want to hire someone to *find* that dog, clean her up and take care of any medical problems she has, on my dollar. Then I want her brought to the mansion so she can stay with me."

"Brown dog, shaggy hair, lice. Got it. Got a name for the dog?"

"I heard someone call her Roseanna once. Not sure if that's really it."

"Ok. Rose-Ann-A. Got it. I've got a top-notch crew of investigators in my contacts. We'll let you know as soon as something turns up."

"Thanks Mitch."

"You got it. Have a great day, Mr. Scaputo."

All directives completed, the Jean machine plunged into his mattress' soft, loving embrace, and gave the finger to the remains of the day.

~ ~ ~

A couple of days later a blank, grey van pulled up driven by two men in solid, white jumpsuits. They claimed to have been sent by Mitch so Jean buzzed them in. One was fat and mustachioed; the other thin with large, protruding ears. They looked like they'd come to supervise an alien cover up in Roswell. Jean suspected there was something odd about these two.

"Hey, I wasn't expecting anyone from Mitch. What's this all about?"

"Sir, my name is Stan Headburg and this is my brother Joel." Joel said nothing, twirling the edges of his long, black moustache between his fingers.

"Hi Stan. Hi Joel. I promise you I don't have any E.T. hidden behind my stuffed animal collection."

"Ha. Ha. 'E.T.'? Good movie reference, sir," laughed Joel.

"I try," Jean replied looking down at the ground.

"Me and my brother ... or my brother and I, yes, are here because of a report of a missing dog," explained Stan.

"We're pet detectives," chimed in Joel.

"Ahhh ... Touché, another movie reference," Jean

observed.

"And what movie is that, sir?" asked Stan. Both of their faces were expressively dull and confused. Stan started to speak, "Wha..." before stopping himself. The awkward silence hung there in the air a moment. Finally Stan cracked a huge smile, "Oh, just kidding sir, we get that one all the time." The brothers busted out laughing like it was the funniest thing they'd ever experienced. Jean quietly furrowed his brow.. There was definitely something odd about them alright.

"Well, come on inside, boys," he invited them, stepping aside the doorway.

They shuffled into the foyer. "Thank you sir but we'll only be a moment. You see we've come to a successful conclusion in the case of bounty number six, five, three, dash nine: the little brown dog called uh...", he paused to look down at the clipboard in his hand, "Roseanna".

It was Jean's turn to smile. He was so overjoyed that he bounced a little on the balls of his feet, "Wonderful! Are you sure her name really is Roseanna?"

Joel chimed in again, "Pretty sure, sir. That's how we got her to come towards us: by calling her name. After a little 'dog whispering'," he mimed quotation marks with his fingers, "she responded. Someone must have loved that dog once."

Stan hesitated a moment, glancing at Joel, then interjected, "But if you don't mind me asking, she looked pretty worse for wear, especially before the doctor got to her. Has she always been *your* dog?"

Jean resented the implication he'd abuse an animal, "Hell no. Fear not gents this was no dog of mine, not until now. She's going to be my rescue operation."

Stan and Joel looked at each other and breathed a sigh of relief. Stan motioned his head towards the van. Joel went outside. When he came back he was holding a leash with

Roseanna in tow. She slinked submissively into the house.

"She's all yours now mister," Joel said, offering him the leash and a small plastic bag filled with supplies. Jean took them both off his hands. "Well sir, that concludes our business here. We'd best be on our way. It's a long drive back to L.A."

"Holy shit!" Jean exclaimed. You drove here all the way from L.A.? I had no idea you'd come this far."

"We go where the money is. You didn't think there'd be pet detectives in Boroughtown, North Dakota did you?" Stan asked rhetorically. He laughed, then stepped through the door to join his brother.

With the brothers gone Jean turned his attentions to the dog. It was the first time he'd seen her in the daylight but he could immediately tell there was a stark difference in her appearance. Roseanna's fur looked cleaner than ever before and for once there were no lice skydiving all around her. Those things the doctors had accomplished were dramatic improvements in their own right. But her full recovery would obviously take time. Roseanna looked terrified to be there. It'd take time to rebuild her confidence, if in fact it could be done at all. Plus, she still had patches of missing fur with scabs layered along the exposed regions of her skin.

The mange, he thought. Sure enough, looking inside the plastic bag there was, among other things, a medication labeled, 'Treatment for the alleviation of sarcoptic mange. Administer 1 pill orally on a daily basis.' He popped out one of the pills and dropped it into his pocket.

"Come here, girl. It's alright. I won't hurt you," he coaxed her to no avail. She pulled back on the leash, trying to run away.

He grabbed the pill out of his pocket, offering it to her with an outstretched hand. She bared her teeth. Clearly this approach wasn't working. He unhooked the leash from her collar and she ran off to cower under the coffee table in the sun room. There weren't any cans of dog food in the bag so he fixed her a plate of scrambled eggs and Cheetos, leaving it in a bowl in the kitchen. Inside the eggs he stuck the pill.

There's only patience now, he hoped, *I'll see you through this girl.*

12

Reconstructed from the journal of Barbara Savoy ...

Barbara sat alone in her room. She'd waited for Jean to call or visit until she was sick to her stomach. Then she waited some more. All she could think to do to pass the time was make more arts and crafts. But since she'd already accumulated a proper pile of paper hearts in the corner of the room, unrequited hearts at that, she'd finally grown sick of that too.

And it made her furious to think that she couldn't go after Jean without her parents getting angry with her. It would be the same old song and dance. No sooner would she head towards the door than old Nurse Glenda would hear the creak of the steps and head her off in the foyer. By now, Barbara knew better.

But once it was different. She'd been staring out her bedroom window one day, mesmerized by seven magnificent golden-winged butterflies fluttering around the rose bushes outside. They were so spellbinding that she just *had* to see them in person. So she bravely, quietly snuck down the stairs and out the front door. She couldn't believe she'd somehow miraculously managed to slip past her nurse's attentions. Unbeknownst to Barb at the time, Nurse Glenda had stayed up half the night prior on a long distance call with her cousin in Cincinnati. Consequently, that afternoon, Glenda had grown so drowsy that she'd fallen fast asleep face down on the kitchen table.

Meanwhile, Barbara carefully approached the rose bushes so she wouldn't scare away her little friends. She got in close enough that the golden butterflies swirled all around her. She bounced with joy, stretching out her palms for the insects to perch upon. After a few moments, eureka (!), one of the little creatures landed right onto her hand. "Hello little girl! You're just as pretty as can be!" she purred. The butterfly moved its tiny feet along her hand and it tickled. Barbara squealed with delight.

Unfortunately, Barb's squeals of joy were loud enough to wake her caretaker. Nurse Glenda, who'd been snoring soundly asleep, awoke with an indignant jolt. Thrusting her chair screeching back from the table, Glenda bounded to her feet, bolting out the door, rapidly zeroing in on the location of her charge's cries. The door slammed shut behind her, scaring away Barb's beautiful, baby butterfly.

"BARBARA SAVOY!" Glenda screeched, "What in the Sam Hill are you doing outdoors, you naughty girl?"

Barb instinctively knew the jig was up and yet she wasn't ready to abandon her newfound freedom so easily, "Leave me alone, *please*," she begged, "I wanna play outside." She fled from Glenda as fast as her stubby little legs would take her, but before she could get very far, Barbara tragically tripped on an overgrown tree root protruding from the lawn. Nurse Glenda wasted no time, pulling the girl to her feet kicking and screaming. Barbara tried to struggle free but Glenda subdued her in a powerful bear hug. The wiry old gal had an unusual strength for a woman in her late fifties. As infuriated as Barb became, she failed to break free. Nurse Glenda dragged her back inside the house kicking and screaming until she was finally, devastatingly able to bolt the door, sealing them both inside.

"I hate you!" Barbara cried.

"That's cause you don't know any better," Glenda spat back in spiteful condescension, "The Devil is smiling at you down in hell little miss. Better change your ways or he'll have you for his own one day. Just you see."

~ ~ ~

Remembering that day still gave Barbara pause about trying to escape again. So she turned up the volume on her pop radio and tried to forget about it. Oh, how she tried. She tried singing at the top of her lungs. She tried dancing wildly; anything to drown the unthinkable thoughts away. But instead, the anger just welled up more and more. She spied her reflection in a tiny mirror on the dresser, picked it up angrily and hurled the damn thing into the bedroom wall where it shattered into shards along the carpet.

Next she set about tearing up all the paper hearts she'd dedicated to Jean. Barbara tore them into tiny pieces. But once she'd finished, she sobbed regretful tears onto the shreds of construction paper she'd once loved so dearly. Procuring a roll of scotch tape from her art supplies closet, she tried to piece them back together. It was difficult to find which piece went where when they were scattered around on top of one another like they were. Her mind calmed and focused during the doing of the task, so much that by the time she'd finished, Barbara steadfastly determined that her imprisonment should not stand a moment longer. She resolved to escape her parents' home once and for all, find a place to call her own- *a life to call her own.*

Barbara strode defiantly down the stairs towards the front door. Of course, Nurse Glenda had heard everything. She was waiting, chest out, hands firmly planted on hips, to stonewall Barb at the foot of the stairs. Little black and grey hairs stood askew of her cranium like she'd recently reached her finger into an electrical socket, "Just where do you think *you're* going?" she spat indignantly.

"Move, Nurse Glenda. I want ... to go ... OUTSIDE!"

"Oh no you don't."

Glenda grappled her with both arms. They struggled back and forth. But this time Glenda's back gave out, allowing Barb the upper hand. She shoved Glenda into a wooden vase stand which toppled over with a thunderous crash. Glenda screamed in pain, "Aghh! My back! My back! You selfish little ... retarded bitch!"

Barbara had rarely heard anyone hurl anything so contemptible directly in her direction. These things were usually reserved to frustrated whispers overheard between the cracks in her parents' bedroom door. *Never again*, she thought. There was no time to waste in leaving. No matter her condition, Nurse Glenda was still a force to be reckoned with. At any moment she might rise from the ashes of defeat like a vengeful revenant to steal away Barbara's hard-fought victory. So Barbara ran further and faster than ever before, heart pounding, past row after row of suburban houses. It was exhilarating. When she'd finally grown too tired to sprint one step further, she stopped. It was somewhere she'd never been before. And behind her, Glenda was mercifully nowhere to be seen. But in front of her? That was the brilliant part. Along the street before her there were the most magnificent golden butterflies scattered as far as the eye could see.

After two and a half weeks cooped up inside the house it was fully apparent Jean finally *had* to go down the mountain into town. The dog needed kibble, he had to sign some papers at the Schroderberg's office, and he was getting sick of his mundane, one-note diet. He picked up the rotary phone receiver and dialed up Marissa. It rang a few times before the line connected. All he could hear for those first moments was a man talking boisterously in the background. Then Marissa whispered forcefully, "Shut the hell up will you." There was a rustling on the line, a cracking sound and then someone chewing.

"Hello? Is this Marissa?" he asked.

"Oh. Hey Jean! How are you, babe?" her voice lit up.

"What was all that noise in the background?"

"Noise?" she thought for a second, "Sunflower seeds babe."

"It sounded like you were at the DMV or something. Some man was talking loudly before you came on the line."

"Oh. *Him*? He's just a cable repairman. He came over to fix the internet and he got on the phone with his wife or girlfriend or whatever."

"Ok. Well I'm planning a trip into town today and I was wondering if you could come pick me up from the mansion."

"No can do today handsome. I swear I'm all tied up. Maybe next time."

"Sure, take care", he hung up and reconsidered his options.

He called up Boroughtown Taxicab Company, the only

taxi service in the country with an all-black fleet of vehicles.* The taxi pulled up to the gate about twenty minutes later. Jean met the driver on the side of the gate outside the property. The driver introduced himself as Anju Pearsongupta. It was the first time Jean had seen an Asiatic Indian outside the Boroughtown

Wal-Mart. In the town Wal-Mart there were so many Indians working and shopping that someone might think they had passed through a portal into New Delhi.

"Pleasure to meet you sir," he said in a very thick Indian accent with his hand stretched out for a shake.

Jean shook his hand, "Nice to meet you, man. My name is...."

Anju cut him off, "You don't even have to say my friend. You are the famous Jean Genie, millionaire lottery winner."

"I guess my reputation is starting to proceed me."

* * *

*Yet another reverent allusion to Boroughtown's bygone oil boom era.

Anju turned back around. Switching the car into gear, he proceeded out of the driveway and around the bend. "Quite so, sir. Quite so," they sat in silence for a while before Anju proceeded with a smile, "You know in my culture the little man is seen as a harbinger of great luck. Many little persons are revered as mystics with great prophetic wisdom."

"Cool. I didn't know that. Do *you* consider yourself a mystic, Anju?" Jean inquired.

A serious expression washed Anju's face. When they stopped at a red light he turned round to face Jean. "I am in a close contact with the unknown, Jean Genie. Mystic visions have run in my family for generations. It sounds like you have something on your mind my friend," Anju turned around, the light switched green and he hit the gas.

Jean sat there a moment incredulously. Then he

consciously relaxed, loosened his body and asked the question which had most been on his mind, "My whole life up until a month ago had been nothing but bad luck. More bad luck and abuse than most people could expect in a whole lifetime. For many years I've had nightmarish visions of an entity I call The Great Ulysses. There's always been a nagging voice in my head that blames all my bad luck on this, this ... thing. And then all of a sudden, 31 years of bad luck comes to an end. I won thirty-two million dollars in the lottery. One of the most beautiful women in town is my girlfriend. I know I should feel unreserved joy but I still feel a pall hanging over my head. Can you tell me what the hell is happening, Anju? I keep wondering where Ulysses went and if he's coming back."

Anju reflected on this a moment before responding, "Your story strikes me less as a direct product of Hindu mythology than something out of the Jewish Torah, the Book of Job specifically. In this story, a god of temptation and a god of jealousy tortured a man for the simple product of a wager. This man, Job- his family was murdered, his livestock were stolen and he was struck with lesions about his skin; all for the pleasure of these two amoral gamblers. Most consider these deities the 'Jehovah' and 'Satan' of Jewish and Christian mythology."

Jean nodded his head, "I'm familiar."

"We Hindus are quite comfortable with polytheism; the belief in many deities," Anju continued, "Many polytheistic religions featured this god of luck or gambling. For instance, the ancient Greeks had the goddess Fortuna-blind, veiled and capricious. But whether we truly speak of gods, apparitions, or something else, completely misunderstood by modern man, the gambler entity has no other parallel in the entirety of the Judeo-Christian canon."

Jean thought on this a minute before responding, "You know I've never put much stock in the supernatural since I was a little boy, Ulysses has really been the only exception. I've never seen a UFO, a ghost, observed ESP or anything like that. But I have seen for myself how harsh this world is on those living in it. Too harsh, I think, for there to be anything good behind the steering wheel. Even this Ulysses, most of the time, is just a phantom feeling. Only the dreams are so real I can't forget them."

Anju pondered this a moment. "An unreal thing we believe can hurt us is sometimes more damaging than a real thing we believe cannot. The trick is to believe in neither the power of the real nor the unreal to hurt us. I've found belief to be the most powerful of things, Mr. Jean Genie."

"Yeah, but what if I actually get hurt?"

"What's worse, the punishment itself or the fear of the pain? We must deal with it in the moment, from all else abstain."

"Thank you for that Anju. That was... helpful. I'll try to remember it next time I have one of those dreams."

The jet black cab pulled up to the curb in front of McCutcheon, McCutcheon, McCutcheon, McCutcheon & Schroderberg. "That will be twenty five fifty, sir. And I will say a prayer for you in your continued fight against spiritual injustice."

"Thank you, Anju," Jean said, handing him a fifty, "Keep the change."

Jean walked to the secretary's desk in the law office. The secretary, a pleasant middle-aged woman, was excitedly gabbing with a friend over the telephone. Her attention was so rapt by gossip she hadn't seen Jean come in and now he was completely obscured by the height of her desk.

"Hello?" No response. He coughed very loudly. This time she'd heard.

"Hold on a sec, Patty," she rested the receiver in the crook of her neck and peered over the desk to take a look,"

Oh my! Patty, I'm going to have to call you back." She placed the receiver back on the hook. "Mister Scaputo, I'm so sorry. I didn't hear you come in."

"It's alright," Jean reassured her. "Can you let Mitch know I'm here to see him?"

"Right away, sir." She picked up the receiver again, red-faced and clearly embarrassed, "Hi, Mister Schroderberg...."

Jean glanced out the office window. It was a sunny day, only a few lazy clouds floating in the sky. Across the street a postman was talking to a housewife adorned in a floral nightgown. They were both sweating profusely in the afternoon humidity. She invited him inside, maybe for iced lemonade or a romantic rendezvous.

From there Jean's eyes followed a bluebird in the park that was hopping around and pecking at the ground, looking no doubt for a worm. Then suddenly the bluebird was obscured by flowing ringlets of blonde hair passing in front of the office window. Jean thought he recognized the face but couldn't believe it was true. Yet who else in town had a face like *hers*.

"I have to run outside for a moment. Tell Mitch I'm sorry and that I'll be right back."

"Oh. Ok, Mister Scaputo."

He flew out the office door, chasing those ringlets up the sidewalk. He caught up to the woman, placing a hand on her thigh. She turned towards him and sighed. It *was* her! "Barbara!" Jean exclaimed with delight.

Barbara's mouth fell open, "Jean?" she asked, surprised. Then before he could answer, her demeanor changed to anger and disappointment, "Jean..." She crossed her arms tight against her body.

"Uh oh," Jean didn't know what to say. If he'd broken her heart he would hate himself forever.

But it only took a few moments before her good nature

set in and she could no longer stay angry with him. She let out a final enthusiastic, "Jean!" and wrapped her arms so tight round him she compressed his spleen.

Jean let out a sigh of relief and hugged her back. "What are you doing out here by yourself, Barb? Since when are you allowed out of the house like this?

She turned indignant again, "Allow-ed?! Allow-ed? I'm a big gurl, Jean; a grown woman!"

Jean wondered if their liaison hadn't set something off in her. "I know you are, Barb. It's just that I've never seen you like this before."

They sat down together on a bench in the park. "I'm tired of bein' tole what to do, Jean. I want to live *my* life."

Jean thought about this a moment, then threaded the fingers of his hand through hers. He let out a sigh, "Does this have anything to do with what happened between us?"

She thought a moment before answering, "No," she replied. But he could see in her eyes that she was lying. She cast her eyes down to the sidewalk. She reconsidered, "Yeeeesss..."

"Do you want to talk about it?" he offered.

"I guess so. It's just my parents, Jean. They tell me I'm speshl, that I'm part of Gawd's plan, but they treat me like I'm too stoopid to live *my* life. I want to have a man, Jean. I want to fall in love."

"Well you certainly deserve it. There's more decency in you than everyone else in Boroughtown put together. You'll find someone who loves you, Barb. I promise you that."

"Real-ee??" She hugged him and rested her head in his lap. "Jean?"

"Yes Barb?"

"I ran away from home."

"You did? Are you planning to go back?"

"Jean, I don't want to go back. I want to be free. I want to have my own life. But I don't have nowhere to go. Can you help me out? Please?"

Jean thought about it for a moment. Of course he had to help her but the mansion wouldn't really be a safe or appropriate place right now. "Yeah, I will Barb. Follow me."

They walked to the real estate broker's office together and picked out a cozy little one bedroom. Jean tipped the agent an extra three hundred dollars to make sure that Barbara could get into the place right away and that it was stocked with all the groceries she could need.

~ ~ ~

Jean showed up half an hour late for his appointment with Mitch Schroderberg. When he re-entered the office, Mitch was talking to a new client: a skinny blonde kid charged with trespassing and destruction of property...for cow tipping. He was listening intently to the client until Jean entered his office. Then he suddenly seemed ashamed to be seen with the boy.

'Alright: enough. Time to get lost you little shit." But while Jean was distracted climbing onto a chair, he held up his thumb and pinky like a phone and mouthed, "Call me," to the boy.

Mitch's desk had one of those Newton's Cradle kinetic energy toys with the big steel balls that were so popular before the turn of the century. There were volumes of leather-bound legal tomes on shelves round the office. *Pretty ordinary office*, he thought at first. But then Jean noticed some pretty strange things as well. A tank containing a solitary crayfish sat on a shelf by the window. Even more unusual was a framed and signed portrait of Yasser Arafat displayed on the mantle of an antique fireplace behind his desk.

"Mitch, do you mind if I ask you a personal question?"

"Maybe; maybe not," he replied scratching his cheek, "Go ahead. Shoot and we'll see what happens."

"Why does a Jew have a signed picture of Yasser Arafat

displayed in his office?"

Mitch thought a moment before answering, as if he couldn't make up his mind, "Because I was raised in Gaza by Palestinian parents. I was a war orphan. My birth parents were Israeli Jews," he answered with an air of sentimentality.

"Sounds like you've lived through some serious shit."

"No doubt. And now that you know where I'm from you know why I get *everything* I want for my clients."

But Jean didn't understand the allusion, "And why is that?"

"Because no one has time to negotiate with people from my part of the world. It would take centuries!" he said with a smile. They both laughed. "Now Mr.Scaputo, if we could get down to business..."

"Sure. Let's do it," Jean relaxed into the leather armchair.

"Well Mr. Scaputo, I've drawn up the papers you requested," he pulled a short stack of papers out of the drawer, "But I'm still at a loss to understand why you'd give anyone so much money without acquiring any kind of asset in return."

"I'd assumed by your reputation that you'd understand," Mitch still didn't seem to get it so he continued, "that I'm being blackmailed in some way."

Schroderberg rubbed a ballpoint pen against his temple. "Ok. So I am to understand that you're giving away two million dollars for nothing? We need them to agree to hand over ownership of that money-sucking diner in exchange for the money. That would give us plenty of cover for the transaction. What do they need it for anyway? They're going to be millionaires."

Jean was blown away by the suggestion. "I don't know what to say."

Mitch swiveled his chair round. He picked up a

beautifully stained cypress wood cigar box from a shelf against the back wall. "Cigar?" he offered.

Jean nodded. Mitch picked one out, cut off the tip and handed it to Jean along with a lighter. Jean took the cigar but refused the lighter. "No thanks. I have my own," he answered, lighting up. He pulled on the stogie a few times until he was able to inhale billows of aromatic smoke.

"Cubans, of course, recently freed from embargo by the United States government," Mitch leaned back and continued, "Now, Mr.Scaputo, I think it's only fair that in exchange for becoming multi-millionaires the Savoy family agree to hand over the property deed to Savoy's Diner."

"What in the world would I do with a diner?" He took a few nervous puffs.

"You wouldn't have to do anything actually. I have another client, Gambini Retail Holdings, which are interested in acquiring a partial stake in this property. They would agree to offset some of your losses, to the tune of seventy-five thousand dollars."

Jean was intrigued, "And in exchange?"

"In exchange," Mitch continued, "they will take over management of the property. The day-to-day operations of the business will still remain the responsibility of the Savoys, should they choose to remain onboard, in an operational capacity."

"That doesn't sound like a bad deal. Everybody wins," he reconsidered, "Well, not me, but at least I lose a little less."

"Indeed, Mr. Scaputo."

Jean felt Mitch had been very convincing, "Sure. If John will agree to that, then let's do it."

"Very well. Excellent decision, sir." Mitch stood up and thought about whether he should explain what else was on his mind. He decided to speak candidly, "And if there are further problems ... if say Mr. Savoy decided to renege on our deal and ask for more money ... my other clients could be very persuasive in changing his mind."

Jean wasn't happy with that suggestion, "No, that won't be necessary. No one will bother that family. Clear?"

"Completely, sir." They shook on it.

14

That night Jean had another nightmare. He was in the backseat of another black taxicab driving down from the mountain into town. But he could tell the driver wasn't Anju this time. The driver had long, flowing locks of white hair, like the mane of a majestic albino lion. Flames burned from the pits of his eye sockets and his beard was a squirming nest of fluorescent snakes. It was The Great Ulysses.

Jean went for the door handles but before he could reach them there was a whirring sound of mechanical locking mechanisms and the bolts went in. He tugged on the door handles in panic but they wouldn't budge.

"Oh, fuck! What do you want from me?" Jean cried out helplessly.

Ulysses turned around to face him with an inhuman calm, "The same thing I've always wanted. In your case the die has already been cast. You picked up a straight flush while The Master was away from the table. But he'll return soon to collect and all debts *will* be paid."

Jean tried to recall Anju the cabbie's advice, frantically repeating pieces of it to himself, "An unreal thing can't hurt me. A real thing can't hurt me. The trick is, the trick is..."

By now they'd reached Boroughtown. The cab was approaching a red light. Without turning around, Ulysses pushed the gas pedal all the way down to the floor. The engine growled into overdrive. Jean screamed as the car blew past the stoplight into oncoming traffic. They were t-boned by a speeding mini coupe and the black taxi exploded into a ball of flame.

Jean woke up in his bed gasping for air. The sheets

around him were soaked. It was already 2 p.m.

Jean rolled out of bed and stumbled to the bathroom. He had a hell of a hangover and his 5 O'clock shadow was looking a quarter past ten. There was a ringing in his ears that wouldn't let up. By the time he'd had a shit, a shower and a shave it was all he could think about. It was giving him a five-alarm migraine. Finally, he managed to labor down the steps and fix himself a glass of vodka and orange juice at the bar. The ringing slowly faded away.

Sooner or later I'm going to have to find something to distract me from all this drinking. At least for a little while, he thought.

Then he heard a faint clicking and cooing noise from somewhere in the house. It sounded like someone had found a baby and was trying to charm it into giving them a smile. Jean followed the noises through the kitchen, through the entertainment room and towards the dining room. He stopped himself. Maybe the dream had left him a little too much on edge. The usual paranoia started to build into something more intense, like the world was full of vampires eager to suck his blood. He crept into the small space between the dining room door and the wall and peered through the space left by the door hinge. At first he couldn't see much of anything at all.

Jean rarely used the dining room because when he ate by himself, as he usually did, it felt too big and lonely. When he ate with guests it was too stately and formal. Still, even he had to admit that it had a certain old-world aesthetic charm. His eyes traced along the top halves of the walls searching for clues. They were a burgundy color that reminded Jean of thick, red adobe mud or a cabernet sauvignon wine (he'd been learning the names). Lined along the wall were regal, silver-plated, antique candle holders which had, at some point, been retrofitted with small, soft lit electric light bulbs. *Nothing out of the ordinary there*. Then he checked the bottom halves of the walls which were covered in attractive ivy green wallpaper lined with checkered rows of white fleurs-de-lis. Still nothing suspect.

Then in the corner of his observable field of vision, Jean noticed that someone was crouched in the room. But the person was mostly obscured from his view by the large oak table and chairs in the center of the room. Then there was a whimper and a snarl from under the table: Roseanna was there too. Finally an arm stretched out into view with an open palm, towards the sound of the dog's voice. The arm wore a black sleeve, rolled back to expose a forearm tattoo of a busty brunette pinup seated precariously on an anchor. Jean let out a sign of relief: it was only Two-Shanks.

"Come 'ere love. I won't 'urt ya," he entreated the dog.

Jean came out from his hiding spot to find the dog lying under the table. Her teeth were exposed in a snarl but her upper lip twitched in fright. Two-Shanks was keeping his distance from her too, playing it safe.

"She's a tough case, isn't she?" Jean observed.

Two-Shanks only just noticed him then, looking up with a start, "Oh, 'ey Jean-O. You could say that again. I feel sorry for the bitch: frightened all the time. I don't know 'ow to get through ta 'er though. She just stays 'idden under the furniture all day."

"Don't give up, Shanks," Jean implored, "I think she'll eventually trust that we won't hurt her and ease up."

Two-Shanks stood up, "'Opefully, mate. Why not 'ave a go yerself? She's been 'ere a week and she's like a ghost 'auntin' this 'ouse: 'eard but nevah seen."

Jean thought about the predicament a moment, "You know Two-Shanks, you're a good man for trying to help her. But I think we can wait beside that table till the cows come home and she'll just stay right there."

"True enough," he shrugged.

"Tell you what: I've got an idea to help her. It may take all day but I have some things to do around the house anyway."

"Sounds good mate. Let me know 'ow it goes, willya? By the way, you 'eard from yer lady love, Marissa lately?"

"Nope but that's one thing I'm aiming to figure out while I wait."

"Awlright. Sounds like you've full deeds for the day. I'm 'eaded into town me self. 'Oping to find a filly to spend me time with for the day. Might bring 'er back 'ere if'n ya don't mind."

"Not at all. Good luck. May Poseidon himself guide your sails and all that."

"Thanks mate," Two-Shanks offered with a handshake.

Jean walked back into the kitchen, poured some kibble into a dish, placed it on the divide between the kitchen and sunroom, and then burrowed the mange pill into the center of the bowl. Next, he cooked a steak, sliced it into thin strips and layered them on top of the kibble to sweeten the pot.

Let's see Roseanna try to ignore this! Now it's down to a waiting game, he thought to himself, climbing onto the sunroom sofa and resting his feet up on the coffee table. He pulled out his 'special' tin from under the table and rolled a fat spliff. Once he'd smoked it down until it burnt the ends of his fingers, he pushed it into the ashtray, picked up the telephone receiver and dialed Marissa.

Riiinnnggg. Riiiinnnggg. Rriiinnnggg. She picked up.

"Hey sweetie. Long time no see."

"Too long, baby. I want to see you tonight."

"Alright. I want to see you too. Seven okay?"

"Sure. Why not go out tonight, have some fun in town?"

"No, baby. I don't think that's a good idea. Do you mind if I bring Bobby and Jerome over?"

He groaned and rubbed the bridge of his nose, "Now that, that is definitely not a good idea. Why do you keep asking to bring those guys over?"

"They're my friends!"

"Well you know I don't like them so stop asking."

She cracked a sunflower shell between her teeth, "Whatever. I'll see you at seven then baby, alright?"

"See you then. Bye."

Jean hung up the receiver and shook his head in consternation, *Stupid bitch. It's not bad enough that you have to fuck these dumb thugs but you want to bring them around and rub my face in it too. Fucking hell!*

He was about to slam his fist down onto the table when he noticed Roseanna slinking into the kitchen and restrained himself. Mustn't scare her away now with any pointlessly loud noises. She hadn't seen him yet. That was good. He lowered himself quietly onto the floor. She'd discovered the dish now. He tiptoed past her while she gluttonously devoured the steak strips, gently closing the door leading out of the kitchen into the entertainment room. Roseanna chomped right through into the kibble, devouring her pill along the way. So far, so good. He crept back along the kitchen tile. Just when he was turning the corner around the counter, the floor creaked and Roseanna's ears perked up. But it was too late. He knelt down between her and the sunroom, blocking her escape. Roseanna bared her teeth in a vicious snarl. She cautiously backed away until she'd trapped herself against the wall. Jean crawled towards her.

"It's okay girl. I'm not going to hurt you. I'm going to explain this to you in a very calm voice. I want you to get used to it because I'm going to be your friend," he took a glove out of his pocket and placed it on his right hand, "One time I applied for disability for my, uh, condition and I got sent for an evaluation with a psychiatrist. Anyway, I got to talking with her about all this pain I have in my head, related to my past. I've actually been hurt a lot, like you. She told me about this medical term called habitul ... uh, habituation. It basically means we're confronted with the thing that scares us repeatedly and it scares us less and less each time we're exposed until we can see that we have nothing to fear at all."

Jean moved his hand slowly towards the dog. She growled even louder. A little bit closer; closer still until just over her head and then ... SNAP! She sunk her teeth through the glove with the tips of her canines, just breaking the skin of his hand. A few drops of blood fell to the floor.

"Ow!" a surge of anger flashed through his head but he controlled it, stood up and grabbed another slice of steak from the pan. Roseanna's nostrils twitched, sniffing the morsel. "Let's try this again." Jean inched his gloved hand towards her once more, this time with a little bribe. Forward, forward, inch by inch. The dog let out a whimper through her bared teeth. Then he was dangling the food just over her head. She turned away from it at first, and then, suddenly ... snapped it from his hand. While she was preoccupied with her snack he removed the glove and rubbed his bare hand along her fur. When she finished eating, she resumed snarling but she didn't actually try to bite him this time. Familiarity had gotten the better of old Roseanna. They sat there on the kitchen floor a while in one another's company.

It was around 7:30 when he buzzed in Marissa. She was wearing a truly flattering black dress, sensuous as ever. But there was something more somber in her expressions than when they last met. "It's really good to see you again. You look fantastic," he told her honestly.

"Thanks. It's really good to see you too, Jean," she replied, shyly looking down at the floor; unusual for someone with her natural confidence, to say the least.

Jean gritted his teeth, working up the courage to speak his mind, "Did you *really* miss me? Because I've hardly heard a word from you in the week since we slept together."

She made a step towards him. "I'm sorry, really sorry, about the way I've been acting lately. You were so good to me and I had a *great* time," she explained, running her fingers through his hair.

"But?" Jean asked pessimistically.

She looked him directly in the eye. "No buts. I think I just liked you a lot more than I thought I ever would. And that scared me because I was only looking for a good time."

She was even more alluring when she was shy. "Wow, I never knew. But that's exactly what I wanted to hear," A wave of paranoia sent shivers up his spine but he pushed it out of mind, "I love you, baby," Jean said dreamily, hypnotized by the magic of the moment.

"I love you too, Jean. Please do me a favor."

"What is it? Anything for you."

"Take me please," she begged, "Right here in this room."

Things were unfolding like a fantasy rather than real

life. Jean smiled and grabbed her hand, walking her possessively over to the couch. They sat down beside each other, hands knit tightly together, staring into one another's faces. Her eyes were a shining hazel with such detail that they could have held galaxies, planets and the secret truth of all life inside them. He noticed her lips were full and red. Vision seemed heightened by the slowing passage of time until he could stop it completely to notice tiny details like a rectangle of light reflected on her lip. A galaxy of neurons discharged in his brain. They kissed each other, hard and full of passion. Then time seemed briefly to freeze altogether.

It felt like the climax of an entire lifetime, building only to this. She stood up and stripped, never taking her eyes off him, until she was standing in all her blindingly radiant, naked beauty. She laid her back flat on the sofa, leaned her head back, "Make me yours. Mount me lover." Jean was light-headed from all the excitement. His clothes seemed to float right off him. He climb on top and pushed himself inside her. "I'm all yours now. Show me you're the man!" she cried shaking her hair. Her arms stretched out over her head like she was poses for a painter's canvas.

"I'm your man, baby!" he replied excitedly.

She cried out in ecstasy as he pounded her young twat. She moaned and convulsed, her hips grinding hot. Her stomach twitched like a powerful earthquake across a once-still valley. After she'd finished, he picked up the rhythm until he felt a rush of endorphins and he'd left his love gift shot deep inside his sweetheart. Then he just rested awhile on her tit like baby Jesus in the arms of the Madonna.

"God damn! You may be a little guy but you know how to fuck me big time, Jean."

He finally dismounted. Outside the sliding glass door there was a wicker basket filled with white pool towels which had recently been cleaned and folded during the new maid's weekly visit to the mansion. He slid open the door, grabbed two towels, handed one to Marissa and began to wipe the sweat and jism from his body.

Freud once speculated that melancholy following post-coital release was akin to a "little death" -the great mountain of fulfilled anticipation, followed by the deep valley of ennui. Though every volume of Freud's work was collected inside the mansion library Jean hadn't worked his way to that particular section yet and so he knew nothing about it. But what came after the great consummation of his love for Marissa was exactly that and he was about to be laid low in the deepest of valleys.

~ ~ ~

Bam! Bam! Bam! Someone was pounding his fist angrily against the front door. Waves of paranoia washed over him again, like he'd felt earlier in the dining room but more intense. There was a stronger logic to it- no one had ever *just* knocked on the front door. They had to get buzzed in first before they'd even get that far. But no one had been buzzed in except Marissa.

Marissa and Jean looked at one another, startled. "Are you expecting anyone?" she asked him.

"Noooo," he drawled loose from his mouth.

"It's probably just one of your friends then; Johnny Two-Sham or Biff got locked outside," she slid her bra back through her arms, hooking it into place in the back. "Why don't you relax, baby and I'll get it for you," she pulled the now-wrinkled black dress down over her head.

But something about that didn't sit right with Jean. Maybe it was the primal, instinctive urge of a man to protect his woman, or maybe it was something more selfish. Regardless he put on his clothing and replied, "No. Wait here. I'll get the door." Jean proceeded cross the floor with trepidation, fear jackknifing his heartrate. All he could hear was the sound of his heart pounding loudly, insistently against the walls of his ribcage. He carefully positioned the stepstool against the door, trying not to make any noise. Walking tepidly up the steps, he reached the summit and peered through the peephole.

Standing out there on the porch were two gigantic gorillas: Jerome and Bobby. They were dressed all in black: Bobby had black jeans, a collared black shirt, and black leather jacket. Jerome was dressed the same except he wore a black t-shirt with a golden graffiti design on front instead of a collared shirt. Their chests looked so swollen Jean considered they might have been doing push-ups in the lawn. He hoped it was just a distortion of the peephole lens that made them look so massive.

Bam! Bam! Bam! Bobby pounded his oversized ham hock of a fist against the door. Jean flinched a little in fright. Dwarves were not cut out to fight.

Jerome scratched his bald, black head. It looked like a bowling ball, shining under the porch light. "Hey Bobby. Did you check the doorknob? Maybe it's unlocked."

Bobby adjusted the front of his leather jacket, "Hey! What do you think I look like? An idiot?"

Jean recalled a terribly tragic detail- he never locked the door. Why should he when there was the locked gate outside to screen visitors? He tried to reach down in time to apply the lock before the Bash Brothers could get inside but he got there too late.

Bobby had already reached down to turn the door knob, "Oh shit. Looks like you were right," he exclaimed. Bobby tried to open the door directly but at first it was jammed against the stepstool, so he drove his shoulder hard against it, sending Jean and the stepstool crashing hard to the floor. The wind knocked out of him, Jean writhed on the ground in pain, gasping for breath.

"I thought you were gonna answer the door, bitch!" Jerome yelled at Marissa. Her demeanor had changed. She was leaned forward on the sofa, expectantly, with her elbows resting on her knees. She looked nervous, tired and ravenous now. Then again, maybe she'd always been and Jean was just too distracted to notice it.

"Relax, dude. We got the little man right there on the floor. Tie him up before he recovers," Bobby instructed Jerome. He dug into the chest pocket of his jacket and pulled out a baggy full of drugs, tossed them to Marissa. She gloved it enthusiastically like it was a last out pop up in the World Series.

Jerome pulled out a short length of rope that had been tucked into the waistband in the back of his jeans. He used it to tie Jean's wrists together in front of his stomach. Jean struggled against the binds at first but when Jerome saw this he reared back and punched Jean so hard he nearly lost consciousness. After that, he accepted that it was safer to go along with these awful events, at least for the time being. Jean got a close look at Jerome while he was tying his wrists. Jerome had a bulbous nose and mountainous biceps. Jean thought he looked like a professional wrestler.

Jerome was about to put a gag over Jean's mouth when Bobby called him over, "Hey J-Money! Give the lady a light, willya? She's ridin' my ass about it right now."

"Sure," Jerome responded, walking over to Marissa, who was intently focused on a thin metal pipe gripped between her fingers, "Finish blindfolding him for me, bro."

Bobby picked the long, folded piece of cloth off the ground. It was his turn to be scanned by Jean while he applied the blindfold. *Any details might help the police later*, he thought. Bobby was a white man with humorless, short-cropped crew cut hair. Bobby was the kind of rigid tough guy who'd probably had a day job as a bouncer, footballer, or military man once. Incongruous with the rest of his austere style was one small, golden ring pierced into the skin around his eyebrow.

Jerome lit the pipe for Marissa. She took a long draw of smoke, then reclined into the sofa, dazed. She finally turned her attention back to Jean. "I'm sorry Jean but you have no idea how much I needed this. Don't worry. They promised me you wouldn't get hurt."

"Like hell," spat Jerome at Jean, "We need you ta give us a little somethin' and we will do *whatever* it takes to you until we get it."

Marissa groaned, "Nooo. You promised," meekly, almost inaudibly, before taking another hit from the pipe. She faded back into the sofa cushions.

How did I not see this? Jean chastised himself, *She's been on the wagon as long as I've known her. Still, she's a recovering addict I've clearly scoped hanging out with bad men. Sad to see her fall so desperately; seems like it's all destiny. The clock is always counting down till anyone in Boroughtown reverts to the worst possible version of themselves.*

Bobby picked up where Jerome left off, "Now the first thing we need from you is just to sign some papers," he spoke as if he were asking nothing at all, "You got the deed to this place roundabouts or we gotta take a ride downtown tomorrow?"

"I've got it here," Jean answered dejectedly. His broken heart was so disconsolate, so filled with melancholy, that his will to fight had evaporated; "There's an electronic lockbox, in the wine cellar. It's inside an old barrel of aged, Irish whiskey. The code is the year of the original distillation: 1876."

"Check on it," Bobby instructed Jerome with a flick of his wrist.

"Yeah, yeah. This better be right or I'm gonna have yo ass," Jerome threatened Jean.

Marissa stumbled off of the sofa towards Jean. Though he couldn't see her he felt her tits pressed against his face when she embraced him. "I'm so sorry, baby. I wasn't very happy. I was bored. I told you my life wasn't going nowhere. These guys they offered me something that makes things better; for a little while at least. I hope if you love me you'll understand, baby."

Bobby laughed condescendingly. "I bet this girl just broke your little heart, huh?" Jean didn't respond. "Why'd you want to fall for her anyway? That girl's been cocked more times than John Wayne's pistol."

Jean hated Bobby so much in that moment but he knew there was a sick truth to what he'd said. "And probably half those times by you. What's the fucking difference?"

"Fuck both of you," Marissa yelled, "Let's just hurry up and get what we came for."

Bobby laughed again. "You said it, mane."

Fifteen minutes later Jerome returned with the deed clutched in his eager grip, "We got that shit, yo!" He pulled the blindfold down from Jean's eyes, "Now you gonna sign," he motioned forcefully to Bobby, "Yo! Give this nigga a pen!" Trapped with no conceivable recourse, Jean signed the deed of Borough Mansion over, of course. "Yo! What about that other doc Jennifer gave you, mane?"

Jennifer, Jennifer, Jean tried to mentally place who they could be referring to. *How many Jennifers are there in Boroughtown?* The answer was: a lot. Still, there was one glaringly obvious selection. But his mind was under too much duress at the time to make the connection.

"Oh yeah," Bobby remembered. He extracted a slip of legal size paper folded into his jacket pocket. Bobby unfolded the slip and slapped it onto the wall beside Jean's head, "Sign."

Jean moved slowly so that he'd have time to see what he was signing. It read:

To Whom It May Concern,
I, Jean Scaputo, wish to formally acknowledge that I

am madly in love with Ms. Marissa Stotgard. I love her infinitely more than I do every dollar in my bank account or every star in the night sky.

As a token of my sincerest devotion, I hereby state my legal intent to bequeath all of my assets and finances into the possession of Ms. Marissa Davis in exchange for a simple agreement that she will give me her hand in marriage at a later date to be decided.

Signed,

Marissa has already written her name onto the document. There remained some space for his signature just above that. Jean reluctantly scribbled his name into the blank.

"Ha haaa!" Jerome laughed, jiving and dancing with jubilation.

Bobby slapped him on the back, "Now we just need one more little old thing and you can get outta here safe and sound. That bank account you got- what's your pin numbah?"

~ ~ ~

Once they'd gotten everything they wanted, Jerome threw Jean over his shoulder like a sack of potatoes, carried him outside and dumped him in the trunk of Marissa's car. After the door closed Jean could hear Bobby yelling about something or other but the sound of his voice came through the trunk too muffled to understand. A minute later the ignition kicked over and the motor hummed to life. Then he felt the car start rolling out of the driveway.

It was perfectly dark there in the trunk as the vehicle rolled down the mountain. Jean had plenty of time to ruminate there in that darkness, anticipating whatever awful fate he would come to that night. The anger, the bitterness spread like a virus through his mind, threatening to consume him. *So much for the American Dream,* he thought. *It was all a conman's scheme. Even as a millionaire, the great role model on the golden hill there wasn't any love for outcasts like me. Only desire. Desire from other people for you and more specifically what you have. And the hunger doesn't stop until it's raged out of control more, more, more across the lives in your orbit like a wildfire.*

How had the Bash Bros got passed the gate? he wondered. Of course they could have climbed over the gate. They might have even acquired his passcode somehow. But he figured the most plausible explanation was that they had been lying down in the back seat of Marissa's car the whole time and got through the gate when he buzzed her in. From there, they lay in wait until he was at his most vulnerable, probably hoping Marissa would just open the door right up for them.

After twenty-five long, anxious minutes in that darkness he finally saw a ray of light slip through the crack in the trunk door. It was light from town no doubt. They'd likely arrived in Boroughtown or maybe even one of the smaller hamlets on the opposite side of the mountain. Sometime after that, the trunk finally opened to reveal Bobby, who was just about the only sight even less preferable than pitch black darkness. Bobby lifted the dwarf out, set him onto the wet asphalt below. It soaked right through the front legs of his pants. From the smell of it he'd been dropped into a puddle of oil and gasoline.

Looking around it was clear they were in a lonesome alley between several derelict buildings, most likely in the seedier part of downtown Boroughtown. There in the alley, Jean and Bobby were all alone except for a single homeless woman snoring soundly asleep under a newspaper by the dumpster.

In the pale, flickering light of a lamppost bulb Jean saw Bobby pull a switchblade from his pocket. When the blade snapped out from its casing, the gleam reflecting from its polished steel shone directly into Jean's right eye.

Inside, he braced himself for oblivion- cursing Ulysses name one last time, taunting the great beast that his power to torment was nearing its end. He also took a moment of reflection, to appreciate the many brief but joyous moments in life- mostly those spent in the company of friends.

Then he remembered a longing he'd felt as a boy watching the long, sepia colored trains rolling down the tracks out of Boroughtown. He had wondered if it was different out there somewhere. Maybe the world was just a series smaller and larger series of Boroughtowns with the same dishonesty, broken dreams, loneliness, greed and heartache. Or perhaps there were some wonderful places out there in the world, where even the strange and the broken could find love. *Now my time has run out and I'll never know for certain.*

But to his surprise, instead of stabbing him through the gut, Bobby grabbed Jean's left arm and cut the binds from around his wrists. Bobby noticed his shock and grinned smugly. "Surprised? We ain't looking for no murder rap. Stay gone, and I mean *real gone*. Then you and I, we won't have no more problem. Trust me, you *don't* wanna see the alternative."

With his ill advice given, Bobby climbed back into the car, kicked over the engine and drove away into the night.

Jean woke up back inside his old boxcar with a familiar hangover, sweating through the fabric of his clothes in the heat of the afternoon sun. There was a mind-fucking case of déjà vu running laps around his head and he seriously wondered if the last month had all been the result of a fever dream. The sweating and disorientation seemed to back up this hypothesis. He rolled over onto his belly to hide his eyes from the bright sunlight against the skin of his forearm. But a sharp pain shot from the black eye he'd received the night prior and disabused any further notions of the kind.

An hour later, he'd woken up enough to head down to the police station and report what'd transpired. A desk jockey took his story and dispatched two plain-clothes detectives to the mansion to investigate. Jean hung around the station waiting for the officers to return. Hopefully they'd set everything right so he could go home and forget all this had happened. In the meantime, there was nothing to do but drink bad coffee the police station had left out for the public. It looked and tasted like motor oil.

The front door slammed open. Four officers stuttered inside, wrangling a meth-addled man covered in tattoos into the station. The man had a black eye. There was blood spattered on his chest; didn't look like his. He screamed against the oppression he felt, bucking and shaking the officers with all his might. The addict's screams echoed down the corridor to the jail cells in the back. Like animals in some Nation Geographic special, the other prisoners heard his screams and started yelling back to him.

"Hey maaaaan!"

5

"Fuck the police!"

"Get 'em killer!"

"Get the keys and let me out! I'll make you rich."

One of the inmates picked up and tossed a piece of his own feces through the bars of his cell at another prisoner. All the prisoners started rattling their bars, screaming at each other in a symphony of agitated noise. Jean noted that the walls of the police station were all white, like a madhouse.

Jean recognized the new prisoner from school. Jacob Mallory- just another hometown boy, was great at chemistry, bad at English, if he recalled correctly. Jacob had a family and a decent job at the power company. That was before he got laid off and his wife left him. That was several years ago now.

Staring at the banal linoleum checker patterns, with the dust of the night's action settling down, the fuller ramifications of recent events finally dawned on Jean. Did Two-Shanks ever make it back last night with his woman and what became of them when he did? And what about poor Roseanna who'd been rescued ever so briefly only to return to the hands of evil men?

When the officers finally returned they informed him that since the "alleged" home invaders possessed a signed deed, the dispute would need to be arbitrated in court. However, noticing the dwarf's bruised eye, they encouraged him to file assault charges. Jean declined on account that there was no use agitating the Bash Brothers, while he was out in the open, leaving himself open to retaliation. In fact, he might have already pushed them too far by contacting the cops in the first place. Just another justifiably paranoid thought piled on a stack of worries and heartbreak.

Riiinnnggg! Ring! Riiiiinnnnggg! The desk jockey picked up the receiver.

"Hello? Yes. Yes. Uh huh. We're in the middle of an

investigation but we've determined the matter will have to be resolved at trial. Sorry, sir. Very sorry. Hold on I'll get him for you."

The desk jockey waved Jean over to the counter. He picked up the phone, wondering who could have possibly thought to call him here. "Hello?"

"Good afternoon, Mr.Scaputo". It was Mitch Schroderberg. "Sorry to catch you at such a bad time. I know things went, uh, mighty rough for you last night."

"Thanks. I feel like I've been dragged through a pit of nails."

"Be that as it may, I need to see in you in my office as soon as possible. Besides addressing your current predicament we have some other, uh...urgent matters to discuss."

"Really? Is it good news or bad news?"

"Hmm. It's really more of a mixed bag. But it is *all* extremely urgent. If you're not doing anything now you'd better come over right away.

"I'm just finishing up here. Give me ten minutes and I'll be on my way."

He hung up the receiver and walked out of the police station. When he got to the offices of McCutcheon, McCutcheon, McCutcheon, McCutcheon & Schroderberg Mitch was waiting there in the lobby to greet him.

"Welcome Mr.Scaputo. Step into my office please."

He walked in and climbed into a soft brown leather arm chair.

"Can I fix you a drink?" Mitch asked. He was a man of consummate hospitality.

"*Yes*," Jean answered enthusiastically, "gin and tonic if you got it."

Mitch nodded and mixed the drink from the ingredients in his liquor cabinet. He dropped two ice cubes into a glass and handed it to Jean who, very appreciatively, guzzled the first quarter of it right off the bat. Jean felt the cool anesthetic wash over his mind. He hadn't noticed how tense his muscles had been clenching until just that moment when they all suddenly relaxed.

"So Mitch, you said you had some news for me."

"Indeed I do. Well, do you want to begin with the good news or the bad?"

Maybe it was the onset of drunkenness but Jean let out a laugh of relief, "I thought people only got asked this question in the movies. I've always wondered how I'd answer. Now that it's happening I'm not sure how to answer. How much news you got?"

Mitch furrowed his brow, "Two good and two bad."

"Ok. I'm feeling a little reckless you know, with having nothing to lose and all. Maybe we go unorthodox and switch it up back and forth: good, bad, good, bad. How's that?"

"Very well, Mr.Scaputo. You're the boss." Mitch leaned back in his chair and lit a cigar. He offered one to Jean but he wasn't in the mood. Mitch took a drag, held it in a few seconds and exhaled. "Well, the best news is that the bank put a stop on the money transfers from last night. They deemed it "highly suspicious" that 32 million dollars would be transferred out of an account at their bank in one transaction. Maybe there's some greed at work in not wanting to close out such a lucrative account. In any case it worked out in your favor. You're still a millionaire..."

Jean clapped his hands together enthusiastically, "That's great news! Now the bad?"

"...technically. You can't actually access any of your money until the bank resolves the transfer issue, which I've already informed them is disputed."

"Ouch, that hurts. What am I going to live on in the meantime?"

"Well I have a few ideas but we'll get to that later."

"At least you're on the ball. I trust you can make

headway there but damn, I think I need some more good news now."

"Absolutely," Mitch concurred. He hit the cigar again, turning the tip cherry red with fire, "The two claimants to the Borough Mansion have felony records a mile long. Granted they're mostly drug and assault felonies, no prior grand theft robberies, but there will be a serious credibility gap. That credibility gap is going to make it very hard for their claim to ultimately hold up in court. That's even against a drunken dwarf."

Jean chuckled and took another quarter of the gin and tonic down his gullet, "I am who I am," He took a deep breath, "and the bad news?"

Mitch took another good hit from his cigar. He savored it so long it gave the impression he was stalling for time. After some long seconds, he slowly exhaled the smoke through his nose in thick plumes, giving him the appearance of some great old dragon of myth. Finally he continued, "I'm ashamed to relate this last bit of news because, as you may have noticed, I pride myself a great deal on my professionalism and the business acumen I bring to bear for my clients. However," he paused again, "I've recently encountered a conflict of interest between yourself and my other esteemed client, Gambini Retail Holdings."

Jean did not like where this was going in the least. It made him nervous and he sweats when he's nervous. He shifted in his seat to retrieve a cigarette from the pack in his left pocket. He lit it as he listened to Mitch further explain the present dilemma.

"Well first, John and Mary Sue Savoy decided to resign operation of the diner citing the supposedly 'unsavory' associates of the new Gambini property management team. Without the Savoys' experienced guiding hands to run the place, mistakes were made. For instance, there were several severe cases of food poisoning which have resulted in a class action lawsuit."

"I'm sorry to hear that. But how exactly does this affect me?" Jean wondered, "I'm only a... what do you call it? A silent partner."

"Yes, I agreed with you. I put that exact point to the Gambinis but they're of the alternate opinion that you're to blame for dereliction of duty. They can be quite persuasive."

"So what are they going to do, kneecap me? At this point they're just going to have to take a number and wait in line."

Mitch chuckled, "Of course not, Mr. Scaputo. Heavens! Just who do you think they are?"

"I don't think I'm coming out of left field when I say that your other clients sound like mobsters."

"So you hear an Italian name and jump to the Mafia stereotype? This is a more politically correct age sir and someone might take offense."

"Well fuck them if they do. They can cry all they want on the Internet as long as they don't break my kneecaps or shoot me in a drive-by."

"Drive-bys are blacks, not Italians, Mr. Scaputo."

Jean busted a gut laughing. He wagged a finger at Mitch. "Now, now you racist old dog."

"Very funny," Mitch responded dryly.

"Anyways, what exactly do the Gambinis aim to do about this situation?"

Mitch hesitated. "Well I probably shouldn't be sharing this with you but the whole town will know soon enough ... and you *are* just as much my client as they are ... Since the 1970's the Gambini family has managed to acquire ownership to approximately eighty percent of the property in Boroughtown. They plan to cite your, ahem, alleged managerial incompetence and the pending class action lawsuit as rationale to demolish all these properties."

"Wait. What?! Why'd they want to tear all of it down?

Just out of spite?"

"No, it's not that I'm afraid. They're interested in turning the entire town, or eighty percent at least, into an oil field. They seem to think that there's still oil underground. It's just been waiting there all these years under the downtown area itself."

Jean shuddered. "This is ... this is madness."

~ ~ ~

Jean left the office in a state of shock. The streets outside, teemed with the bustle of small town life- people went about their activities completely oblivious to the harsh fate that would soon await them. Everywhere you looked there were plenty of the typically dull folks you'd see downtown around this time of day every day of the week. There were two debonair businessmen contrasting one another's ties, in what seemed to Jean like the epitome of bourgeois banality. One tie had purple polka dots and the other a more reserved turquois. Speaking of ubiquity, of banality in American life, there were also some middle-aged mothers speed walking babies in customized and accessorized strollers. Everything was multi-tasking now- *how else could you achieve the maximal social accomplishment necessary to attain a sense of self worth?* These women were unwitting exemplars of the 21st century American woman, working herself to death just like the men always had and squeezing in time for childrearing as an afterthought. Every second of every life stuffed to the gills with work, social climbing, or reproduction. You could count on these types to be out there buzzing about like worker bees in a hive, each fulfilling his function and reveling in his or her allotted station. Especially at this time of day, just after 4 p.m: This was the time when most Boroughtown folks began their ritual exodus from the workplace doldrums- back to the isolation cells they called their homes to receive the propaganda they called entertainment. But I digress.*

There were some outsiders around too, pockets of resistance that society hadn't yet figured out how to suck the marrow of humanity from. A few teenage boys in fast food uniforms were skateboarding in a parking lot outside the jobs they hated. They were trying to impress a girl in tight jeans and haltertop. The plucked strings and yowls of the itinerant musician were drifting from the park. He was poor but there was freedom in his art. There was courage. There was truth. *Would all these people have a place to go when the dust settled on the New Boroughtown oil patch?* Jean wondered.

~ ~ ~

* This is a time of government and corporate surveillance of phones and internet, politically correct censorship, one-sided, ideologically overzealous political messaging in the media, drastically increasing social isolation and a self-policing citizenry, drunk on schadenfreude, tearing other people down for the slightest of indiscretions. You can't describe early 21st century America without mentioning how much it looks like 1984.

Jean was becoming numb to the whole charade. Amidst this mundane din, he could only bring himself to stare dumfounded and half-interested past the rows of cement buildings towards Bison Lake. Situations had become too drastic to even face reality as it was. But a chance occurrence snapped him back. Just then a familiar pair of misfits walked through his field of vision, disrupting the daze. It was Two-Shanks walking Roseanna-dog across the street through traffic, the two of them sticking out against a world of convention like mustard stains on a white dress. Jean was so happy to see his friends alive and well after all that had happened. He thought he might cry or try to kiss them both.

"Two-Shanks! You old dog! And Roseanna..."

"You old dog?" Shanks offered with a sly grin.

"Yeah literally," Jean chuckled, "I'm so happy to see you both," he cried out, jogging in their direction.

"Oy, mate!" Two-Shanks respond.

Jean patted the calf of Shanks leg with joy, and then, more cautiously gave Roseanna a rub on the back. She didn't bite or even snarl this time, although she still looked unsure of his intentions. *Kindness is still a new experience for her*, he figured.

"Did you end up back at the mansion last night?"

"Aye. That's where I got the dog."

"So what happened? My mind's been worried sick all day that they might have hurt you or Griff... or even Roseanna for that matter."

"You see me 'ere fit as a fiddle. Griff? I saw 'im noddin' off near the tracks earlier. You mentioned the people what took over your place. Who are *they* exactly, Genie? The only one I recognized was your girl, Marissa."

"The two charming thugs you probably saw there are named Jerome and Bobby. I haven't been able to figure out exactly what they are to Marissa. Friends? Boyfriends? Drug dealers? Sex studs? It makes me fucking shudder to think about it. All I know is she's had them around for a while and they've been playing some sort of angle on her as long as I've known them. I really had no idea it was anything this dangerous until they showed up on my porch unannounced and started talking with their fists."

"Yeah, I vaguely recall seein' them 'fore but couldn't put names to the mugs. What 'bout the blonde?"

"Blonde? There wasn't any blonde as far as I know. I don't know who that might be. She must have shown up sometime after they booted me."

"Dunno the timin' mate but me an' the ole lady, Maybelline shown up around midnight, didn't see ya in sight."

"Yeah, I was long gone by then. Tell me what happened. Exactly."

"Alright but let's take a seat somewhere first mate. I can't handle rehashing this awful shite under the burning sun without a few in me. You got any cash on ya? I dunno if they took that from from ye too."

"Thankfully, yeah. My lawyer gave me a line of credit. Gods know how I'll pay him back if I lose my court case."

"You're charged with somethin' too mate?"

"No, it's a civil trial about who takes possession of the mansion and the lottery winnings. Don't worry about that now. What I mean is that I've recently discovered some information about who my attorney's in league with. My gut tells me it's a real dangerous organization and I'm not sure I'll like what happens to me if I can't pay them back. But shit, there's so many ways this goes south now it's just a matter of whether I take the bus or high-speed rail."

They decided to walk over to The Last Call. Although Outlaw's was the real good time, boogie joint in town and The Dew Drop Inn had the best, most empathetic bartender, The Last Call was much closer and supposedly more relaxed about dogs hanging out on the floor. Besides it had a rather... unique charm all its own.

17

Jean and Two-Shanks swung open the old-fashioned saloon doors of The Last Call. They took their seats towards the back in a dark, comfortable booth and waited for the bartender. It had been ages since Jean had been in this bar. He'd always thought it had a really cool atmosphere but rarely frequented it because it held quite a tragic aura to it as well. There was an air of death about the place that appropriately fit its fatalistic namesake.

The Last Call bar was decorated from corner to corner with the wreckage of airplanes from the early twentieth century. Mounted along the walls was a propeller from a Sopwith Camel, the hull of a Curtiss JN-4 emblazoned with an American flag, the cockpit seat of a 1921 Kinner Airster and many other interesting bits of antique aviation paraphernalia. It's truly a sight to behold.

The place has a certain mystique that's bred a notoriety reaching far beyond the limits of Boroughtown. In fact, over the years, The Last Call has become a popular stop for eccentric aviation aficionados traveling the great American highways and byways. But that fascination has as much to do with its macabre history as the oddities that make up its décor. It's a history that dovetails appropriately into the wider series of rumors surrounding madness in the Borough's family line.* Jean had heard the story many times over and it still gave him chills.

The original owner of The Last Call was a woman named Beatrice MacDonald who just so happened to be rich Old Man Borough's beloved niece. Beatrice was a red-haired young firecracker who idolized the great aviatrix

Amelia Earhart. She kept a scrapbook of press clippings**
commemorating each major achievement in Earhart's
storied career: when she broke the women's altitude record,
her solo flight across the Atlantic in 1928, her receipt of the
U.S. Distinguished Flying Cross from Vice President
Charles Curtis in 1932, and even some favorable reviews of
her best-selling books.

When her old Uncle Bill passed on in the Winter of
1922, Beatrice benefited from a large inheritance endowed
to her in his will. With that prodigious capital she realized
her dream of attending flight school and dedicated her
burgeoning career as an aviatrix to her uncle's memory. Her
single-mindedness, even obsession, in pursuit of her goals
quickly had her lapping every one of her peers in terms of
both knowledge and ability. All of her instructors
commended her prodigious talents. She could loop the
loop, fly for remarkably long journeys with the patience of
a saint and she broke every speed record set by the male
students attending the academy.

After graduation, Beatrice felt a supreme confidence to
be as bold as her aspirations could take her. She purchased
a spunky monoplane and flew all around the Middle and

~ ~ ~

*No, Old Bill Boroughs was far from the only one. If you
want the full rundown of insanity in the (probably inbred)
Borough family line you'll have to check out the historical
tome, *Bad Times in the Badlands: Deranged Tales of Small
Town Life in Boroughtown, ND.*

**Now residing in the Boroughtown Historical Society
Museum.

Southwest United States- from the badlands to the Rio
Grande, past The Great Lakes to Niagara Falls, over the
Grand Canyon and into the border town of Tijuana- making
a living escorting gaggles of gaping tourists for high pay and
low living. She was legendary- a prodigious drinker and

even more prolific lover of strapping young men across these United States. Wherever she happened to lay her head for the night there was a new adventure and a new beginning. Among the pilots who'd seen her fly in those days, she was considered an aviatrix very nearly the equal of Amelia Earhart herself.

Then in January 1939, as Beatrice was sharing a plate of grits and eggs with a handsome cowboy in an El-Paso diner, she heard word over the radio that Amelia Earhart had disappeared somewhere over the central Pacific Ocean. She started crying uncontrollably. Anyone who'd ever known her could attest to how unusual it was for the resilient young woman to act this way, in public no less. A psychological feeling of great weight had descended on her shoulders, so traumatizing that it prohibited her from flying her plane back home to North Dakota.

Instead she had her love struck cowboy drive her back home across five state lines to Boroughtown. In those days it was expected that a man would go to the ends of the earth to look after his woman. But it was a different time then. Nowadays a woman might consider him a "sexist" or a "chauvinist" just for insinuating that she might need his help. Or even worse, she might reduce the motivation for his affectionate sacrifice to a ravenous ploy for sex. But I digress.

In the vulnerable emotional state she was in on that trip, she finally slowed down enough to take notice of her cowboy's love for what it was- real as bare skin on skin contact and as steady as the rising of the moon and stars. When they returned to Boroughtown, she convalesced in her bed for a month, pouring over all her clippings of Earhart's achievements. Her cowboy waited by her side hand and foot until she was at last psychologically well enough to leave her bedridden cloister. They got married several months later and settled down. During that time they shared a profound love. And as the cowboy stood by her, she acknowledged his commitment while she learned to struggle with her illness. They shared a happy, loving bond for over 40 years, a bond which shone glimmers of radiant light even through the darker times to come.

But as time passed on and hope for Earhart's survival diminished with each passing day, Beatrice swore to never fly an airplane again. In the coming years she drained her small fortune purchasing pieces of airplane wreckage, first from WWI military collections and much later, by bribing state police officials for the remains of local airplane wreckage. She'd monitor a little CB radio mounted on her work desk day and night. As soon as a wreck was reported over the police band, she'd fetch her cowboy to drive her to the site of the wreckage. Sometimes they'd arrive in time to save some survivors and escort them to the hospital. But more often than not all they could do was scavenge the bloody steel remnants of the crash. At first she was appalled by the gruesome sight of the bloody corpses strewn about the crash site but over time even that ceased to faze her. Depleted of almost all her inheritance and desperately requiring some form of revenue, she invested her every last remaining cent in building The Last Call saloon, which she decorated with the voluminous contents of her morbid collection.

By now the original owners and management have long since either died out or reached the age of retirement. The current bartender, Angel, had never personally flown an airplane but she *was* an Air Force brat from a long line of fighter pilots. That gave her some useful experience for the job. Plus there was a distinctive style to her that meshed well with the joint. She wore a patch over one eye to disguise a mutilated eye injured, not during combat, but during a childhood firearm accident. Her neck was adorned with a variety of Native American beads bought from some of the nearby reservations. A nasty looking bowie knife was sheathed at her hip. She looked perfect for her role there. But if it seemed too good to be true, it was. The problem was that Angel wasn't happy where she worked and she didn't even attempt to conceal her anger about working at The Last Call. Aviation was *daddy's thing*, not hers, and she hated the man.

Angel sauntered over to the booth Two-Shanks and Jean had taken in the back. She flipped out a pad and pen. "Hiya Shanks. Hiya Scaputo. What'll it be boys?"

"Whiskey sour for me, love," Two-Shanks answered.

"Same for me, Angel," Jean dug into his pocket and handed her two twenties, "In fact, why don't you just bring us the whole bottle?"

Angel's eyes grew wide as saucers. Forty dollars was downright bourgeois in this shithole she'd been scraping her living in. She grinned, "Sure thing Mr. *Millionaire*." She let the words roll off her tongue with spite, a taunt dripping with malice for Jean and his fortune. But he didn't pay it any mind since she was well known for being a surly cunt to everyone. Not that popular consensus against someone ever meant a damn and it certainly doesn't negate the validity of an opinion. But it can be comforting to remind oneself of negative popular opinion when dismissing an irritating person, for good or ill.

Anyway, Angel snapped back from her rebellious posturing to her function as a worker drone, grabbing a full bottle off the shelf for her two thirsty clients. She stared them in the eyes for some reason as if she was about to issue a challenge. On her way back to the table her hips swayed provocatively from side to side with the various accouterments she wore shaking with each confident step. Angel had swagger, at least you had to give her that. But it was a loose, drunken swagger really.* She very nearly tripped over Roseanna, who'd taken up a spot on the wood floor of the dingy old bar.

"Hey! You no good punks brought a dog into the bar? I almost dove face first over the damn mongrel!" she screamed.

"Whatcha yappin' at us for love? I've seen both a Siberian Husky and another ole grey mutt loungin' round 'ere on the bar floor on right many occasion."

Angel slammed the whiskey down on the table. The fur on Roseanna's back stood up. She growled softly to let Angel know she was ready to defend herself with violence if necessary.

"That's a lot different. *Those* dogs are the *owner's* and they're *bar dogs!*"

"Huh? Maybe you can explain to us paying customers exactly what the difference is between regular dogs and bar dogs!" Jean demanded.

"The difference is that bar dogs know how to move around the floor. They know how to stay out of the damn way so you ain't tripping and causin' accidents all over the fucking place."

Jean implored her to let the dog stay. "Take it easy, will ya Angel? We didn't mean anything by it. Lord knows the dog didn't either. She's had a rough life just like the rest of us here. Why don't cha catch her a break babe?"

To demonstrate that Roseanna could stay out of the way, Jean pulled her up onto the booth's seat by the leash. Roseanna wasn't happy about taking orders in this newly submissive role and turned her ire towards her new master. But Jean understood well enough that he'd have to win her over here or she wouldn't continue obeying him in the future. Fortunately one of the

~ ~ ~

*Angel was never one to let professionalism stand in the way of a good time at work.

previous customers had left a stale tortilla chip sitting

on the table. Jean offered it to her. She barely took a moment to sniff it before gluttonously accepting the rapprochement. After devouring the chip she rested her chin affectionately on Jean's leg and closed her eyes for a nap.

"See there she is restin' loik a babe. Let it slide, Angel. Please?" Two-Shanks pleaded.

Angel sighed, "Alright. Keep her out of my way and she can stay. But don't mess with me. You don't lose an eye like I have without becoming one tough high-strung bitch." She must have thought Shanks had given Jean an incredulous look because she continued, "Don't believe me? Have a look for yourself!" She flipped back her eye patch revealing the scarred crater that remained beneath. While Jean and Shanks were stifling their gag reflexes, Angel grinned menacingly, flipped her eye patch back in place and sauntered back to the bar to clean some dirty glasses.

Two-Shanks whispered, leaning in, "Definitely tough and definitely a bitch, just not necessarily in that order." Despite his troubles Jean managed a chuckle. It sure was a relief to have a good friend sticking by him during these dark times. "There 'e is," Two-Shanks encouraged. *There* was the legitimate glimmer of hope he'd wanted to inspire, "We'll find a way to fix this sitch,* mate."

"Yeah ... sure. So let's get down to business. Tell me what you saw last night."

"Well," Two-Shanks lit up a smoke, "I was strikin' out wit' the fillies at Outlaw's so I called up me ole lady, Maybelline. Oh yeah, we're kindsa seein' each other now mate."

"Congratulations man! Good for you."

"Yeah, thanks. Anyways she drove us up to the mansion. When we got there the gate was wide open, real unusual-like. So we's got out and knocked on tha front door. Before long a woman answers from behind the door, 'Get out! We ain't acceptin' no visitahs!"

"Did she say it exactly like that?"

"Course not, mate. You know I've been livin' in this sinkhole for half me life and I still can't imitate your bloody accents. I'm a cockney lifer, yeah? Anyway, I thought you 'ad a woman ovah so, just jokin', I answered, 'Open up. It's the police!' Must not o' been a bright gal to open tha door for a British sounding cop in North Dakota but thankfully, that she did."

"Was the woman Marissa?"

"No mate. I nevah seen 'er before in me life. She was 'bout five foot six inch tall, blonde 'air, pensive cat's eyes and the noicest pair a tits me ever seen in..."

Jean had to stop him. Shanks had a habit of overdoing it sometimes. "That's enough," Jean poured a shot of whiskey into his glass and swallowed it down, "I know that woman. She's the one who tried to steal my ticket the night I won the lottery. She called herself Jennifer but I doubt she gave me her real name. Ok. So what happened next?"

"Well she said, 'You ain't a cop' because... well, I ain't."

Jean grinned, "What gave it away?"

"For one thing I was a bit too drunk even fer a Boroughtown cop," he laughed, "Then when I asked, 'Where's Jean?' she tried to shut the door in me face. But I moved quick and jammed tha door open with me boot. I looked past 'er and saw three otha' figuhs. Two a them were burly meat sacks I din' recognize (I'm guessin' these was Jerome and Bobby) and the third was yer girl Marissa, only she looked a lot worse for wear than I'd evah seen 'er. She 'ad blood drippin' from 'er lip and a soulless, dead look in 'er eyes. She was 'ittin some kind a pipe and the black one was cuppin' 'er titties. Meanwhiles tha white one was..."

"I get it, believe me. Anything else?"

"Not really, mate. When tha bruisers finally noticed me, I took Maybelline by 'er 'and an' we got the fuck outta there."

Jean didn't know what to make of it. "Jennifer" was in on it too? That woman just wouldn't leave him alone. She'd become like a pit bull lock-jawed onto a bone. Jean was drowning in all this bad news he couldn't do anything about. He got to staring into the labyrinthine pattern of metal in an old Ford Tri-Motor engine on a shelf near the restroom. Those bars, thick and thin, curved in and around one another. Studying those patterns, it mesmerized him. His head went dizzy and his stomach nauseous.

"What's the matter, mate? Too much whiskey?"

"No, not that. I'm just not feeling so good," Jean answered. He slid out of the booth, grasping Roseanna's leash.

"You gonna be alright?"

"Yeah, I think so. Maybe I'll just take Roseanna for a walk outside to clear my head. See ya around."

"Oi," Two-Shanks answered.

Jean pushed open the saloon doors and walked out of the bar. He hadn't gone far before he noticed the unnatural quiet. Strangely, there were no cars driving or people walking in the streets. The itinerant musician's strings and yowls had gone silent. No birds were hopping around the park as they usually did either. Something in the atmosphere was hued and hazy, a mellow orange cloud hung over.

Hanging from the lampposts were banners depicting a sinister looking cowboy, his face obscured by a ten gallon hat tipped down over his eyes, leaning against an oil tower spouting oil. A much wider banner strung between two buildings in the middle of Main Street. It read 'Black Gold Festival'. An incredibly chill northern wind blew, shaking the fabric of these signs and rustling the leaves of the trees.

The wind must have carried the scent of some distant food source because Roseanna cut out in a lightning sprint. She forced Jean to the ground in a collapse so powerful it loosened the leash from his grasp. She went racing off down the street. Jean pushed himself back onto his feet and ran after her but he was so much slower than her and getting winded. She'd gone completely from his sight in a matter of seconds, leaving Jean behind, profusely sweating and gasping for air.

Jean doubled over to catch his breath. He felt like he might vomit. Spittle involuntarily dripped from his mouth onto the pavement. Then, out of the corner of his eye, he caught something flying through the street. He looked up the block towards the intersection. It was a newspaper which blew in his direction until it came to a stop wrapped tight around his ankle. He picked it up with trepidation.

The headline read, "BOROUGHTOWN OUTRAGE". The article below explained, "Citing revenue needs associated with a class action lawsuit and new tests indicating the potential for oil exploration around populated areas of Boroughtown, millionaire Jean Scaputo and his partners Gambini Retail have set large swaths of the town up for demolition." It continued on like that until at the end of the article, "Due to these extenuating circumstances the Black Gold Festival has been canceled until further notice. City officials cited the inappropriateness of celebrating oil exploration at a time when it happens to be placing so many residents in dire straits. Several emergency meetings flared up after a swath of eviction notices were posted throughout the downtown area. Concerned citizens have organized themselves into a brigade, vowing to take their demands directly to Mr. Scaputo, by any means necessary."

Attached to this article was a photograph depicting the outrage at the community meeting. There was an elderly woman seated in the picture with a big globe of permed white hair. Her hands were trying to wipe away the tears streaming down her cheeks. Beside her was a man in his fifties, furious, his buttoned shirt torn open, fist punched against his hairy chest and baring his teeth like a feral ape. The furious man was issuing an anguished call to arms in front of a baying crowd.

Inside the body of the article itself, Jean found a much smaller photograph of the large wooden event stage the town had made for the festival. In the foreground there was a black sign staked into the ground which announced in red letters, 'Canceled'. What really caught Jean's attention was that the stage in the photo looked identical to the lynching platform in his nightmare of The Great Ulysses.

Jean's pulse quickened. The all-too-familiar paranoia began to thicken. The degree of his troubles had seemingly mounted so far that they'd breached the clouds of reality themselves into the realms of the absurd. How so many things could have gone wrong was beyond rational comprehension. It defied logical sense. With the phantom lynching platform located merely across the square from where he now stood, it was clear that he'd literally stepped right into his own worst nightmare.

Right then and there Jean came to a critical decision. He resolved to face his existential fiction head on, no matter what terrors might await. There's only so much punishment anyone can take before they either lie down to die or try removing the straight razor of injustice from against their throat. He steered himself, though filled with fear, near the cul-de-sac across the street where the stage had been erected. Jean inspected all directions of the eerily deserted square, certain that the ominous silence belied a looming danger ready to pounce from some street corner. When he reached the other side, he spied the lynching platform lying at the dead end of the street. A hanging rope was the only ingredient to completely transform it into a death machine.

As Jean stared in disbelief at his ultimate terror, an ominous hum filled the air. It was a hum very much like the approach of a distant swarm of locusts. He whirled around to see what it could be. Approaching in the distance, up Tulliver Street, were all the missing townspeople. They'd congregated into a violent mob. *A lynchmob?* he worried. There were so many of them, crammed shoulder to shoulder in five or six rows, stretching from sidewalk to sidewalk. The Furious Man was on the job. He spotted Jean straight away and pointed him out to the mob. The mob stirred about like a nest of angry hornets; fists shook, people shouted strings of angry invectives. "For what you've done *you'll hurt!*", "Traitor!", "Get that little jerk!" Everyone was yelling so loud and gnashing their teeth. The speed of the mob picked up to a steady march for justice, quickened by communal hatred and bloodlust.

Jean tried making flight up Tulane Boulevard but another type of mob barred his escape: thirteen Mafiosos, looking for a scrape. *This fucking sucks*, Jean thought. In their fists were weapons like baseball bats, Molotov cocktails and brass knucks. Jean noticed how much closer they were to him than the Boroughtown citizen brigade. But the Mafiosos hadn't made a straight line to the square. The Mafiosos stopped to wreck everything in their path. One picked up a metal trashcan, smashed it through a retail store window. Another lit a napalm-drenched Molotov cocktail and threw it into the building. One gangster ferreted out a screaming man hiding inside an appliance repair center, shook him for all the cash in his wallet, broke his nose with a baseball bat.

With two opposing threats approaching from Tulliver and Tulane, Jean turned towards the only path of egress that remained: Eucalyptus Avenue. Eucalyptus led to the town's small factory district. He could hide in one of the old buildings abandoned during the recession. But before he could even cross the intersection, he heard an ominous clacking of hooves echoing from that direction. It stopped him in his tracks, paralyzed him with fear.

Jean squinted because the sun shone in his eyes. He was just able to make out the surprising scene beyond the glare: A massive, muscular white steed galloped up Eucalyptus, the rider that imposing figure of Ulysses himself. Ulysses' brilliant locks of white hair flowed behind his head. Venom dripped dread from his beard of snakes. Tempestuous hellfire flared from his eyes. As his steed charged forward, rivulets of blood fell from the sky. Clenched in his mighty fist were links of long, metal chain. Chains fastened to cage-locked facemasks of masochistic penitents, dragged behind in procession. Stunningly these ragged, pitiable men were furiously flagellating themselves with stinging whip cracks. Crimson tears of blood streamed from self-inflicted gashes on their backs. Jean was confused, *Now he's got white liberals too? We're all doomed!*

Next, followed Ulysses' hordes of monsters, a sinister, rhythmic chant surged from their order. The chant, some kind of ancient Latin verse, burst from inhuman lungs of Lotus Eaters and Laestrygonians alike like a curse, "Exsurge .... Domine ... Fortunae,*" ad infinitum. Upon inspection, the cyclopean Laestrygonians instilled fear by sheer size alone. Massive footsteps shook the earth with force to shatter stone. A horde of hag-like Lotus Eaters: stringy-haired and hunchbacked, sharpened their bladed talons for attack. Sparks flew; their talons grew as sharp as knives. The Lotus Eaters leered at Jean with savagely determined eyes.

All three groups descended simultaneously upon poor Jean, cornering him hopelessly against the death machine. Backed against its wall, he had nowhere to go but up. So he backpedaled up steps cautiously, one by one, anxious eyes kept on all the action at once. Any one of the mobs could have torn him limb from limb. Why didn't they all just begin? It seems he had one saving grace. They embraced a mutual hate; an enmity towards each other as much as towards Jean. So they leered mean at the base in a Mexican standoff, each afraid to pay that first bloody cost.

* It means something like 'Arise, O Lord of Fortunes'.

Finally, at Ulysses' behest, several Lotus Eaters shambled forward, coalesced inside the Boroughtown crowd. Glimmering, otherworldly spores secreted from bulbous sacs along their rough skins. The "good people" of Boroughtown froze in their tracks like mannequins. Was this the work of the spores entirely? Or perhaps those folks were completely paralyzed with anxiety. In either case it was a monstrously terrifying sight to behold. A notably ugly Lotus Eater unfolded its fist, revealing a small, delicate flower. With sinister glower, it pinched the petals of that flower between the tips of its talons and fed it into the gaping mouth of Furious Man. The rioter looked doped, a fattened calf. A Laestrygonian picked up the dazed man. Then, I swear this is all true, the beast bit into Furious Man's head like it was a leg of lamb!

The mobsters, who had not been sedated by the spores, were watching all these events with pure horror. One of the skinny ones, panicking, smashed a Molotov cocktail against the feasting creature's frame. The Laestrygonian burst into flames. Its pained screams were so horrid that windows around the block shattered to pieces. This violent event was the catalyst that finally sent the whole scene careening into savage melee. With its talon, a Lotus Eater quickly gouged the skinny Mafioso through his right eyeball, straight to the back of his skull. His allies rushed in for vengeance, beating the Lotus Eater to death with their bats.

"An unreal thing ... a real thing ... the trick is, uh ..." Jean tried to steady his mind long enough to recall Anju's maxim.

Ulysses dismounted his steed and walked unperturbed through the violent maelstrom. His masked penitents kneeled to the ground until they turned into three beautiful women: a redhead, a blonde and a brunette. They stared right at Jean. He recognized them as Marissa, Barbara, and his kind benefactress from the park. Mitch was there too, exhaling plumes of smoke from his nose. His facial features were contorted into those of a dragon. It seemed almost everyone had come to send him off into the great beyond. Ulysses deliberately ascended each step of the lynching platform. The three women stood up. The fabric of reality seemed to glitch a moment and their features changed to static expressions of terror.

"The trick is, uh ... the trick is to believe neither the real nor unreal can hurt us." Ulysses clenched his fingers around Jean's throat, squeezed and lifted him off the ground. With his free hand, Ulysses reached out an outstretched palm. A length of chain flew through the air into his hand. WHOOSH! He slung it around a post and looped it into a noose. "He doesn't have the power to hurt me."

Ulysses fitted Jean's neck into the noose. As Ulysses released him into its cold, steel grip Jean closed his eyes, exhaled and tried to clear his mind. He focused it with renewed concentration on removing the metaphorical razor from his throat. He had time for one last try, this time with a germ of the good stuff: *true belief*.

"He doesn't have the power to hurt me."

~ ~ ~

Jean landed on his knees. They stung with pain from the impact of the fall. Yet the pain let him know that he was still alive. It produced the most joyful feeling he'd ever known. He looked up. The length of chain had disappeared. Oh, the elation! Beyond the stage everyone had stopped in their tracks, motionless and calm. Not on account of any narcotic spores though, no, because even the Lotus Eaters remained perfectly still. Jean looked to Ulysses. He was staring back, contentedly, like some New Age mystic. The fire in his eyes had simmered, his muscles were completely relaxed and the warrior's hostility vanished. He was still "Great" to behold in size and strength, yet all around much less fearsome.

"Um, hello? Ulysses, can you hear me?"

"I can," Ulysses answered. His booming voice contained a surreal vibrato, like a leaf blower forming words inside a well.

Jean got back up on his feet. "Can you tell me what's happening?"

"You have ceased our impetus for attack."

"Me? How's that exactly?"

"We await your command, of course."

"Oh, riiiight," it took a moment to click, "Right! You have the power that I allow you. Something like that?"

"More or less."

Jean found it funny to hear the dread Ulysses talking so colloquially (so much like himself). "Will you ever attack me again? Like maybe I lose confidence in my ability to control you one day..."

Ulysses took a step forward, "If you allow it."

Jean held up his hand to stop him, "No! That won't be necessary."

Ulysses halted, "As you wish."

Jean studied him in silence a moment, the hunted to the hunter, "So, uh, what are you exactly?"

"Maybe you'd better find a therapist to answer that question."

Jean found himself surprisingly indignant about Ulysses' response, "Don't talk back to me. You await *my* command, remember?"

"Yes. It's true."

"Besides, I don't want to see a shrink ... Just give it your best guess."

"Alright," Ulysses pondered, stroking his snake beard. "I guess I'd call myself an embodiment of your fear. Even though you'd of had a fucked up life anyway, I'd still claim responsibility for kicking your ass a good, solid thirty-five percent of the time anything has gone wrong."

"Does that mean the second I feel any intense fear you're going to come right back after me?"

"Not necessarily. Everybody has fear, pessimism and self-doubt in their lives. Yours has snowballed so much that you've anthropomorphized it into being and imbued it with the faculties of a god. That takes some serious neuroses."

"That, that actually makes a lot of sense. Maybe I should ease up on myself a bit."

"Does it? It was just a *guess* after all."

Jean smiled, "Well it was pretty astute. I think you may have missed your calling as a psychologist, Ulysses."

"I was *this* close to just diagnosing you with schizophrenia, but what do I know."

In an instant, everyone vanished: Ulysses, the Laestrygonians, the Lotus Eaters, the Mafia and the entire, riotous populace of Boroughtown. Jean stood there, peacefully listening to the wind howling down the cement canyons of the deserted town. Then that vanished too.

He woke up in the boxcar, with Roseanna curled up beside him, and smiled.

"**P**ull!" Bobby's voice echoed down the valley. Jerome flung a porcelain dinner plate like a discus over the railing into the sky behind Borough mansion. BAM! A rifle shot rang out, smashing its target into hundreds of pieces. The fragments rained down like snowflakes onto the valley floor. A strong wind carried a flurry of the smaller pieces back onto the porch.

Jerome covered himself from the debris by ducking his head into his hands. "Hey! Motherfucker! Try shooting it once it gets *away* from the damn house!"

"Try throwing it farther you stinkin' pussy!"

Jerome reared back like he was going to punch Bobby in the face but Bobby didn't flinch. He was the one with the gun after all.

"Whatever, man."

Jerome fished another fine china dinner plate out of the cardboard box resting next to his feet. "Watch this motherfucker." This time he backed up, got a running start and twirled himself around 360 degrees before hurling the plate across the valley with all his might. The china flew so high into the air Bobby had time to wait until it started to fall.

"Go on. Shoot it!" Jerome yelled.

"Who the fuck do you think you are man? Hercules?" Bobby raised the firearm to eye level and fired. BAM! The plate exploded on impact. "You going all out like we at the Olympics or some shit."

"Damn!" Jerome exclaimed, "How you always hit it like that?"

"I never told you, bro? I was the skeet shooting champion of the Army Rangers Kandahar Division in '07 ... *and* '08."

"You lyin' mane."

"Nah bruh. I swear on my mother's life."

"For real? Damn. Let me take a shot at this shit." Jerome wrestled the gun out of Bobby's grip. He released it with some reluctance.

"Aight if you think you're up for it man. But I'm tellin' ya, it ain't gonna be no cake walk like that."

"Whatever," Jerome loaded and cocked the rifle, "Throw it."

"Pull," Bobby insisted.

"What?!"

"Weren't you paying attention at all, J-Money? When you want the disc in the air you yell, 'Pull', okay?"

"Sure, whatever ... Pull!"

Bobby flung the fine china over the railing just like it was the clay used in formal skeet shooting. Jerome aimed and fired. The shot rang out over the valley, rustling some birds nested in the branches of a Black Walnut tree... but the shot went wide. The fine porcelain fell to the ground and smashed onto a bed of rocks.

Unbeknownst to either Bobby or Jerome this dinnerware, which they'd raided from a collection in the dining room, originated from the private collection of the Chinese Emperor Wanli. Emperor Wanli reigned for 48 years during the Ming Dynasty, far longer than any other emperor during that period. The dinnerware they were destroying was the very definition of priceless antiquity.

"Damn! I missed that piece of shit."

"Haha! Not so easy is it?" Bobby gloated.

"Just give me another. I'll get it."

Viola Davis watched them through the sliding glass door from inside the house. She slammed a highball down her gullet. *The mind numbing stupidity of these men!* Truthfully she hated her new business partners. *At least the dwarf was reasonably good in bed,* she thought. *Maybe I should have just done a long-term seduction- marriage without prenup followed by a quickie divorce. Damn that would have been so much easier.*

Viola, known throughout the shadier circles of Boroughtown by her nom de guerre "Jennifer", cursed herself for taking the more difficult route. She'd been caught in the act by her mark, a dwarf, who'd managed to wrestle the fortune literally right out of her hands. *Oh the humiliation!* But she wasn't a quitter. No, not her. She was her father's daughter through and through. That is to say a stubborn bitch who would never, *ever* quit until she got what she wanted.

So when she found these two lummoxes at Outlaw's and they explained how they had the dwarf's woman wrapped around their fingers, she knew it was time to pony up for round two. In fact, it was shocking to her that they hadn't already put a plan in motion themselves. It seemed that she'd have to do *all* the thinking herself ...

There they were sitting at opposite end of the bar from her. It was her classic setup but she didn't see much potential in them as marks. Therefore, they weren't worth her time. But they were so loud she couldn't help but listen in anyway. She knew better than to turn her nose up at free information.

"We was just driving along and this chickenhead says, "Pull over. I need some dick or I'm gonna *die.*"

Sounds like a lie, she thought.

"So we spit roasted the ho," Jerome guffawed, spitting out a swallow of his beer in the process.

Viola was disgusted, "Aren't you two proud of yourselves? How much more romantic can it get than taking advantage of a lonely crackhead?"

"Just who da fuck do you think *you* are?"

Viola had been content over at the opposite end of the bar, as per usual, sipping her favorite margarita. But these buffoons made her lose her cool; rookie mistake. Nothing disgusted her more than men who took advantage of women. Of course, it didn't happen to bother her that her game was pretty similar. She didn't have *quite* that degree of self-consciousness.

"Don't worry about me. Low class thugs have got nothing that would interest me."

The bartender started to get nervous about the vitriol stirring up, "HEY! Why don't you all calm the fuck down?"

"Shut up!" Bobby, Jerome and Viola yelled at him in unison. At least they'd managed to agree on something.

"Sure. *Whatever.* I just work here. Tear each other to pieces for all I care," the bartender threw his rag on the bar in disgust and walked away.

"Listen bitch. You think *we're* low class? Then how come we got Mr. Millionaire's crush waitin' on our beck and call? She wouldn't even give that midget a taste."

"Fucking loser."

"Yeah we got more class than a millionaire."

In the world Bobby and Jerome come from "class" meant nothing more than a simple formula: how much money you had at a given time plus how much power you could exert over those around you. That philosophy wasn't totally alien to Viola either. In fact, she never made pretensions she thought the sentiment was vulgar. She simply actualized the philosophy *better* and *smarter*. The profit angle was paramount to her game. And it clicked in Viola's head almost immediately.

"Wait. Maybe I had you boys all wrong."

"Damn straight."

Viola scooted over to the stool beside them, "So you boys are dealing drugs to the dwarf's woman?"

"She ain't never been the dwarf's woman. He just fell in love with her."

"Fucking dumbass."

"So the feeling wasn't mutual?"

"Hell naw. She was holding out for a real man," Bobby jabbed Jerome in the gut.

"So it was an unrequited love. Interesting. Very interesting."

There it was: the profit angle. The dwarf was in love. Men in love are always blind to a woman's shortcomings ... just long enough to fleece them anyway. She'd exploited this very weakness on many occasions. The whens, wheres and hows started to thread into a magnificent tapestry in her mind. She spelled out the plan in terms so simple even these idiots would understand: convince Marissa to romance the dwarf, get him to drop his guard and then steal every red cent he owns.

Now here she was in the mark's illustrious mountain mansion. So she didn't have the money. It would come. In retrospect things had gone about as well as they possibly could given the information she had at the time. The bank had been the only foil. How could Viola have known about their safeguard policy? If they'd given her access, for even a moment, she'd have emptied the entire account and fled to Cuba. She'd be dirty dancing with lusty Latin men and sipping cold beverages by the beach until the heat blew over. To hell with the house, she could buy another anywhere in the world.

Jerome and Bobby had begged her to let them kill the dwarf but she held her ground just like daddy taught her. She knew that there was a world of difference between facing a murder conspiracy rap and leaving him alive. Alive there was plausible deniability. It could've all been a "disagreement over a financial transaction".

Viola stepped out onto the porch. Jerome still hadn't

managed to shoot one of the dinner plates. "God damn it. Throw it slower, mane!" he exclaimed with frustration.

"There is no 'throwing it slower'. Ain't you heard of gravity, mofo?" Bobby retorted.

"What? You can't even hit one little old plate, Jerome?" Viola jibed him. She looked into the cardboard box filled with dinnerware, "My God. Do you halfwits even know what you're shooting at?" She rubbed the bridge of her nose. "You know what? Fuck it. Hand me the gun."

Jerome reluctantly handed the rifle over, "Shit, this is gonna be good." He looked over at Bobby with nervous laughter. But Bobby wasn't laughing. He respected... better yet, feared this woman. That's what kept her safe from them.

Viola's father, a Texas cattle rancher, had taught her all about how to handle a rifle. He used to kill time by throwing old tin cans into the air for her to shoot as target practice. Viola steadied the weapon against her shoulder, "Pull!" she shouted. Bobby hesitated. "I said PULL!" Bobby reached down, grabbed a plate and hurled it high over the valley. BAM! Viola's bullet struck the corner of the plate, smashing one half while leaving the other intact.

"Ha!" Jerome yelped.

Viola reloaded with the coiled reflexes of a rattlesnake and fired again. Her second bullet hit the remaining piece, shattering it into little bits of porcelain.

"Damn," Jerome concluded.

There was movement inside. Out of the corner of her eye, Viola noticed Marissa shambling down the stairs like a half-dead zombie. Her balance was off. It looked like her knees might buckle and she'd go tumbling face first down the stairs. Viola shoved the rifle into Jerome's gut and ran back inside. She held out her arms to embrace Marissa. There were black circles under her eyes. Her skin was white as a ghost.

"Help me, Jennifer. I made a big mistake. Tell him I'm sorry."

Marissa had been apologizing to a phantom over the last two weeks. Sometimes, in a fever, she'd mention him by name, "Jean... Jean. It wasn't my idea. You've got to believe me, Jean."

Viola thought she sounded positively haunted. "It's okay, honey. I've got you. I'm going to take care of you now," Viola soothed Marissa, laying her down comfortably on one of the couches. She'd been in bad shape ever since Jerome and Bobby had run out of crack rock. She was addicted to it. Once the withdrawals started, Marissa started giving in to hysterics: screaming out throughout the night, threatening to leave the mansion in search of a fix and clawing her nails at anyone who dared stand in her way. The Bash Brothers had run out of their own supply a week ago. Without the fortune in hand, they'd simply refused to spend any of their own money to resupply.

The cheap bastards are jeopardizing the score, Viola thought.

"Please, Jennifer. I need a shot or I'm going to die," Marissa begged.

Yes, that's right ... a shot. Of heroin. Without Viola's knowledge Bobby had begun shooting Marissa up with his remaining supply. The "logic" behind it was that he still had heroin in supply. He could shoot her up with it for now and avoid spending money on crack until the trial was over. It was an effective way of keeping Marissa high and under control. Now the poor girl longed for that too.

Marissa wrapped her frail arms around Viola's neck. Viola tore them away and stormed back out onto the porch. The Bash Brothers were taking a break between rounds of skeet shooting to chug shots of whiskey straight out of the bottle. *No, that isn't dangerous at all*, Viola thought, *These great, big bull males always think they're going to live*

139

forever.

"Your girl in there is fiending again."

"So fucking what?" Bobby retorted.

"So fucking what? So fucking what?! We have a court trial in a couple of days is what. We can't have our *meal ticket* dope sick and half-mental from withdrawal is what."

"Oh," Bobby grunted. He reached into his pocket, procuring a thin syringe case and a small white bag of dope. Viola snatched them up.

After a short stop in the kitchen, Viola returned to Marissa's side and cooked up the drug on a metal spoon. Pumping it up into the barrel of the syringe brought to mind a memory of her beloved father. What a strange life she'd led ...

It was back on the ranch in her youth. Little Viola had a favorite calf she'd named Lilly. She'd raised and doted on it from the moment she'd watched it pop out of her mother, covered in amniotic fluid. But during one of the cattle drives, Lilly wandered off. She was nowhere to be seen when the rest of the herd was rounded back into their pen at night.

Little Viola cried and cried until daddy could stand no more. He pulled her up onto a horse alongside him and they rode off together in search of the prodigal calf. The search was long. Night fell. The temperature grew cold and hostile. Daddy had to wrap her in a protective shawl for warmth. But she refused to give up and so did daddy. He would have done anything for his daughter. It took hours, into the misty twilight under threatening storm clouds, but they finally found the calf. She'd wandered onto an adjacent neighbor's property and gotten her leg caught in a coyote trap. She was baying and crying while blood dripped down her leg onto the desert sand. Viola ran up and threw her arms around the calf while her father worked to release it from the trap.

"It's going to be alright, girl," she tried to sooth it. The calf's big, dumb eyes just stared at her with such fear and melancholy.

Father led the calf over to their horse, using the opportunity to inspect the severity of limp in her gait. Father reached into his saddlebag for a syringe, filled it with veterinary grade tranquilizer and injected it into the animal's hide. Lilly began to grow tired. She laid down to rest in the dirt.

"See, girl? We're going to make it all better," Viola told the calf.

Father was strong. Whenever he had something to say, he said it without hesitation. But yet he hesitated here, "Viola, honey ... Lilly's not going to be able to make it home. She's too injured. I'm going to do something ... something I have to do ... something I wish you didn't have to see."

'What do you mean?" Viola asked.

"I'm going to have to put her down, baby."

Viola began to cry. "No, daddy! Don't do it! Just give her some more medicine!"

"She would live the rest of her life in pain. We have to put her down as an act of mercy. To keep her alive, on a cocktail of drugs, would be no life at all." Viola latched onto her father's leg in an attempt to stop him from carrying it out. But she was just a little thing compared to her big, strong father. He dragged her along to the horse, where he retrieved a pistol from within his satchel. "Baby, please try to understand."

"Never!" she screamed.

Father shook his head remorsefully. "I'm sorry, Viola. Please forgive me." He cocked the pistol, pulled the trigger and buried a bullet into Lilly's skull, killing her instantly.

They rode home that night in an uncomfortable silence that had never existed between them before. Of course, Viola *did* eventually get over it and had long ago forgiven her father. But something about the incident had left a scar in her mind that never quite healed. Viola shook the memory from her mind and shot the syringe full of heroin into a vein in Marissa's arm. Just because she'd gotten over the way Lilly died didn't mean she'd taken daddy's advice from that night to heart. *What would he think if he could see me now? He wouldn't like it, that's for sure.*

Viola sat down on the carpet and eased her back against the base of the couch. She allowed herself a moment to breathe a sigh of relief. Maybe now she could finally relax. BLAM! Fat chance of that it seemed. Another shot rang out. Viola turned to check it out. Jerome had finally managed to hit a plate but hit it when plate was still overhead. Bobby didn't have time to look away. The pieces rained down with terminal velocity into his face.

"Aaagh!" he screamed out in agony. A jagged shard of porcelain had lodged into his left eye. Bobby withdrew into an animalistic panic. In a fit of blind rage, he rushed forward and clotheslined Jerome over the balcony.

"Fuuuuck!" Jerome's voice trailed off into something like a Wilhelm Scream. He landed with a sickening crash and thundering snap of bone.

Viola ran back outside, past a whimpering Bobby, to gaze out over the railing. Jerome was crumpled into a bloody heap in the valley below. Several of his teeth were knocked out. His right leg was twisted in an unnatural position with a bone sticking out just below the kneecap. He looked awful, but at least he was still alive.

"Heeelp meeee," Jerome gasped with strain through injured lungs.

"Fuck me." Viola was exasperated. She turned to Bobby who was going to be no help. He was hyperventilating. "Now listen, Bobby. I know you're not going to like this but I've got to pry that shard out of you before things will get any better."

"Mmm-hmm," Bobby whimpered.

Viola tore a piece of fabric from her dress. She stuffed it into the palm of his hand.

"When I count to three I'm going to pull it out. I need you to do something for me. You've got to clot the bleeding with this cloth immediately afterwards or you're going to bleed to death." Bobby nodded. He knew this already from his military training. Viola hovered her hand just above the shard.

"One..." with the other hand she handed him the bottle of Jack Daniels, "Two..." Bobby guzzled so much that he had to gasp for air, "...Three!" Bobby dropped the bottle. Viola gripped the porcelain shard and tore it out of Bobby's eye.

"Fuuuuck!!!" he screamed, flailing about like a madman.

"Put the cloth into your eye socket!" she reminded him. Crimson blood was flowing into pools on the wooden porch. He was too frenzied to understand. Viola picked up the glass bottle of Jim Beam and smashed it over his head. Bobby dropped like a sack of iron. She extracted the cloth from the palm of his hand and plugged it into the eye socket for him. The bleeding mostly stopped. She looked back over the railing. Jerome had somehow crawled to his feet and begun limping back up the hill towards the porch.

Great. Now I've got to help a cripple with a broken leg and internal bleeding. She hadn't even had time to find and prep a decent lawyer for the trial. There was no time for this! *What the fuck is happening?* she wondered. "What did I do to deserve all this BAD LUCK?!" she screamed at the top of her lungs. A strong, cold northerly breeze blew down from The Great White North. The irony of her words escaped her as if they were blown away by the wind itself.

20

In the days leading up to Jean's civil trial, the Boroughtown Standard published a series of articles smearing him in every way known to man (while inventing some new ones for good measure). Meanwhile these same columns were unabashedly rooting for the convicted felons who'd stolen his home and fortune.

For instance, "Psychologist Mary Albright speculates that Jean Scaputo's actions are overcompensation for his diminutive height. And let us not forget that even his parents disowned him. What bitterness he must feel for the human race. What kind of love could a man like that have for his community?"

And another for good measure, "Truthfully, most Boroughtown residents haven't got much love for the defendants either. When you get right down to it Jerome Ridland and Robert Lampe Jr. are both felons with a nasty history of assault, possession of amphetamines with intent to distribute and petty theft. They're the kind of men we don't want to think about living in the same community with our beloved family members. Although to his credit, Robert Lampe Jr. is a veteran of the United States Armed Forces. To make matters even seamier, their entourage includes an ever-present blonde named Viola Davis a.k.a. Jennifer Anastasia, a woman convicted on numerous counts of fraud and theft.

Despite all this, many residents say they view these individuals as their champions, the lesser of two evils, compared to the greedy misanthropy of nouveau riche millionaire Jean Scaputo, a man leaving generations of residents homeless for the first time in their lives."

When the morning of the trial finally came, Anju arrived at 7 a.m. sharp to the Royal Sunset Hotel on the outskirts of town. Jean had sprung for a hotel room the night prior in order to sanitize himself like any citizen in good standing with the judiciary would. His regimen included a thorough shave, brushing of the teeth, wiping his ass after every shit, and eating three square meals (delivered by room service). He capped it all off with a proper haircut in the lobby's barbershop while perusing the propagan ... sorry, I mean to say "news", in the national papers. In the morning he dressed himself in a snazzy suit and tie outfit recommended by his attorney.

Anju met him out front. "Greetings, Jean Genie. You look like a new man." He opened the passenger side door.

"Dressing sharp and feeling dull, brother. But mark my words: I'm going to win this thing." During the ride over he continually fidgeted with his tie. It felt strange having something purposely wrapped around his neck. When they arrived at the courthouse, Mitch met him out front with a briefcase tucked under his arm.

"Tell me we're going to win this thing, Mitch."

"We'll see."

"We'll see? That doesn't exactly inspire me with confidence."

"What can I say? They have signed documentary evidence. Our case hinges entirely on the credibility of their character. Plus, I'm assuming they've hired legal representation PR work on their image, just like I've done with you. We'll just have to see." At that moment, a luxurious stretch limousine pulled to the curb in front of the courthouse.

"Speak of the devil." A chauffeur walked around to open the door. Mitch and Jean couldn't believe their eyes.

Mitch grinned just a little in the corners of his mouth,

"So far so good. I'll see you inside."

When the defendants walked into the courtroom there were gasps from the peanut gallery. Bobby had so much gauze and bandage wrapping around his head and eyeball he looked like a living mummy. He moaned like one too. Jerome limped into the building on crutches, with a thick plaster cast on his right leg. There were unsightly bruises along his neck and arms. There was something odd about the appearance of Jerome's teeth too. They looked plastic, like dentures grandma used to wear in the seventies. And finally, there was Viola Davis (Jean had only recently learned her real name through the Boroughtown Standard). By all accounts, she wasn't banged up like her co-conspirators but she looked stressed, anxious and sleep deprived.

The judge, an elderly black man with graying hair, shuffled into the chamber. He was hunched over, facing down onto the tops of his shoes. His neck did not move more than a couple centimeters in any direction, suggesting a severe arthritic condition. Everyone in the room stood to pay their respects. "The honorable Judge Bryce Howard presiding," a stone faced policeman announced. The judge took his seat and everyone else followed suit.

The old judge took a moment to observe the folks in attendance. When he saw the defendants, his lazy eyes grew large as quarters. "Are the defendants sure they wouldn't like to postpone this trial to a later date?"

Their attorney stepped forward. "That won't be necessary, your honor. We're prepared to have our case heard today."

He was a slick Bismark-based attorney. Jean recognized him from a series of commercials aired during the local news: Mark Harrison. The man was never seen without his signature look: pomade slicked hair, wearing a yellow and purple polka dot tie. A typical Mark Harrison commercial started out in black and white. There'd be a woman driving during rush hour traffic in downtown Bismark. She's applying lipstick with the aid of a vanity mirror. Distracted, she rear ends a Cadillac. She gulps hard, accidentally swallowing the lipstick right out of its tube. From her passenger side window we can see the Cadillac veering off, smashing through the guardrail and rolling down into a ravine.

"I'm ruined!" the driver laments, burying her head in her hands.

Just when all seems lost, there'd be a knock at her door. Standing beside her is Mark Harrison, smiling like the Cheshire Cat. She rolls down her window.

"No, you're rich!" (That was his catchphrase.)

Cut to a black background. Mark Harrison steps into frame. 'We'll get you *YOUR* money, whether you deserve it or not." He points dramatically to the camera. Fade out. *This* was the attorney they'd hired.

Judge Howard set a pair of reading glass onto the crook of his nose and read from a pile of papers on his desk. 'Let's cut to the chase folks. We've all been subjected to the media circus surrounding this case. It boils down to your clients," he pointed to Mark Harrison, "claiming Mr. Scaputo has signed over his fortune in exchange for an agreement to marriage."

"That's right, your honor," Harrison interjected, "We have documentation signed by Mr. Scaputo."

The judge motioned Harrison forward and read over the slip of paper Jean had been forced to sign. "How do you counter this evidence, Mr. Schroderberg?"

Mitch stepped forward. "We contest the validity of this agreement based on the fact that my client signed it under threat of physical violence."

"Do you have any evidence to support this claim?"

Mitch offered him a dossier of photographs

documenting Jean's injuries as well as reports from a thorough physical examination, "Here is a detailed description of all of my client's injuries sustained on the night of the burglary."

"Objection, your honor! My clients have not been convicted of any crime."

"Objection sustained. Mr. Schroderberg, you will abstain from making any unsubstantiated claims of criminal misconduct."

"Sorry, your honor. Here is the police report from the night of the "alleged" burglary," Schroderberg handed the evidence over to the bailiff.

"This does raise some interesting questions. Why did your client decline to press charges in the matter?"

"Judge, Mr. Scaputo feared violent reprisal for undertaking legal action. Robert Lampe has threatened my client's safety on several occasions."

"These are very serious accusations. How do you respond, Mr. Harrison?"

"I'd like to remind the court of the very, very serious doubts surrounding Jean Scaputo's credibility," Harrison answered. Mitch was taken aback by this stratagem. Harrison had decided to undercut Jean's own best argument by using it first, "The Boroughtown Standard has done a marvelous job reporting the ignominy of Jean Scaputo. It is virtually beyond dispute that he is an antisocial lout who has turned his back on the traditional family values honored in this community. Jean Scaputo is a voyeur, frequenting the town's pornographic theatre. He is a drunkard cited numerous times for public intoxication, a rabble rouser charged with disturbing the peace and a misanthrope whose name is absent from the rolls of *any* of the fine Boroughtown churches."

"Objection, your honor," Mitch cut in, "My client's religious affiliation is not germane to these proceedings, nor an acceptable basis for discrimination according to the United States Constitution."

"Objection sustained. You will refrain from any further insinuations about Mr. Scaputo's beliefs or lack thereof."

"Apologies, your honor. I just thought you'd appreciate the value of religious belief to personal character, since you've personally been an upstanding church deacon for over thirty years." Harrison winked at the old judge. The judge stared at him stoically.

"And what lengths have your own clients gone to show their religious piety?" Judge Howard asked.

"Ahem. The character of my clients is not under assail."

"Ahhh. Would you like a rebuttal, Mr. Schroderberg?"

It was the perfect volley. Mitch practically leaped from his seat to pass the next round of documents to the bailiff. "On the contrary, assailing your clients' credibility is my primary purpose." The bailiff dropped the stack in front of the old, black judge. "No doubt you're already aware of the defendants' extensive criminal records, which have been thoroughly listed in the press. I just want to illustrate these crimes a little better."

Mitch motioned to a paralegal who'd been waiting in the back for Mitch's signal. The paralegal rolled forward a projector while Mitch carried forward a white screen. The bailiff dimmed the lights a little. The projector flashed its first image onto the screen. It was a gruesome photograph of a man's injuries. He looked terrified. There were black and blue bruises all along his face. He had a broken nose, twisted to one side. Several of his teeth were missing, although unclear whether due to violence or long term drug use. The remaining teeth were rotted off, black stumps or malformed and yellow.

"This is Lee Wayne Fitzgerald. He was a regular customer of Jerome Ridland and Robert Lampe Jr.'s methamphetamine business in Truth or Consequences,

New Mexico. These two "hustlas" put this man in ICU for a month after he smoked some crystal meth he'd been contracted to sell for them. Half that month he was in a coma. Doctors weren't sure he'd ever wake up. This is legally substantiated by guilty verdicts: aggravated assault, possession with intent to distribute; you can see these verdicts documented right before you in the police reports.

The paralegal switched to the next slide. It was a side-by-side comparison of a shirtless Lee Wayne Fitzgerald before and after his methamphetamine addiction. He'd lost about seventy pounds between subsequent times the photos were taken. Emaciated wouldn't even begin to describe it. Lee Wayne looked like a Holocaust survivor. The judge tried to turn away in disgust but was unable to on account of his arthritis, "God bless it!" he cried out.

"And one more for good measure," Mitch pushed forward.

The next slide was of a young woman no older than fifteen years old. She was in a shipping container filled with many other ragged and desperate looking young women. "This is a photograph of Lee Wayne's daughter, Priscilla. It was taken immediately after she was recovered by authorities, along with other sex slaves, hidden inside a shipping container in Cambodia. While her father was in his hospital bed, unable to make payment to Robert and Jerome, he let some of his buddies use her for spare cash. One thing led to the next..."

Another slide: a headshot of Priscilla Fitzgerald, same angle as the one of her father. Like him, her teeth were rotten and mangled. Two generations destroyed by the same disease. "Priscilla was used and abused. I can only imagine the trauma she had to endure. When she came to Robert and Jerome for help, instead of bringing her someplace where she could receive counseling for sexual assault, they saw in her just one more eager customer. This photograph is from just one year after she started using these "hustlas" crystal. A year after that she ended up sold down the river. The ones that sold her have never been caught." Mitch looked Jerome square in the eye. Jerome looked down at the floor.

"Now, lest we forget their pretty, young accomplice, Jennif ... er, excuse me (Viola Davis is it?). I direct your attention to her own less-than-illustrious past as an accomplished fraudster."

Viola's glance shot him daggers. "Yes, she's conned quite a few people in her day. But there's one mark that's just heads and above all the others, wouldn't you agree, Viola?" The next slide was the mugshot of a Latino man with a thin moustache. "This is Felipe Calderone. He was a ranch hand on a ranch co-owned by Viola's father, Johnson Davis and another man, Samuels Jefferson. Viola and Felipe became lovers in the summer of 2007. Together they hatched quite the plot. Viola seduced Jefferson and convinced him to liquidate many of his most valuable assets, included his stake in the ranch. He invested the proceeds into a shell company run by Felipe's cousins in Mexico."

The projector whirred, shifting to the next slide. It was of a frail, old man seated in a wheelchair. He had a bushy moustache and wore a trim cowboy hat. "This is Johnson Davis, Viola's father," Mitch explained.

Viola was furious, "Don't bring

That's your right, ma'am. But since we're on the subjects of crime and credibility where ... in the world ... did all your injuries come from?" him into this, you bastard! I'll ki ... mmmff." Harrison wrapped his hand over her mouth just in time to muzzle something she'd regret.

"Sorry, Viola," Mitch continued, "I know this is hard to hear. Despite whatever crimes you've committed, Ms. Davis, by all accounts you love your father very much. Mr.

Davis' ranch collapsed without the financial backing of his partner but Viola had accounted for that. She intended to transfer a sizeable chunk of the ill-gotten gains back into her father's account. Two things escaped her machinations. Number one: Jefferson had recently invested his life savings into the ranch in order, ironically, to provide for Viola's future. Samuels had proposed a massive expansion plan to substantially increase their share of the beef market throughout the southwest. And second: Felipe planned to betray her all along. He ran off with the entire sum, leaving both Viola and her father destitute."

The little, black judge shook his head, "My, my girl. Is that true?"

"You don't have to answer that," Harrison cautioned.

But Viola wasn't listening. Schroderberg had known exactly where to stick the dagger and find her heart. "You know nothing; not about me, not about my father," she seethed.

"Your father worked his whole life for what he had. Now he can't even afford the taxes on his home. *You* tell *me* what I don't know."

"He's goading you. Don't give in to it, Viola!" Harrison cautioned.

Undeterred, Viola continued, "I did it all for him. Don't you see, you self-righteous ambulance chaser? I pursued the dwarf and his stinking money for *him*. It was all for him."

"What is it *exactly* that you did, young lady?" the judge followed up. This time Viola was composed enough to keep her mouth shut. "Don't want to answer?

Harrison put a stop to that, "My clients have no comment on that your honor. It's a totally unconnected personal matter."

"Is that so? Because it looks like your clients are violent thugs who can't even keep their hands off of one another.

I've seen enough to make my ruling. The property, the bank accounts and all other assets revert back to Mr. Scaputo, effective immediately." Mitch had been right all along. The Bash Brothers' case was sunk by the weight of their rap sheets. The judge had seen through them and their dime store lawyer.

Unsurprisingly, the town's residents were less than enthusiastic about Jean's courtroom victory. The trial, which had already been a veritable circus, erupted into chaos. When the judge ruled in Jean's favor, there was screaming and crying from the audience in the gallery. The old lady with the snow globe of white hair, who'd become something of a symbol for the town's sense of victimization, fainted right out of her seat. She would have hit her head smack on the floor too if she hadn't been caught by a sheriff's deputy standing nearby.

Protesters, covered in black paint, burst forth from the rear chamber. Many of them carried signs like, "We're drowning in youre oil", "Toss the miggett" and "Hell is two good for you Scaputo". The young radicals charged up the aisle to the front of the court. One of them was a bushy-bearded young man in thick-framed glasses with long hair tied into a bun on top of his head. He made a straight path towards Jean with ill intent in his heart. Fortunately, the sheriff had already been drawn to the radical by his overwhelming stench of patchouli oil. The radical tried to get his hands around Jean's throat but the sheriff deftly shot a Taser dart into the man's stomach. The young radical fell to the ground shaking like a leaf, with 50,000 volts coursing through his body.

State police managed to tackle several others from the same collective. But some of them got through, overwhelming the insufficient police presence. One was an unkempt young woman wearing denim overalls covered in sloganeering buttons. She rushed the judge's stand. All the

Jason Kessler

judge could do was impotently smash his gavel against its block. The radical grabbed the judge's microphone and screamed, "This is a fucking miscarriage of justice. The system is broken. Let's all tear it down and start again. End the oppression!" Once the police had secured her friends in handcuffs they came for her. But she was quick and nimble, leading the police on a pretty absurd chase throughout the courtroom. They finally managed to corner her and the sheriff slipped his crackling Taser against her bare midriff. She dropped to the floor in convulsions just like her patchouli brother. While the deputies led her out in handcuffs she managed to scream out an anguished, "Fuck you, you racist pigs! Black power!" It baffled most in attendance because first, there were hardly any black people in Boroughtown *to be racist to* and second because *she herself was white*. Jean shrugged. *Well, she did have dreadlocks. Maybe it's an honorary thing.*

Jean wondered if the protestors were aware of the irony were attacking a man who'd been homeless and penniless for most of his life. He'd been spat on, ignored by the system; exactly the kind of individual these protesters supposedly championed. He would have even agreed with them about abuses of power, if he'd not known how very wrong they happened to be. But because he knew completely of his own innocence, the protestors' blind, unthinking vengeance appeared as clearly misguided as it truly was. It was a product of capricious emotion over logic; a raging force of nature like a hurricane, tsunami, asteroid collision, or ... a human cult; nothing like the kind of righteous justice they'd intended.

Bobby, Jerome and Viola slipped towards the courtroom door under cover of all this chaos. On Viola's way out, Mitch grasped her firmly by the arm, "Go home, girl. Go home and make things right with you father, while there's still time left." She nodded solemnly. She'd been bad but she wasn't heartless or stupid. Boroughtown was a dead horse and all she'd left to do there was kick around a few bones. She turned to Bobby and Jerome, "Fuck this. I'm going home to Texas."

155

21

Jean left the courtroom triumphant, so joyful to have dodged the bullet. Waiting outside in the wings were Shanks, Pete, Griff, Jolene and Maybelline. Beaming, they all hugged him tight. Jean couldn't quite stop smiling ... until he sighted Marissa, waiting forlorn and alone on a bench. Her fellow henchmen were nowhere to be found. They'd bound off without her and she'd nowhere to go. So she just sat there glowering at the show Jean's friends made of celebrating. Noting Jean's stare, doting on her with pity, Marissa burst into guilty tears.

"Thank you, guys," Jean said to his friends, "I'll meet you all back at the house for some beers." Leaving their company he took a seat next to Marissa. She turned her back. So he placed his hand on her shoulder. She shook it off.

"What's next for you?" he broached with concern.

She turned round to face him, red-faced, mascara running down her cheeks, "Don't pretend like you care after what I did!" she reproached.

Jean offered her a cigarette. She wanted to brood on yet was too hard up to decline rapprochement. She took the cigarette and he lit it for her too.

"There is no *next* for me ... but I don't need your compassion," she finally answered, "I gave up my apartment and job to move into your mansion. Now I'm out on the street with no money. Funny how I let those dickheads talk me into that phony plan. I never should have let them turn me into a junkie, man. I should have stayed strong," her countenance turned dark, "Jean, I have a craving that's tearing me apart inside. Maybe you could slide me a little money, you know, for old time's sake."

"Sorry, girl but I can't do that. Damn! You had it all: you were clean for so many years. Open your ears, you need rehab, a steady job ... you've gotta get clean and get back what you've lost."

Marissa nodded perfunctorily. She didn't have the willpower to stick with therapy, yet. "There's something else ... one of them got me pregnant, Jean," she dropped her face into her hands and began crying again.

He rubbed her back for comfort. "Shit," he sympathized. Then a truly scary thought hit him, "Shiiit. Could it ... be mine?"

"I don't knooow!" she bawled.

"God damn. Well, we'll need to get you off drugs and do a paternity test and get you off the street and..."

"STOP! Jean. Stop." Marissa let out a sigh and dried her red, glistening eyes. Their gaze rested sadly beautiful and hazel on Jean, expressing a depth of sorrow he'd rarely seen in his entire life. "The baby's dead, Jean."

He was floored, "H-how? How did it die?"

"I'm not sure. It was probably the drugs," she seemed to decide on the spot, "But Bobby, he got rough with me one night because I didn't want to fuck him. He hit me real hard..."

"Christ," Jean didn't know what else to say. She threw her arms round his back and cried the collar of shirt into a damp rag. "I'll make sure you're alright. I'll have you flown out to California, to one of those really exclusive rehab centers. They'll take good care of you there. You're going to be alright. Will you *promise* me you'll go?"

She finally consented; nodding and repeating, "I promise ... I promise ... I promise ..."

"Then it's settled. You're *going* to get better."

"You really are a good man, Jean. I know that must not

matter, coming from me."

"Please. No more talk about the past for a while, sweetie."

They agreed to meet one another in Boroughtown Park in two days at 7pm on the bench near the fountain with a little cherub on top. That'd be enough time for Jean to research treatment centers, make a reservation for her and buy a plane ticket. Jean went online and found a top of the line, well-reviewed, $50,000 a week rehab center called Voyages in Rancho Mirage, California. He reserved her the "as needed" package at Voyages and booked first class passage from Fargo to Los Angeles on Atlantic Air.

When the date of the meeting arrived, Jean showed up to the park fifteen minutes early, sat down on the bench overlooking the fountain and waited. The little cherub's spit stream made a sooth gurgle at the foot of the pool. At first Jean listened to this innocuous sound with wonder. As time dragged on, it became monotonous, irritating. After half an hour he was worried sick about Marissa and wondered if she'd show up. Maybe something had happened to her. An hour passed then two, three and four. Jean waited until his eyelids grew too heavy and then he fell asleep right there on the park bench. In the morning he woke up all alone save for the itinerant musician, who'd already arrived and begun playing Leonard Cohen's 'Suzanne'.

Through the next month, Jean kept an eye out for Marissa; contacting the police, scanning the crowds whenever he walked through town, even hiring a private investigator to turn up leads. Nothing turned. But she still came to mind sometimes in his quiet moments. When she did, he wondered what it would have been like if she'd had the baby, his baby, and they'd carried on that way together, making a life of it.

ACT 2

1

Around this time, Jean began detailing his thoughts and adventures in a memoir. What follows is a minimally edited version of the ensuing events, in his own words.

I felt it was an appropriate time for change. The worm had indeed turned. Nowhere was there left any great challenge, physically or spiritually. Fickle love had withered and fallen dead like the autumn leaves falling upon the lawn. Ever one to retreat inside myself in moments of great change, I celebrated my courtroom victory with an aged bottle of bourbon (I promised myself it would be my last for a long, long time) from the cellar and night of killer rock and roll blasting from the stereo.

Yes, fortune had changed me. The removal of monetary pressures had opened me up to the finer pleasures in life. Reading the great works, bedding beautiful women, articulating my thoughts in the memoir you now hold before you. It somehow seemed nobler to sit around enjoying such pursuits now that I was a rich man. I was growing smarter, deeper as a result of these changes. Yet, on the flipside, I felt I was growing softer too, like some spoiled trust fund baby.

I picked up the old rotary receiver from the telephone

in the sunroom. Ring- Riing- Riiinnng!

"Hewo?" Barbara answered.

"How are you, girl?"

"Jean! I'm watching the kitties play in the alley."

"Did little Stripey have her babies?"

"Oh yeah. There were seven of them. All wet. Dey couldn't see a thing!"

"That's great, Barb. You took them all in I guess."

"Ooh nooo, Jean. Dey need to be free, Jean."

"Just like you, huh girl?"

"That's right. Just like me. I set out tha creeaam. Blackie, Whitey, Stripey all come and go as they please."

"That's great, hon. You doing anything tonight? Roseanna dog and I would really like to see you."

"Are you back in your house now, Jean?"

"Yes. Everything's back to 'normal' now. Don't worry about it. I'll call Anju and have him pick you up in time for dinner."

"Ok. Can we has some crab cakes and chocolate sundaes?"

"Absolutely, dear. See you later."

"I'mma so excited, Jean. Bye bye!"

I appreciated her more now. She made me feel loved, almost human. In truth, I knew that at this moment in my life, despite victory over my enemies, I needed companionship more desperately than ever. I'd seen the ugliness, ignorance and vindictiveness of the human mob firsthand. I'd begun to question my own humanity, believe my own press.

My beating at Jerome's hands had left me convalescing with a lazy eye and slight limp. The delicious drama of the situation was too much to resist reveling in: the hated midget with the limp and oddly spaced eyes avoiding the fury of the villagers from the security of his mountainside compound. I found a copy of the old horror film standard,

Johann Sebastian Bach's Toccata and Fugue in D minor and punched it into the stereo. "Dadada-dum, dadada-dum...."

Jean Genie, the melodramatic Universal Studio's monster looked over the balcony from his mansion of hate and stifled the impulse to crush the people of Boroughtown as asked, no .... demanded that he would. They had lied on, defamed and cheated me whether I was a despised hobo on the streets or a jealously envied man of wealth and privilege. I knew what it felt like to be hated like Stalin was hated, like Hitler was hated, like the first gays with aids were hated in the 1980's. I wanted my oppressors to feel the consequences for their base natures; the natures that singled out vulnerable pariahs like me for scorn and derision.

That is why I needed Barbara, Shanks and Pete. They were the only ones who had ever loved me. Roseanna entered the room, rubbing her haunch against the back of his leg. *Well, the only human who loves me at least.* I reached down to scratch her favorite spot on the lower back. Roseanna's leg kicked excitedly.

The splitting headache I felt was from alcohol withdrawal. It made the rage too easy. But I'd promised myself to take a break for a while after the trial was over. Poor blessed Marissa and her addiction had struck that note in me. A wave of nausea suddenly roiled through my corpulent belly. I went running outside, retching a plate full of scrambled eggs and Cheetos over the balcony (through the trellis technically). I took a gulp of water to wash it away, leaving a sickly sweet flavor on my taste buds.

I laid down on a lounge chair and tried not to think about a drink. I kept reminding myself that I needed to take a break from the stuff. Too much crazy shit had been going down. I needed to find some mental clarity in my life, put things in order. But it was overwhelming sometimes. The mind could be cleared for a little while but then my hands would begin to shake and the temptation became unavoidable.

All I'd have to do to show those bastards was not to lift a finger at all. I could fix a milky White Russian or three, wash them down with a port wine. Once the bender started I could just keep right on partying, forget about fixing the situation with the Gambinis in town. When I finally sobered up the wrecking balls, bulldozers and immigrant laborers would be well on their way to tearing Boroughtown apart, brick and mortar.

For now there was still hope. The wreckers had already come to the porno theatre and had now moved on to tearing down an old gas station and an historic five and dime. But the permits hadn't come through yet for the coveted residential properties. Most assuredly they'd come by early next week. Mitch was working against the clock on towards a solution. The Gambinis were business people after all. He was convinced they could be reached with a lucrative business offer that would halt their demolition.

I threw himself onto the soft goose down mattress in my bedroom. I couldn't relax. Though my eyelids were shut sleep would not take me. A daydream fantasy, borne of a spiraling tension-headache took hold of my mind. It was Romania, the 15th century. Mist and fog floated across the chilled morning air. It was a valley. The air stank putrid. A lantern, hung from horse drawn carriage, cut through the fog enough to make out large wooden spikes jutting out of the ground. There was a Judas cradle, a spike driven straight up a man's ass through his mouth. And more skulls adorned on spikes besides that. Some still carried flesh in various states of decomposition. This was the historical land of the dread count, Vlad the Impaler. *It could be returned again here in Boroughtown. Long live the reign of Vlad the Imp,* I thought.

Boroughtown ... the bastards had dragged my dead mother into it. Reminded me how little love lost there was between us. They'd lionized the thugs who drugged Marissa too, effectively ending her life (even if she'd survived she was fucked). Jerome and Bobby ... hell, Viola too ... were still out there somewhere sucking air. And all my money couldn't do a damn thing to put an end to them.

While Mitch was working things out with the Gambinis I was left in the lurch with a dangerous obsession. I couldn't stop worrying about the mystery of Marissa's disappearance. The whereabouts of Jerome and Bobby bothered me too. They'd left me alone so far but how long before disaster came knocking on my door once more? All my tactics had so far amounted to nothing more than grasping at shadows. But early one morning, at the end of a sleepless night, I formulated the kernel of a plan to save Marissa and regain my grit.

A few months back I made a trip into Leafier, the sleepy hamlet on the opposite side of the mountain. I was on a particularly turbulent bender when I stumbled into the mercantile store for fuck-knows-what reason. Through the alcoholic haze I became enthralled by a shiny, chrome short band radio scanner. It'd been prominently displayed in a lighted and locked sliding glass case next to a stack of artisan sorghum syrups. At the time the $368 price tag was far too expensive. But now, I could purchase it with only the spare cash in my wallet. I sent Two-Shanks down the mountain to pick it up for me.

Shanks brought the radio back to the mansion and set it on a little writing desk in the small study by the laundry room. It was a room no larger than the small apartment bedroom I'd slept in as a child. I felt comfortable there. When I first clicked the radio on, a yellow light glowed through the room's darkness and a shrill white noise erupted from the speakers. I adjusted the knobs until the noise subsided. I clicked the scan button. The frequency went up and down without any sign of human life broadcasting anywhere in the badlands. I'd have time to wait it seemed.

The idea was to monitor the police and emergency medical bands for clues that might lead to Marissa. Jerome and Bobby might have gotten off from the law but they had to be desperate now. They were out on the street, without the cash they'd been promised, nursing grievous injuries. With any luck they'd remained in the area and get picked up on a drug charge trying to pull their finances back in order.

It took about four or five minutes of listening before the radio picked up its first bits of chatter. It was from the CB of a trucker rolling down the interstate.

"Big Bertha this is Flying Echo. Do you read me?"

After a few moments, a husky-sounding woman responded, "Flying Echo, this Big Bertha. I read you LOUD and CLEAR. You coming in for a pit stop, hon?"

"That's a big affirmative. I'm running hot out of Tucumcari and I got some dirty oil needs changing."

"Ooh, that's my speciality, daddy. Pull on into the garage. I'll get you cleaned out."

"Ten-four. Over and out."

The task was a lonely one. I fucked up and brought along a bottle of Old Grand-Dad to keep me company (this self-control thing would take time) along with an ottoman so my little legs wouldn't swing while I sat in the study chair. I scolded myself for falling off the wagon so soon but how I else could I distract my mind during the deafening bouts of silence? The last thing I wanted was to hear my own thoughts right now. Like: How stupid was I for trying to help this woman who'd betrayed me so hurtfully? All I can say for myself is that, at the time, I was still new to the affections of beautiful women. I wasn't at a point where I could admit to myself how foolish it was to continue yearning for her. So I took a drink.

Eventually, I heard a female emergency dispatcher radioing for help. "Hey Chris. You finished that heart attack yet?"

"We're en route to the hospital as we speak," answered the EMT.

"Well, when you're finished with that we got a woman pulled over to the shoulder on Route 11, near the 25 mile sign for the Rez."

"Oh yeah? What's her condition?"

"She hit a deer. The thing pumped its hoof through the windshield and broke her nose. She's seeing triple and wants to get checked for a concussion before she drives home."

"I can swing it but it'll be about 25 to 30 minutes."

"10-4. I'll let her know."

Why should I even bother? I wondered. But I knew that I didn't have it in me to give up. Although Marissa had betrayed me and delivered me into the hands of dangerous men, I'd seen the regret in her eyes. I'd seen serious addiction before too, when I was on the streets. I knew how it could make you a slave to some unscrupulous dealer's whims. I took another swallow of whiskey, cursing myself for the hypocrisy.

"Any officers in the Tulane district? We've got a drunk who left Outlaw's disturbing the peace. He was singing 'The Star Spangled Banner' at the top of his lungs in a residential area and may have urinated on one of the city councilor's flower gardens."

"Drivin' by Outlaw's right now dispatch. I'll give it a look."

It was pretty quiet after that for the next few hours, just a few more reports of petty stuff. I had no doubt that there was more serious crime lurking beneath the veneer of tranquility. But Boroughtown police were too understaffed to start a war they couldn't win. Some corners were too dangerous to shine a light into, particularly after the latest depression brought in an influx of predators with bags of crack, smack, ice and strange new designer synthetics. So most of the public averted their eyes, fearing the police couldn't protect them from reprisals.

I had to fix a strong cup of black coffee to stay awake. It wasn't until exactly one minute after midnight that I next heard something that caught my interest. One minute the scanner was surfing the radio waves like usual and then, all of a sudden, it hung on a particular frequency. At first there was nothing but static from the speakers. Then in a hushed voice, a tired-sounding man began repeating, "Delta ... Oscar ... Alpha ... Delta ... Oscar ... Alpha ..." When the man finally coughed and switched off his microphone, there followed four minutes of clicks I vaguely recognized as Morse code. This was all very strange since there were apparently no military bases in the area.

Maybe it's coming from across the border in Canada, I wondered, *or maybe it's just some burnout sending messages to the Mother Ship.* There were some serious weirdos hidden away in the badlands outside of town.

The man switched the microphone back on. He said only three words, "Radio Outpost Centauri." Then a sleepy old song from the forties began to crackle over the airwaves. "Somewhere, beyond the seeaaa ..." I switched the dial back to scan and continued my search.

Nothing else of much note happened for the rest of the night. By the time the morning light began to shine through the curtains I had, good and drunk, lain my head down onto the desk and drifted to sleep.

The following afternoon I took Roseanne to meet Barbara and Bambino in the park. I couldn't travel safely alone any longer so I paid Shanks and Griff, the former Green Beret, to guard me from harassment. They kept out most of the riff-raff. Still, hecklers called me some familiar names: freak, midget, fucker, asshole. One of them even managed to nail me in the head with a crushed up soda can. Griff made an example out of the marksman, dropping him into a painful submission hold.

Barbara's little pup Bambino, was nearly twice the size since I'd first met him and had no compunction about leaping all over the older dog, much to her dismay. Roseanna resented the pup's lack of respect Bambino showed to her, the grizzled matriarch. At least they both had Barbara's full adoration.

She suddenly turned serious, "I miss my fam-we, Jean". There was isolation inherent to freedom that she couldn't have guessed at when she first left her family home.

"There are a lot of people that feel alone out here in the real world, Barb. Especially the ones who are different like you and I."

"I want to be free ... but I want people to love me too," Barb lamented.

I encouraged her to take an arts class or do Special Olympics, make some new friends. I promised to be there whenever she'd need me.

"If you had it to do over again, would you have stayed with your parents?" I finally asked.

She thought about it a while, stroking Bambino's fur.

Then she turned back with resolve in her eyes, "No. What's over is over, Genie. We go forward now."

~ ~ ~

After the ride home, I paid Anju to stick around. Have a car on standby might come in real handy with my dirty new business. In case anything turned up I'd have to move fast, maybe faster than the police. As soon as it grew dark I waddled into the study with a dusty bottle of gin found under the cellar stairs. I flipped the radio switch and the speakers buzzed back to life again. I poured myself a strong drink.

It turned out to be one hell of a busy night. Friday night: where a hundred dreamers wake up to their REAL LIVES, find they want nothing to do with them. So the age-old ritual begins: ravishing our various delights until we can momentarily lose our own reflections in the mirror. Things would begin as they always did with the crowds going out for a buzz or for love. Then there would be heartache, too much money would be spent. There'd be shame. Some of the victors would take things too far, taunt the wounded. Then as the night dragged on there would be desperation, victimization ... dominance of the weak by the strong. Everyone parties to kill their past, knowing there'll be a Saturday morning out there to sleep it all off and live again.

A trucker with a thick Mexicali accent was first the first voice on the scanner that night, "Any gringos out there looking for trouble?"

"What'chu say, boy?" *Someone* was angry.

"I got a real problem with you white boys tonight. My abuelita got sent back to Mexico yesterday, holmes. This is her home now, not Mexico, you fuckers."

"So what spic? Good riddance."

"Yah, yeah; spic, wetback, beaner. It's been 7 years since we crossed the border. We're every bit as American as you now, 'boy'. So yeah, I'm looking for a fight."

The female dispatcher interrupted, "Do you know who you're talking to, ese? That's 'Zyklon' Ben. Whatever you're haulin', haul ass out of here because the poh-lice don't want to have to clean your carcass off the canyon floor at 3 in the mornin'."

"Stay out of this PD!" Zyklon growled, "Let the beaner make up his own damn mind."

"Wait a minute. Are you police? Is that the *official police response*? Fuck me." The Mexican musty have thought better of it because I never did hear any more from him.

Then there was silence for a while. I had time to think about where I'd heard the name 'Zyklon' Ben before. He was one of the more successful ice merchants in the county; did business with truckers. That's why he always kept a CB around, for the old-timers who'd rather eat shit than use a cell phone. I considered whether Zyklon might have a business relationship with the Bash Brothers but nah. Zyklon was a committed, card carrying white supremacist and wouldn't even supply a white hood like Bobby if a black man like Jerome was making profit off it at any end of the chain.

Roseanna sauntered into the study and curled up next to my chair. I scratched behind her ear and lit a cigar, awaiting the next transmission. And come they did. By around 11 p.m. the reports came in so steady that police stopped responding to all but the most serious dispatches.

"Someone hit a mailbox on Theroux."

"We've got a late night baseball game on Cascade. A man collapsed on the diamond after taking a knee to the ribs."

"Couple of horses out for an evening stroll by Route 2 ... *without the company of humans*."

"The resident of the house on Theroux went out to check on his mailbox. An ex-boyfriend was lying in wait;

assaulted him with a baseball bat."

"Copy that. I'm on my way."

I scratched my behind. Maybe nothing would ever come of this. Maybe they were all in the wind already. I poured another stiff drink. My vision was already growing hazy. The gin had me so disoriented that I barely noticed when the radio hung. A digital clock on the desk shone in red numerals, 12:01. *Oh yeah. This thing again?* I checked the frequency this time: 463. 8500. A microphone clicked on and the Tired Man repeated a new code, "November ... Whiskey ... Oscar ... November ... Whiskey ... Oscar ..."

Then followed four or five minutes transmission of Morse code, just like the night before. I understood none of it. I just sat back listening in awe.

"Radio Outpost Centauri."

I'd been dreamily watching stars shining in the night sky between an opening in the window curtains. Abruptly, a blues lick kicked in the door on my reverie. "Hot air hangs like a dead man, from a white oak tree ..." The song played on, "Dark night. Dark night. It's a daaaark night ..." I finally got up and set the radio back to scan.

"There's a hallucinating female outside the packing plant. Police have tried subduing her with Tasers but she is resisting and has rammed through a wooden fence."

I thought I'd heard it all but was shocked. *The addicts are resisting Tasers now. Jesus! Since when can they do that?*

"There's been a robbery at the Hometown Pharmacy on Sioux. Be advised the perp is probably a tweaker. He stole the entire supply of cold medicine and beat the pharmacist within an inch of his life. Officer, please respond." *No one was answering. The Boroughtown PD was already swamped.* "Hello? Anyone there?" *Damn it! This one was going to fall through the cracks!*

I picked up the microphone, hesitated briefly, found the

right words and pressed the talk button. "Can I get a description of the suspect, dispatch?"

There was an anxious moment of silence. A bead of nervous sweat rolled down my forehead. *If they don't buy it I'm pretty sure they can trace these things.*

"Hello officer." *Yes, they bought it!* "The suspect is a white male, mid-thirties, 6' 2" with crew cut hair ... Oh yeah. Get this: he has an eye patch."

Bobby, I thought immediately. "Any idea which direction he was headed, dispatch?"

"No clue. There were several witnesses at the scene; best start with them."

A-ha! It had to be them. I swayed out of my chair but tripped drunkenly over the ottoman, landing face first onto the floor. It hurt bad. *This, this has to change,* I thought.

Of course Anju, ever loyal, was waiting patiently outside by the car. He was watching a Bollywood musical on the car's dashboard monitor and talking loudly with a relative on his cell phone.

"Are we ready, Mister Genie?"

"We sure are, Anju."

"Excellent, sir." He returned to the person on the other line. "Majoola, I'll have to call you back later. Yes, I love you too."

I climbed into the back seat. "We're going to the Hometown Pharmacy on ..."

Anju interrupted, "Fifth and Sioux. Yes, I know it exactly. Right away, sir."

"Anju, I want you to step on it. We've got to get there as fast as humanly possible. All your legal bills are on me if you catch any trouble." I passed two one hundred dollar bills to the front of the cab.

Anju snatched the bills and hit the gas, "I have the speed for your need."

The sleek black automobile spun out of the driveway,

hanging tight around the curves of the sleepy mountainside road. Anju recited a Hindu mantra for safe travel without obstacles or accidents.

"Krishnay Vasudeva Haraye Parmatman ..." and so on.

I had the window down so I could feel the onrush of the cool, fall air against my face. I love that feeling. It sobered me up a bit for the business to come and gave me a respite from the choking, pungent smell of incense in the cab. In contrast, outside smelled like conifers. It was a safe smell that reminded him of childhood, a sweet distraction from the fear of rushing headlong towards a dangerous criminal.

"Any more trouble with the Ulysses, Genie?" Anju asked.

"So far, so good. I just keep repeating your advice like a mantra."

When we arrived at the pharmacy there was already an ambulance parked outside. By the looks of things it had only just gotten there. EMTs were lifting a stretcher out of the back. Inside the pharmacy, the victim had managed to crawl up to the storefront where he'd marked the glass with a bloody handprint. A trail of his blood smeared along the ground too, all the way back to the rear pharmacy counter.

He was too badly hurt to recognize other than to say he was a balding white man in his forties. The features of his pitiful face were disfigured by a grotesque purple swelling about his eyes, mouth and cheeks.

The EMTs finally reached him. "Can you tell us your name, sir?"

"Mmm-mmpphh!" he garbled, too swollen to speak.

"Ok. Just take it easy now, sir. We'll get you out of here."

Obviously, the poor man would be of no value to my investigation. I stepped out of the cab and looked about. As the red lights of the ambulance rotated through the dark night they illuminated the faces of several mortified onlookers. A witness had to be among them. The nearest to me was a young man in a checkered button up shirt. He looked terrified by the bloody tableaux before him, yet his macabre fascination with the tragedy wouldn't allow him turn away.

"Excuse me. Did you see what happened here?" I inquired.

"What's it to you, shorty?"

"The guy in there is my sister's husband. She's worried sick. I told her I'd figure out what happened."

The young man scrutinized my face. He seemed to recognize me but said nothing about it. "Um ... no, I didn't see nothin'... but my wife ..." He stuck his thumb out in the direction of two frightened women commiserating beside the ambulance.

"Thanks, buddy." I left him and approached the two women. From close up I could tell that it was a blonde and a redhead. The taller of the two, the blonde, had her arm wrapped around the redhead's shoulders for comfort. I recognized the redhead. She'd given me money on occasion when I used to panhandle in Boroughtown Park. Beautiful girl.

"He kept telling the attacker, 'Stop. I'll give you whatever you want.' But the psycho just kept punching and punching like he'd just done the thing to get his damned animal violence out," she sobbed.

"Excuse me. The man in there is a friend of mine," I lied, "Did either of you see what happened?"

The redhead nodded, "Is he going to be alright?"

"I don't know to tell you the truth. But if you can tell me which way the attacker was headed you'll help bring the animal that did this to justice."

She pointed, agonizingly up 5th Avenue West; the direction nearest the Boroughtown city limits.

"Anything else? Any detail might help."

She sobbed and shook her head 'no'. "He wasn't exactly

a man of many words." I'd turned to walk away when she spoke again, "Wait. I remember something else, come to think of it. There was a black man with dentures behind the wheel of the getaway car. Sorry, that's all I know."

"Thanks. For what it's worth, those men who did this have an innocent woman hostage. You might have just helped save her life." The redhead nodded and I returned to Anju's cab.

"Any luck, sir?"

"Head west up 5th. That's the way they were headed. And drive slowly. All we can do is hope they left some clue behind."

"You're sure it was them, sir?"

"One hundred percent."

"Any sighting of the woman you're looking for?"

"Unfortunately, no. She might not even be with them any longer for all I know."

Most of the buildings along 5th Avenue were abandoned and in various stages of dilapidation. 5th Avenue used to be filled with thriving offices. Half of them got knocked out of business by Reaganomics in the 1980's. Just after the 90's resurgence when it looked like everything was on its way back the 2008 Depression wiped out two thirds of what remained.

Under lamppost light we saw a massive, stark naked black woman running up the street. She must have weighed 300 lbs. Her enormous flopping tits spun around in circles as she ran. Her girth must have been an incredible burden yet she was sprinting as though possessed with the superhuman stamina of an elite athlete.

"Oh, sweet Shiva! Protect my eyes from sin!" Anju prayed.

"Sweep back around," I ordered him, "Shine your lights into the buildings."

Anju angled the front end of the car and switched on the

high beams. Many of the buildings had broken windows. Light shown all the way back inside, to the cinderblock. There were torn out fixtures stripped of copper wiring by thieves, low-hanging asbestos from the ceilings, dusty three-legged desks, even a few Cold War era IBM computers.

But the only recent signs of life were the graffiti scrawled onto dead relics of that bygone era: "Jester" sprayed onto the old library, "Bzrt" on a mom and pop office supply store. A stone eagle statue that once proudly perched over the entrance of a legal justice center, now sat crumbling from teenage vandalism and age.

"My name is Ozymandias, king of kings: look on my works ye mighty and despair!" Anju remarked in a hushed voice.

"Huh? What's that?"

"Just something I read in grammar school as a boy," he answered in hushed tone.

Empty soda bottles, potato chip cellophane wrappers, and used needles were strewn outside the dwellings. Some people still lived here. But there was no point in rousting whatever living dead haunted these modern mausoleums. Bobby and Jerome weren't there. I could feel it in my gut.

"Enough of this. Let's keep going."

Anju steered us back onto 5th Avenue. We drove right on past the 'Welcome to Boroughtown' sign and parked on the shoulder. In the distance stretched the distant buttes, standing silent watch over the gulch, awaiting the end of the scurrying things which had claimed so much of their kingdom. The fresh air was brilliant. But there wasn't any clue to be found but the open road.

Mitch called the next morning with a renewed enthusiasm, "I did it, buddy boy. It wasn't easy but the Gambinis are willing to deal. They're sending Giovanni Portico, the founder's nephew. So they mean business."

"You're a bloody magician, Mitch. Without you I'd be six feet under. I've never been five feet in my life so that's saying something."

Mitch chuckled, "Don't get your hopes up just yet. We're still going to have to do some strong arm negotiating. For heaven's sake make sure you're there on time: Tuesday, 5 days from now, at 7 a.m. in my office. Giovanni is an impatient man, you don't want to be even a minute late. He's had men beaten for less."

"Ok. I'll make a note of that right now," I pulled out my notebook and jotted the information down.

"Oh and one other thing while I've got you on the phone: word is you went out last night investigating a robbery on 5th Avenue ..."

"That's right. How'd you know about that?"

"You'd be surprised the kind of things you hear when you're not shut up in the house all day, Mr. Scaputo."

"Touché. It's not like I'm cramped. My house basically has its own area code. Still, I take your point."

"I know the investigator I hired isn't exactly blazing a trail to your missing girlfriend ... but what you're doing is borderline suicidal. What are you going to do if you find her with these men ... these dangerous men ... who just beat a store clerk to the brink of death?"

"I don't know exactly. It depends on the situation. I'm

hoping they'll leave her unattended and I can just, you know, sneak in and out."

"You're betting your life that they won't catch you. What then ... if they catch you?"

I fidgeted, tapping a bulge protruding from the side of my chest. "I've got a ... I've got a gun."

"This is the kind of thing I was afraid of. This isn't a movie, Mr. Scaputo. You're not trained to use a firearm. In the real world, novices aren't marksmen and accidents happen all the time. Innocent people get killed. I won't be able to get you out of trouble so easy then."

"Hopefully it doesn't come to that, Mitch."

"Just the same, I think you'd do better with some protection. I know a real killer, ex-Mossad assassin. You wouldn't believe how brutal a killer can be when he feels God is on his side; the real crème de la crème. He doesn't come cheap but let's face it, you can afford it."

"How long would it take him to get here?"

"Well they're all in Israel right now, so not tomorrow, but I could have a team waiting for you in the office after our meeting with Portico."

"Ok, Mitch. Do it. But if anything comes up before then I can't promise I'll wait."

"You won't regret your decision. And otherwise... good luck."

I hung up the phone. There was another bit of planning I needed to do for the day. There'd been two nights in a row in which I'd come across the strange Radio Outpost Centauri while surfing the airwaves after midnight. Every night it broadcast the ominous letters and mysterious Morse code. Of course it couldn't possibly have anything to do with my search. Still, I wanted it explained all the same.

The only person I knew that could interpret those messages, if they weren't just gibberish, was Griff. Finding Griff might be another matter. He wasn't a man of rigorous habit and his schizophrenic episodes often landed him in some unusual places. When I found him he was digging through trash in the Salvation Army dumpster. His arms were cradling a child-size bowling pin shaped like a grinning clown.

"Hello?" I tried to grab his attention, "Griff, what have you found?"

Griff looked askew at me through the sliding plastic door. "The gates of Heaven admit their perfect children."

"Alright." I was hoping not to spook him. Better play along.

Griff climbed out onto the pavement with the doll. Beside Griff's feet I noticed several electrical wires connected to a car battery.

"What are you working on there, Griff?"

"Exorcising the devil," he unsheathed a Bowie from his belt and began hollowing out an orifice in the clown's crotch.

"Say, Griff. Did you happen to learn any Morse code during your time in the army?"

"Dut-dut-dutta-duh-dut-dut. I was communications officer..." Griff jammed a phallic bit of circuitry into the clown's new orifice, "...so yes."

"Fuckin' A right. Want to stay with me at the mansion tonight? I've got booooooze."

Griff hooked the circuitry up to the car battery. He was staring at me with unbridled madness burning in his eyes. After a moment his eye started to twitch. Smoke rose from the clown. Burning plastic fumes choked the air, with the first flickers of flame consuming its cyber-phallus. Griff smiled at me, never averting his penetrating gaze. Then he soiled himself.

~ ~ ~

Griff smelled a dead thing, post-mortem. When we arrived at the mansion I strongly encouraged him to wash up. He didn't take the hint. Instead he walked into the billiards room to roll balls around the table like a child. That's when I ordered the filthy bastard to take a goddamn shower. While he was cleaning up I threw his soiled clothes in the wash.

It was a little early to switch on the radio so I poured a drink for myself and one for Griff too. Then I waited. It was lonely without Marissa around. I don't like thinking about that any more than I do about Ulysses. There must be something to spend my money on to keep these thoughts from my mind: a Tesla sports car, an A-list Hollywood actress (moonlighting as a six figure prostitute), a soothing drug available only on a mountaintop in Tibet, or a barbaric act of sado-masochistic violence attainable only to the highest bidder.

By the time Griff came downstairs (dressed in my favorite fucking bathrobe by the way) his clothes had had time to be washed and dried. He took so long I think he must've fallen down or masturbated in the shower. Anyway, once he was dressed he seemed more civilized by a mile. It rubbed off on his demeanor too. Once he took that drink with me he was downright serene; so much so that I ended up inviting him into the radio room with me for the night. What the hell, right? I could use the company. So I got Griff to help me drag a chair into the room for him to sit on. The nearest we could find was a leather Osaki "massage chair" inexplicably stored in the adjoining laundry room. It was heavy to move. I instantly regretted the decision but it was too late to turn back now. Griff had already fallen in love with the strange contraption, even feeling a ... kinship. I realized it had to be retrieved for him or I'd never get another moment's peace that night.

Anyway we got situated in the radio room and I fired her (the radio) up again. Griff started rolling himself a makeshift cigarette from a tin. It was filled with cheap tobacco and the brownest, dirtiest weed I've ever seen in my life.

At once, the radio spat out a sonic fuzzball: the first dispatch of the night. "This is it, Lt. Jeffers. We were able to find the clearing at the base of the mountain. The bones are there beside the cave just like the hiker reported."

"Is there any imminent danger, Lieutenant? Are you in need of backup?"

"Negative, but I'm going to need a forensic unit out here. Maybe we can match this to one of our missing persons."

"Copy that. Sending a team out to you now."

Could it be her? I'd pray to Ulysses himself if it would affect the outcome. Of course I'd considered that that outcome was a possibility. Hell, I'd even say it was a likely one after she'd been this many days missing.

Griff lit up his dirt weed cigarette. It smelled awful; like holding your face near a pile of burning leaves. I asked him to take it outside. Graciously, he obliged without doing any weird shit first. Small miracles I guess. There's no denying that Griff is one strange cat. But I swear he's a very decent individual when you get to know him; even heroic if you judge the guy by his distant past.

He'd told me his story before. It was rambling and scattershot like everything he does nowadays. Very schizophrenic. Funny that; supposedly he didn't used to be this way. Griff is a Boroughtown hometown boy. Someone knows a bit of his story here and someone else knows another bit over there. When you distill the commonalities in the various accounts you begin to get somewhere near the truth.

Growing up, Griff was always a bit eccentric, just this side of sanity. But he had a genius for electronics. He'd spend hours in his parents' basement, tinkering with computers and lifting weights. He was truly a gifted and driven young man and people took notice. After high school the United States Army welcomed him with open arms. They trained him in communications, sent him to cut his teeth in Europe decrypting diplomatic transmissions. Brussels, Paris, Berlin; the USA had faith in their new wunderkind and in return he exposed the dirtiest secrets of power players on the world stage. But personally, Griff never felt at home there. The carefree sexual reverie of socialist Europe disgusted his virginal sensibilities. The wanton, joyfully horny women of the trendy nightclubs in the Old World scared him. Even as they threw themselves at any man with a uniform and a steady paycheck he turned them down, secretly wondering if he might be queer. Instead of indulging like his peers, he preferred to frequent the bookshops, the quieter pubs near the suburbs, or stay at home rapt with his technological experimentations.

After five years of this, the Army had new mission orders which required his immediate relocation to Bogota, Columbia. When he arrived the commander informed him that he'd be leading an effort to disrupt a burgeoning alliance between left-wing FARC rebels and Rojas, the most powerful drug cartel in the country.

"Why does this concern the United States Army?" Griff asked. "These alliances are formed and torn apart internally all the time. We could just wait it out like we always do."

"One word," the commander answered, "Burundanga." It was the first time Griff had ever heard of the drug known colloquially as "The Devil's Breath". Evidently the nature of the FARC/ Rojas alliance was based on mass production and distribution of this incredibly rare and dangerous drug.

"We must stop this drug from getting into the hands of criminals and terrorists bent on hurting the American people, Lt. Griff," the Commander went on to explain further, "Burundanga is nicknamed 'The Devil's Breath' because an attacker can simply blow a trace amount of the drug, ground into a fine powder, into a victim's face and they'll be mesmerized. Within minutes of contact victims lose every trace of their free will, appearing coherent to all around them, walking, talking ... but inside- a mental slave. After taking this drug, some have emptied their bank accounts or pillaged their own houses for thieves. But these are relatively minor crimes compared to the drug's potential on the scale of geopolitical warfare, Lieutenant. There's no telling what acts of terror a sociopath could achieve with enough Burundanga at his disposal."

"Ok, you've got my interest, Commander. How does this whole operation go down?"

"Glad you asked. The FARC guerillas control stretches of jungle occupied by peasant farmers. FARC coerces the farmers into growing Borrachero trees from which burundanga is derived. They set up camps beside the farms so they can oversee the peasant refinement of burundanga leaves into Devil's Breath. Once an order is sent from the Rojas in Bogota, product FARC loads up a truck and ships it out."

Because there were no phone lines in the Columbian jungles controlled by FARC they had to rely on old TELEX networks to communicate with the Rojas in Bogota. It's kind of like a fax because you send a message on one end and it's printed out on the other. The difference is that instead of using phone lines to transmit data it uses the old telegraphic system. Griff decided his best mode of attack was to intercept the coded TELEX messages, break their cipher and transmit messages of his own, calculated to sow strife between FARC and the Rojas. This way he could effectively crumble their alliance from within.

He spent the first week installing and calibrating the equipment. By the second week he'd begun intercepting FARC transmissions. At the end of the first month he'd cracked the cipher. Because of the irregularity of contact between the two sides it took longer for him to begin mimicking 'the kinds' of things they'd say to each other. But once he had he'd send tactical messages that wreaked havoc on their whole operation: a massive over-shipment of product, a last minute change to an incorrect drop point, a subtle but cutting insult to men with hair-trigger tempers. As soon as they'd incorporate counter-measures to avoid his sabotage, the army would use a secret mole to put Griff back out in front.

It was a long slough, about two years of hard work. During that time, Griff settled into something approaching a normal life. He became well known in the neighborhood: his favorite deli, the café where he'd stop for coffee in the morning and the little restaurant where he'd stop for drinks at night. In the waning days of the operation Griff finally met a woman. He'd taken an outdoor table at his favorite restaurant, Ultima Llamadas, washing down empanadas with ice cold beer. He noticed a golden-skinned Columbian beauty making eyes at him from a table across the patio. Griff's pride was unusually strong on account of success at work. The FARC/Rojas alliance was crumbling before his eyes, all thanks to his masterful sabotage. He felt horny; felt loose. Griff found himself inviting the voluptuous woman over to his table for a drink.

"Carmelita," she introduced herself.

Carmelita was flirtatious, rapturous. She laughed at more of his jokes than anyone ever before. She stroked his ego with finesse. Carmelita was like a drug. When she suggested Griff take her home, he was unusually brave. It all felt like a dream. *Of course this is what happens next*, he thought.

Griff took Carmelita to his flat. He wasn't sure how all this was supposed to go down. He'd seen videos but that didn't tell him much. When Carmelita asked, "May I freshen up in the little girl's room?" he guessed that was his cue to get undressed.

"Sure," he answered. He got completely naked, folding all his clothes in a neat pile on the dresser drawer, with his underwear on top.

When Carmelita came out of the restroom, to his surprise, she was still fully clothed. She let out a guffaw when she saw Griff lying there naked. He was terribly embarrassed. He wasn't sure how he was supposed to behave. For God's sake, a woman had never even seen his penis before.

Carmelita pulled out a baggie of white powder. "Do you mind if I do a line before we get started?" she asked.

"Go ahead," he acquiesced. What the hell, right? Cocaine was everywhere in Columbia and it wasn't The White Lady he'd been chosen to stop after all. Griff sat across from her while she carefully set out a line of the fine white powder on the table top.

"Please," she motioned for him to take the first line.

But Griff wasn't comfortable with such licentious behavior, "No, I shouldn't."

"Are you suuure?"

"Yes, it's not for me," he curtly replied.

"Fine, suit yourself." Carmelita leaned her face in towards the powder ... and blew a cloud of it right into Griff's face. She took a filter out of her purse and covered her mouth while Griff hacked and coughed. The realization hit him too late: he'd been struck by The Devil's Breath. Everything faded except for the increasingly seductive sound of Carmelita's voice.

"Hello, Lt. Griff. Follow the sound of my voice. The more you fight it, the more burundanga I'll have to use. I don't want to run the risk of killing you, Lt. Griff." But it was a moot point. Griff was already in a trance so deep that it threatened to swallow his soul. "Don't be afraid. I'm here to introduce you to your new self. Your mind will now be divided into 17 complimentary parts: one is the child which existed before you were even born, the second is a being living in a solar system never before detected by human eyes, the third is a brilliant but insane scientist, the fourth is a lustful psychotic (like the one that brought me here tonight), the fifth a heroic Knight of the Round Table...." She went on to describe all seventeen distinct personality archetypes. When she'd finished the incantation she punctuated it, "Goodbye, Lt. Griff with regards from the Rojas clan." Then she left out the front door and out of his life forever.

The following afternoon Griff's commanding officer retrieved Griff from a dank jail cell in downtown Bogota. He'd been picked up walking naked through a crime infested ghetto, muttering to himself. He was lucky to be alive. Granted medical discharge, the Griff who returned home to Boroughtown was not the same man who'd left seven years ago. And that's the story of Griff, as well as I can figure it. He gave a woman his heart but she took his mind instead.

Griff came back into the radio room and gave me a little smile. Poor bastard. I wonder if the real you, the whole you, is still down inside somewhere. Just then, a little bit of saliva dripped from the corner of Griff's mouth onto his shirtsleeve.

~ ~ ~

It was about twenty two minutes later until I heard another dispatch from the search team, "Dispatch, this is Johnson with the forensics unit. We've investigated the scene at the base of the mountain." I apprehensively braced myself for the worst.

"Do we have an I.D. on that missing person, Johnson?"

"Yeah, we do. Anyone missing a farm animal?" he answered sarcastically.

"Excuse me?"

"These bones are from a cow, dispatch. We really need to train these damn hick PDs. Forensics isn't driving into the counties every time Deputy Fife gets spooked."

"**C**hrist, EMT needed ASAP. It looks like an attempted suicide on Markus Ct. Woman; 60 years old, took enough of meds for a permanent nap."

"How many?"

"The whole bottle. And that's not all. Ligature marks around the neck. The arteries are opened in her left and right wrists. She'd be completely bled out by now if the neighbors hadn't used her bed sheets to staunch the bleeding."

"Shit. All that and she's still breathing? Old bird covered all her bases and still comes out looking like The Terminator."

"Not funny. Move your ass. She's come too far not to make it now."

There were many times when I contemplated suicide. It was the nights drunk on melancholy and failure that clocked me like a freight train. Some folks get traumatized real bad in life that even the good days feel bad as hell. For me, it was the beatings Ambrose gave me, the betrayal of my mother, the taunts from my fellow man, the humiliating rejections of my desperate love. Somehow you still end up being able to manage most days and the trauma recedes into a shadow, a dark spirit you never quite forget. You might think you do, for a while, but then it returns, always returns, the most loyal companion anyone ever had.

So there you go, depression, suicide are the cocktail you brew when you can't leave your poor soul in peace. I could be cute and say alcoholism is my slow suicide but I just like the taste. I wouldn't do it ya know? Suicide. I wouldn't want the bastards to see me quit. Still, I'd bet there are plenty who greet death with a sigh of relief. Is that suicide too? If you wouldn't keep going ... even if you could?

What brings me down is the baseness. The bestial nature of my fellow man. Hollywood taught us that we're all bound for greatness. But what is greatness? Is it when Mister Hollywood, beautiful & pompous, recites splendid soliloquys written ... with the passion of ugly men like me. He's told where to stand, how to act, with a 100 person orchestra swelling in the background. All for you sweet prince. Handsome prince. That's how the modern plebe views a "great" man.

Throughout history, most heroes are the villains who've most thoroughly killed off opposition; made sure only "the right ones" lived to tell their story. Most of the top dogs these days are born into it: the handsome man, the rich man, the charismatic man leading other men, who dominates women's hearts. Or the woman does all these things and more; knows how to use her body, how and when to cry. So where does that leave the average man? He's either submitting to authority with a bottle in his hand or possessed by the killer drive for "greatness": beating the other heroes. To defeat anything and everyone in his path like a grizzly bear, tearing out the throat of weaker grizzlies ... to lead the pack & fuck the best females. Our analog is greed, war, perfection and we eat it up. We eat the weak. Like me.

I hate them for it but I'd do the same in their position. To get the reward: the love, the respect, the sex we all crave. God I hated them for their ways. Yet I hated myself more. There was no other way. I wanted to die. But here I am anyway, *surviving*. And they'll love me now, for my money, I guarantee it (as sad as that is). The ones like Viola or Marissa were the worst, greediest of the bunch. Most would be satisfied to just fuck me for money as the endgame.

Instead they had to be so prideful, make it hard and rip me off. They wanted to take the cash and split... fuck tall, dark and stupid on a boat off the Greek isles.

Sucker. Sucker. I know I've been played for a sucker and here I'm still wiping up her ass, saving her life. Mister good guy. Mister nice guy. Fuck it all to hell, I'm not ready to die. There better be a karmic hit of ecstasy waiting for me somewhere down the line. I save this bitch and I'm gone. Like Bobby said, REAL GONE. Fuck Boroughtown. Fuck the human race. You're all to the highest bidder and I've got plenty to spend. Look out world; world of fucking animals. You world of fucking whores, children of whores, begetters of whores ... ad infinitum until the sun burns down from the sky.

~ ~ ~

By this point, small town Saturday night was kicking into full swing. Maybe it was partly "Full Moon Fever" but Saturday night was putting Friday to shame. It sounded like an asteroid was about to hit and the citizens of Earth had collectively decided to burn the motherfucker down. Literally in some cases – a house on Sheen burned to a crisp after a meth lab exploded inside. Two good ol' boys stabbed one another over a woman at Outlaws'. One of the inmates at the town jail raped his cellmate. The other prisoners (who were forced to watch) began flinging their feces at one another between the cells. There were 3 heart attacks, a seizure and a stroke; four cases of domestic violence and five car accidents. Two horses (which had been wandering on the loose now for days) finally made it into town. They were currently running down Broad St. One drunk puked on an old lady stopping for gas at the Chevron. Another drunk fell into Bison Lake, almost drowning. The woman who resuscitated the drowning man stole his wallet ... and on and on and on. But there was still no sign of Marissa. Then, like clockwork, the scanner hung on 463.8500. It was

12:01 A.M. on the dot. Buuuuzzzzz went the static.

"Hey Griff! Listen up. This is it!" He'd been slouched over chewing at his fingernails. The Osaka massage chair was humming along as it vibrated against his muscles. Now he straightened himself out, leaning in towards the radio.

"Zulu ... Zulu ... Zulu..." spoke the Tired Man. Then there was Morse code: Dut-dut, Dut-dut, Dut, Dut.

"Paper," Griff said. He spoke so low I couldn't be sure I'd heard him correctly. Then, again, "PAPER!" this time he yelled it so loud I thought he was having an episode.

"Alright! Keep your shirt on," I dug the notebook out of my pants' pocket, handing it over to him. He scrawled a grid onto the notepaper and plopped some dots down within its borders. Then he chicken scratched some characters in the top margins.

The Morse stopped .... "Radio Outpost Centauri". A waltzy piano melody started up followed by a sultry horn section, "Couple of jiggers of moonlight and add a star, pour in the blue of a June night and one guitar..."

Griff wasn't saying anything. As a matter of fact, he seemed enraptured by the big band song on the radio, nodding his head in time with the beat. Naturally I grew impatient with him, "Well? What was the message?"

"They were coordinates. See these numbers?" He pointed to the chicken scratches at the top of the page. "These are longitude and latitude."

"What's the grid for?" I asked.

"It's a rough map of the area. See this area in the middle-left quadrant?" He pointed to one of the dots on the left of the page. "This is the location it pointed to, in the uninhabited grasslands." Fantastic! I wanted to see what was out there. "Alright, I'm going to check it out. You coming with me, Griff?" He nodded affirmatively.

I grabbed my coat and stepped outside. Anju was waiting there. The clouds in the sky were dark and foreboding. Anju pointed upwards, "It's about to rain any moment. Get in the car quickly, my friends." No sooner had we loaded into the black taxi than the first droplets of rain spattered across the windshield. "So ... where will we be headed tonight? Chasing down the trail of another corner store holdup man?"

"No, not tonight I hope. I'm not sure exactly where we're going yet, only that it's outside of town to the west, in the grasslands."

"Is that all we have to go on?" Anju asked.

I looked at Griff and motioned for him to answer the man's question. Griff unfolded his notepaper, showing it to Anju and said, "Here's a rough map with the coordinates. The grid corresponds to the Boroughtown surrounding area."

"Got that Anju?" I asked.

"I think so," he pulled a folded map out of the glove compartment. He opened it up and overlaid the grid sheet on top of the map. Anju raised an eyebrow, "This *is* in the grasslands. I think I know the general area."

I patted him enthusiastically on the back, "You're the man, Anju. I'll plug the coordinates into the GPS on my phone too."

As we sped off down the mountain a real downpour started up. It got so bad you could hardly see more than a few feet in front of the cab. Anju slowed us down to a crawl to ensure we didn't ram headlong into an oncoming vehicle. I was more concerned we'd accidentally careen off the road and explode on impact at the base of the mountain. *Is that a real thing or does it only happen in the movies?* I wondered, fingers crossed I'd never have to find out.

Slowly but surely Anju got us to the area he'd describe, about 10 miles outside of town. Watching the GPS, I had him take a right off the highway onto a road heading deeper into the prairies. Shortly after that we took another right onto an unmarked gravel road. This road took us towards a picturesque valley, dimly visibly through the pummeling rain shower. There were three clay buttes atop a small hill. Midway up that hill stood a lone elm tree. The branches of the elm swayed violently, beaten steadily as they were by the gale winds of the storm. As the car approached this tree the GPS on my phone started going haywire until the device scrambled and turned itself off. We were close to our destination but without the GPS guidance I couldn't tell exactly *how* close.

"Stop the car, Anju."

He pulled over to the side of the road and, in an uncharacteristically bad spot of driving, rolled the tires down onto a thick, gooey plot of red mud. "Fuck!" Anju exclaimed. "I mean 'Oh My!' I apologize for my language, sir."

"That doesn't look like it'll be easy to pull out of."

"I'm so sorry, sir. Would you like me to get us out?"

"No that's okay. We'll stay here a moment."

The tree was very close now. I watched it, gathering my thoughts. It appeared downright valiant in its lonesome stand against the oppressive force of the wind. There's no beating nature but we can each hold our ground for a time. A savage streak of lightning illuminated the night sky, terrifying a skulking badger. It ran down the hill, behind cover of a skunkbush.

I don't know what came over me next. I felt a compulsion. Opening the car door, I hopped over a high stream of rainwater flowing outside the vehicle, landing onto the wheatgrass of the prairie. The ground was squishy and wet, soaking right through to my socks. I started running.

"Hold on, sir. It is not safe right now!" Anju yelled.

But I couldn't help myself. Something sacred, something integral to the very core of my being drew me towards that tree. It was an animal instinct beyond conscious thought. With each step, the ground beneath my feet crackled with an electric energy. My hair stood on end. Then just before I reached the elm, a bolt of lightning seemed to jolt right from the very sky above, rending the elm in half. The ensuing blast knocked me backwards, right off my feet, and I started tumbling down the hill. I tried to halt my descent by bracing my arms against the mud. Before I could get any traction the side of my head struck a rock ... hard. From that point I slipped in and out of consciousness for a time. I have vague memories of opening my eyes three times. The first time my lids opened I saw the two halves of the elm engulfed in flame. The second time I awoke, I witnessed The Great Ulysses standing over my helpless body. I began to panic a little inside. Griff and Anju were screaming from somewhere off in the distance. The third and final time, I was being lifted off the ground by a bespectacled man with stubble and long, dirty blonde hair. Then I lost it all for a while in the blackness.

I awoke on a dirty old mattress in what appeared to be a disheveled research station. I saw computer monitors, old coffee mugs, and newspapers strewn about the floor, metallic shelves and file cabinets galore, walls covered with maps or scientific diagrams, and a dusty calendar of swimsuit models from 1988. I could hear muffled yelling from somewhere to my left. I stood up, groggily. There was a window across the room. Through it I saw Anju and Griff seated in an ocean blue glass tile room. They were silent. The yelling came exclusively from the man with the long, dirty blonde hair, who was pacing in front of them in a state of severe agitation.

I got up quietly in order to escape the stranger's notice. It wasn't hard to stay out of sight. I was barely had to duck to remain below the opaque metallic walls of the room, well below sightline. There had to be an exit somewhere. I waddled forward to do a little reconnaissance. The research station was built into the cliff face of a canyon. The front wall of the room was almost all glass. I pressed my forehead against it and looked down. The view went straight down for about a hundred feet into a rushing river. It made my head dizzy just to look. The canyon was between two massive buttes in what must have been the badlands near where I'd lost consciousness. The rain was still falling in torrents outside. It poured so hard that a hawk, pummeled by droplets, was forced to land mid-flight onto a root-branch protruding out of the canyon walls. Since it was still raining, perhaps I hadn't been under for that long after all. Either that or the storm was worse than I'd anticipated.

At first it seemed like the entire station was just this smallish office space before me; filled with computer mainframes, radio transmitters and other paraphernalia. There was a bookshelf with some mystical-sounding books (like *The Sacred Mushroom and the Cross* and the *Theophrastus Redivivus).* But on closer inspection it was much more than that. There was a bolted metal door in the rear of the room. It looked important. Maybe *this* was the exit back to the surface. I snuck over to it, checking over my shoulder that I hadn't been made by our longhaired captor. I lifted the lock, turning the handle in towards myself. Then, with a little pressure it opened right up. Inside was a corridor, like something you'd expect to see in a military base. It was hard to make out through the darkness inside. But every 50 yards or so there was a pair of blinking red emergency lights on either side of the hallway. This went on as far as the eye could see. I realized this corridor could have stretched back for miles. Maybe even underground of the very spot in the grasslands where I'd passed out in front of the elm.

I stood there a moment, frozen in time, pondering my predicament. If I went down the corridor I might be able to find an escape door, hatch, or whatever kind of exit the installation had. It could be that I'd make it back to the highway and bring back help for my friends. I took a step through the threshold. But wait ... then again I could get lost wandering the tunnels, only to return empty handed. By then all that might be left of my friends would be the violated remains of their corpses. For that matter, this vicious-looking reinforced steel door might be sealed shut from the other side. Or worse yet ... this installation could have lethal countermeasures for intruders. I might end up bullet-riddled, gasping for breath in the darkness, watching the blinking red lights fade to black.

I decided that there was no other choice but to confront

our host and find out what was going on. Sure, he looked agitated, unstable even. He was yelling and wildly gesticulating with his arms, all a blur of flannel shirt sleeves. But maybe it was all a misunderstanding. We can talk man to man, come to an understanding like the civilized humans we are. I stood on my tip toes to grab a hammer resting on one of the metal shelves. You know, just in case he came out raving about his dead mother or putting lotion in the basket, I could pop him a good one in the kneecaps. Then I tapped on the glass and scurried out of sight, positioning myself beside the doorway. The door flung open and the man's startled eyes went straight toward my hammer.

"Mother," he stammered. I drew back my hammer for the blow, "...of God!" He ran back inside and ducked behind Anju screaming, "He's got a hammer. Tell him to put that thing down!"

"What?!" I shouted.

"Put down that hammer before you hurt someone... SIR!" Anju reproached me.

I'll admit I was confused. Here I was about to save my friends from a madman and I end up getting reprimanded for being a psychopath. "Does he always react with such... primal aggression?" the man asked. Griff and Anju shrugged.

A rush of blood flushed through my cheeks. I relaxed the tension in my arm, cautiously stooping down to place the hammer on the cement floor of the laboratory. "Are you quite alright now?" the stranger asked condescendingly. I nodded reluctantly. It wasn't often I allowed someone to speak to me like a child (a mortal sin against a dwarf) but I was embarrassed enough to admit I deserved it.

The stranger stood up and unclenched his shoulders. "Come on inside then. I've been waiting for you."

The room was austere, with only a few chairs. The stranger offered me one of them and I took a seat. I noticed an adjoining studio at the far end of the room. It was filled with radio transmitting equipment. "Are you the one who's been transmitting the pirate radio signals just after midnight?" I asked.

"Yes." I expected him to continue, yet instead he pulled out a comb from his breast pocket and started combing his hair.

"Well? What's the meaning of all this? Why were you broadcasting the signals? Why have you abducted us? For that matter, why were you in here flailing about like a madman?"

Anju came to his defense, "Genie, Mister Albuquerque here has been a complete gentleman since we arrived. He even made us some warm cocoa." As evidence, Griff lifted a steaming Styrofoam cup of the stuff. A thin chocolate moustache accentuated his lip. "But, I hope I'm not being too rude when I say that our host is a bit … eccentric."

I looked Albuquerque right in the eyes with dread skepticism. To my surprise I didn't see the chilled, shark eyes of a deceptive psychopath. I saw the bags under his eyes, the jittery twitch of a dogged obsessive, holding onto caffeine reprieves to stave off slumber. This was my Tired Man.

"So … Albuquerque?"

"Just call me, Glenn" he responded, still threading the comb through his long hair, like it was a compulsion.

"Glenn, I've been listening to the radio scanner every night this week. You could call it a hobby of mine. Every night at 12:01, just after midnight, I hear your voice and the DutDutDut of your Morse code. It was driving me man with curiosity. My pal Griff here listened in and translated the coordinates you were broadcasting. Well, here we are now. You called and we came. So tell me, what's it all for?"

"I've been waiting a very long time for someone to respond to my transmissions," Albuquerque answered, "I'm a researcher for a U.S. intelligence service you've never heard of."

"Oh yeah? Why not?"

"Because no one else has either. I've been researching here in Boroughtown for the last 17 years, on matters of the arcane sciences. As I explained to your friends earlier, I'm deeply embarrassed about how things have played out. You were making a beeline for the coordinates I put out and I was watching you all the time from my monitors. And then you suddenly veered off into an area of intense electromagnetic power during a lightning storm. The kinds of devices I have operating under that grassland are nowhere near safety compliance ... uh, at the moment."

"So what are you? Some kind of geologist?"

"Funny you should mention that because this research station was initially built into the cliff face for that exact purpose, but no. I'm a theoretical physicist dealing with macroscopic scales beyond anything found in traditional academia. Let me ask you a question. Have you ever noticed how many of the certifiably insane drift into this small plot of land you call Boroughtown? Perhaps you should consider that this isn't just random chance. No, not random chance: that it's a celestial event happening at such a macroscopic level it is nearly imperceptible to our own limited senses."

I noticed I was starting to get a headache. At first I thought it was just my idiot mind trying to keep up with the professor but then I realized what it was: alcohol withdrawal. I needed a fix ... *bad*. But I tried to keep up with the program. "Do you have any idea how that sounds, buddy?"

"I assume that you're aware of how dogs, cats, bats, whales and other animals can detect sonic frequencies that we cannot."

"Of course. Say have you got a drink somewhere around here?"

Albuquerque ignored my request. "Well did you also know that these variances exist even within the sensory capabilities of our own species?"

"What, you mean like ESP & such? That's a load of bull. There's no evidence whatsoever for something like that."

"Let's leave aside anything controversial for a moment. It is an undisputed fact that teenagers can hear tones that grown adults cannot. This is just a single example."

"So what does that tell you?" I asked.

"It tells me that a micro-evolution has occurred. A genetic mutation unique to Boroughtown, possibly passed down through the extended Borough family line."

"That includes an awful lot of people in these parts."

"Indeed. Come let me show you in a way that might make more sense to you," Albuquerque jaunted out of the room.

"You comin' Anju?"

"I'm not feeling so good, sir. I think I'll just wait here and keep an eye on our friend." Griff, as usual, sat silently.

I got up and followed Albuquerque back into the main room. On the back wall near the reinforced steel door was a series of computers and monitors. Albuquerque punched in a line of code. This loaded up a program which displayed a global scale, topographical map of the Planet Earth. I noticed something strange about it right away: all of the landmasses were clumped together in one large supercontinent. The left side of Africa plugged in to the right side of South America, the right side of North America into left side of Eurasia and so on.

"This is Pangea approximately 180 million years ago. All of the various continents we now know were joined together as one. As you can see there is no topographical evidence of human environmental impact." He punched in a few more keys and time on the simulation sped up exponentially. The first thing I noticed were the continents drifting apart into their present configurations. I was increasingly aware of an agitated, anxious feeling poking at the frayed ends of my consciousness. Perhaps it was an awful secret trying to make itself known beyond the defense of my good reason.

"Say, Albuquerque ... you wouldn't happen to have a drink around here somewhere would you?" I asked tapping my finger against the metal tabletop.

"Sorry, I'm strictly a psychedelics man," he noticed my shock, "For research purposes of course." He took the comb back out of his breast pocket and tapped it against the screen. "Here we are at 3,000 BCE and if we were to *zoom* in," responding to his voice the program did just that, "we can see the first complex civilization of Sumer in ancient Mesopotamia."

There was architecture there; homes, temples, gateways, libraries, statues, and for the first time, human beings themselves, scurrying about like ants. "What is the point of showing me all this?" I finally asked.

"*World view,*" the screen zoomed back out again. "We're almost there." Albuquerque ran the comb through his hair again while we waited. Not a single hair on his head was amiss, yet he continued guiding it straight back across his head. "As you've seen, the population really started to grow steadily around 12,000 years ago with the invention of domestic agriculture. But then we get to modern civilization in the 20th century..." Albuquerque leaned over to an old cassette player and hit the 'play' button. It was cued to Wagner's Ride of the Valkyries. "Dum-ta Da-tum Dum..." He'd obviously given this presentation a bit of thought. It was very dramatic. Boom. There was suddenly a topographical explosion of suburbs, bridges, Great Walls, Eifel Towers, cultivated patches of farmland, high rises, slums and everything else that modern human civilization entails. It all bloomed from the earth like flowers.

"Like fungus, eh?" Albuquerque asked.

Or like fungus, I thought. "Sure, I can see it. What's your point though?"

He minimized the topographical program and brought up a time-lapse photography video of fungi growing along a forest floor. "My point," he tapped his comb against the screen, "is that *we are the fungi.*"

"For what purpose?"

"We are aiding in the evolution of a much larger living thing. Think about it. Each of us is like a single cell in the fungi, so tiny in comparison to the whole that it. Each of us think that we're operating autonomously when we're really serving a much larger purpose."

"I get you. Kind of like how our own bodies are composed of all these kinds of living bacteria and viruses, right?"

"Precisely. Now you're getting it."

"But you still haven't explained why Boroughtown *specifically* interests you or why you sent out the invitation to find you here."

"All in due time. First: why Boroughtown? Just as some parts of the body are specialized for breaking down chemicals, metabolizing proteins or whatever, Boroughtown has its own unique function in this hypothetical celestial body."

"Hypothetically?"

"Um, yes. There is no way to prove it conclusively ... yet. As I say, this is all a theoretical event happening at such a macroscopic level that our own senses are wholly inadequate to comprehend it."

"All this is possible, I'll grant you. But, no offense, there's no way you could ever prove anything. If all of this is beyond the ability of human beings to sense, what makes you any different?"

"Prove, no. But *sense*, yes. You see, with the technology

available to me within this station I have not just sense but ... meta-sense. Where others think singular thoughts, *I* have access to *all* the thoughts. These systems (Display analysis) comb through the content of cell phone calls, social media posts, police blotter, psychiatric and legal documentation for clues." It seemed the good professor and I had not so dissimilar pastimes. "There is a content analysis of these data points occurring as we speak, looking for commonalities and hidden themes within the milieu. Not only that but I have eyes and ears throughout Boroughtown and beyond (Visual grid)." Row after row of surveillance footage lined the screens. "Every gas station, church, highway, neighborhood, diner, rest area, parking lot, or tourist trap is wired with hidden video cameras."

"Hold on. You see *everything* that goes..."

"We're not done here," he interrupted, "I've been generous enough to answer all your questions so far. Well, I've got a few of my own."

I scratched my ass and thought about it a moment. What the hell, I figured. "Go ahead. I don't suppose it'd hurt anything."

Albuquerque dug a clipboard enthusiastically out of a messy drawer. He seemed genuinely excited. "Fantastic. Let's get started. One, do you have a history of psychiatric disturbance or substance abuse?"

"I'd have to say yes, I do."

"*Very* interesting," Albuquerque checked off a box, "Two, have you experienced any hallucinatory visions?"

"Yes, unfortunately."

"Did these visions involve extraterrestrials, gods, succubae, incubi, extradimensional beings, or ghosts of the departed?"

"Uh-huh."

"Interesting. Very interesting," Albuquerque squinted at me, "Have you ever been an attendee at the Bohemian

Grove gentleman's club?"

"Er, no. What's that?"

"Tsk-tsk, forget about it," Albuquerque shifted his reading glasses. He'd lost his place on the sheet, "Ah, here we are. Do you ... have any involuntary reactions to hearing the word 'iridescent'?" He squinted again, examining me carefully for some kind of change I could not detect. "*Iridescent*," he repeated.

"Hmm, I guess not." But I looked myself over just to be sure.

With an unexpected, mercurial passion, Albuquerque slammed the clipboard down onto the table. "Agh. What a disappointment! You started out with such promise." He buried his face in his hands.

Albuquerque looked so crestfallen that I felt an irresistible urge to try and console the man, "Come on now. Three out of five ain't bad."

But it didn't seem to work. "This is science, man! It must be precise."

"I don't know what to say. I'm just sorry it didn't work out for you." But my sympathy had its limit. After all I had my own agenda to look after. "Say, while I'm here maybe you can help me out with a problem of my own. My friends and I ended up here while searching for a woman. Her name is Marissa Stotgard. She's 5' 6", slender, long brown hair. With all the uh, "meta-senses" you've got going on here maybe you ... possibly ... could help us determine her whereabouts?"

Albuquerque flew into a rage at the suggestion, "No. No. No! I simply do not have time for trivialities when the evolution of universal consciousness is at stake." But I couldn't give up the ghost easily. This might be the best chance I'd ever have to find Marissa. I'm no human communications expert but I knew there had to be a better way to placate him. "The calculations were so clear. How could I have been so mistaken?" he sobbed. All the color and passion had drained out of his face.

"Well, Professor Albuquerque that may be true. But I wasn't even the one who deciphered your message."

He stopped sobbing and looked up at me. The color even returned to his cheeks, "You... you weren't?"

"No, actually that was my friend Griff over there." I pointed him out. "He's something of an expert in communications, like you are. And you want to talk about a guy who sees things other people don't? Holy shit, he's your man."

Albuquerque wasn't as pleased by this news as I thought he'd be. "Oh, damn it. You mean the silent one? I questioned him for over half an hour without eliciting anything more than vague gibberish. That just won't do."

A-ha! I'd drawn a handful of aces. The God of Fortune smiled on me that day. "Professor, my man, you only have to know how to make him comfortable first. Lt. Griff can speak plain English just as clear as you and I."

The professor perked up again. "Then bring him in here immediately. *Make him* talk to me."

"I absolutely can do that for you, Professor Albuquerque. I just need one little favor from you first."

"Hmph. The woman, huh? What did you say her name is?"

"Marissa Stotgard. M- A- R..."

Albuquerque plopped down onto his swivel chair, rolled up to the desktop computer and typed her name into a database. Within seconds a picture of her appeared on the monitor, along with her vital statistics and last known coordinates by time and date.

"This is her, yes?" he asked. I nodded affirmatively. "Her last geolocation was two nights ago in Kippowaya. She's been tagged in that general area 83% of the times she's been located over the last five days."

"Hmm. Safe bet then." Kippowaya: a ghost town just beyond the Boroughtown limits is about a twenty minute drive from town. It was an oil drilling outpost, founded by Old Man Borough during the early days of the boom, then abandoned around the turn of the last century. The thing about Kippowaya was that it wasn't only a place that people worked. They slept there, drank there, went to church and schooled their children there. There's a two-story bunkhouse, a saloon with glass beer bottles walls, a small church, a post office, school and various other buildings. All these were deserted a long time ago, to the best of my knowledge. "Albuquerque, maybe you can tell me why she would be in an abandoned ghost town."

He shook his head, "Abandoned, no. No, not for some time."

I tried to interject with some questions but he'd have none of it. "Bring in your friend. I want to speak with him immediately. I won't address another thing with you until you bring him to me."

I could tell that he was digging his heels in on this one and I didn't want to spend all morning arguing, so I retrieved Griff from the "interrogation chamber" (at least it was in my mind). When I entered the room I noticed Griff had found some loose maps lying around the room and begun scribbling grids on top.

"What you working on, pal?" Damn it. I didn't mean for that to come out as condescending as it did. For whatever else he is, Griff is a fucking genius and we wouldn't even be here without him. But I realize that I'm a fucking idiot. He was so spaced out he ignored me anyway. If this is the way he's going to play it, the timing couldn't be worse.

Anju was more helpful, "He's been working on this ever since you left the room."

Suddenly Griff's eyes snapped forward to meet my own, "Did you know that Jupiter is ascendant at this time of year?

Every place on Earth has either a 'mother' or 'daughter' location somewhere on the planet. Do you want to know where our location's 'mother' is?"

I *hate* astrology. It's all a bunch of nonsense gobbledygook. "Not really. But that guy in the other room; he would *love* to hear all about it. That's why I've come to get you, because he *really* wants to talk to you about your maps ... and uh, some other things."

"No, thank you. That guy ... is a crackpot."

I had to cover my mouth to keep from laughing in his face. This was from the guy who was just talking about astrology? "Listen Griff, will you just talk to the guy for me, please? He's told me where the girl is and I've kind of promised him you'll answer a few questions in return."

Griff reluctantly nodded his head, "Fine. But I spent enough time being prodded by the military shrinks. If I say, 'No' it stops. No questions asked. Have I got your word that you'll back me up?"

"Absolutely, man. You've gotten me this far. I'm behind you all the way."

"Ok."

I looked over at Anju. He was giggling like a bangdu about something on his smartphone screen. "Sure you don't want to come with us, Anju; see what all the hubbub is about?"

"No thank you, Jean Genie." He held up his phone, grinning, "I have the Wi-Fi password."

Griff scooped up his maps. "You won't need to bring those, Griff," I said.

"You never know what prying eyes might do with this information." He motioned towards Anju who was singing a Bollywood show tune under his breath. I sighed.

When we approached, Albuquerque was combing his hair in the reflection of an old computer monitor. He whirled around when he saw us approaching in the glass.

Looking Griff over he demanded, "Tell me you've at least been to the Bohemian Grove."

Griff looked down at me for approval and I nodded. The Griff hesitantly answered, "I've personally witness the robed ones burning Care beneath the Altar of Moloch in the pale moonlight."

Albuquerque's face lit up with childlike enthusiasm, "You're the one," he beamed. Noticing the crumpled papers in Griff's hand he asked, "What have you got there?"

"These? Just the gibberish of a crazy person," he muttered.

"Nonsense! Explain it to me, Lt. Griff," Albuquerque insisted.

"Well," he continued shyly, "the alignment of the planets clearly show a relationship between this research station and a dominant pair in..."

Professor Albuquerque was literally leaning forward on the edge of his seat, "Yeeess? Where?"

This was my cue to interrupt, "So professor, the corridor behind the reinforced door leads back to our taxi?"

"Yes, of course. The 23rd door. Take the left-hand path at the fork ... Oh and be sure to disarm the security apparatus at the console on the inside wall; code is 9112001."

"Do you want us to wait up for you, Griff?" I asked out of abundance of caution. He was just as hooked as the professor, a perfect pairing.

"No, I'll find my own way back. Go on."

Albuquerque could hardly contain himself, "Ok, now. Enough of that. Go on, Lt. Griff before I lose my patience."

Griff was only too happy to oblige him, "See the grid I've drawn on this map of Southeast Asia? It corresponds to a 'parking garage' near the United Nations Building in downtown Bangkok..."

I waved Anju over and we made our way down the

corridor to the 23rd door. Behind the door was an upward silo containing a ladder heading straight up for about fifty feet to an escape hatch. We climbed on and on sweat dripping, muscles aching, until we reached the hatch. I turned a circular lever within its center and it opened up into the grassland. Nearby I could see both the charcoaled remains of the lonesome elm and our jet-black taxicab (which we'd still have to push out of the goddamn mud).

7

Mitch Schroderberg called the next day to discuss our agenda, "Mr. Scaputo, I cannot stress how important it is that you arrive on time for our meeting with the Gambinis tomorrow morning."

"Don't worry, Mitch. I'll be there," I reassured him. I fiddled with a pack of cigarettes in my breast pocket until I was able to get one lit between my lips. "You know that we found her last night? Or at least we know where she is."

"That's great," he replied without actually sounding like he gave a damn, "We'll tip the police off and..."

"No, no, no. The people she's with; they're stupid animals, Mitch. If they get to feeling trapped I'm sure that they'll do something rash like hurting her. I'm going to get her tonight, along with Griff. We'll talk sense into them, bribe them, whatever it takes if we can't just outright sneak her out."

Mitch's voice grew irritated as I'd never heard it before, "That's ... that's an *astonishingly* bad idea. As I've said, you MUST be at this meeting tomorrow. Nothing can go wrong now. Hundreds of people are counting on you to do the *responsible thing*. Besides that, you'll have our Mossad associate at your disposal inside three days..."

I took a long drag of the smoke. I hated giving bad news. "From what I know about the place she's at, Kippowaya, it would be dangerous to leave her there for even a single night longer than necessary. It's not up for debate. I'm ... only telling you because you have a right to know, in case something goes wrong."

I could hear Mitch's teeth grinding from the other end

of the connection. "Fine," he replied, terse and angry, "Moving on, I thought you'd appreciate some company so I took the liberty of contacting 'the agency' for another companion. She'll be arriving at the airport within the hour."

"Really?" I grew excited and a little nervous. I hadn't been with a working girl since I'd started seeing Marissa. I didn't figure it could hurt anything. "Er, good idea, Mitch. Send her on over."

"She's a brunette from Prague. You'll like her. Maybe, for the sake of us all, she'll manage to fuck that ambition out of your head."

That afternoon I admitted to myself that I needed reliable transportation on a more permanent basis and that I'd never do better than the loyal Anju Pearsongupta. When I called him about picking up the girl I offered him a generous retainer to acquire his services full-time. Thankfully, he accepted.

"Thank you so very, very much. You have my deepest gratitude. Oh and one other thing, Genie. Sometime earlier this morning I returned to pick up Mister Griff."

I was relieved. "Great news, Anju. Is he alright?"

"Yes sir, but I think you really must speak with him immediately. He has some new information from the distinguished Professor Albuquerque. I rarely speak against your plans, sir but this once I must beg you not to go."

"Come on. It can't really be that dangerous can it?"

"This I cannot explain exactly. For that you MUST speak to Mister Griff. But I can tell you: your plan is not only a little dangerous. It is a very stupid to thing to try. I'm so sorry to have to say this. " To my surprise I could hear Anju weeping on the other end of the line, "And, to tell the truth, I've grown to see you as a brother, Mister Genie. I... I do not wish to see you die."

For someone who'd never known what it was like to

have a real brother I unexpectedly, reflexively shared a bit of his emotion, "Anju, I'm touched, really. I promise that I'll speak to Griff about it. We'll come up with a good plan, you'll see."*

* Despite being the quintessential Midwest United States town, the story of Boroughtown is also the success story of immigrants like Bobby Two-Shanks, Mitch Schroderberg and Anju Pearsongupta. Much has been made in the press about American hostility to immigrants but this is demagogic hogwash. I sincerely wish for my readers to view this novel as a love letter to immigrants who've done things the right way: entered the country legally, integrated with the culture and otherwise shown respect to their new home.

I flipped on the stove and cracked some eggs into a pan. While waiting for the iron to heat I noticed the sound of crinkling aluminum cans in the very outer limits of my perception. I gandered out the rear window towards the direction of the sound. At first, I wasn't able to discern anything out of the ordinary. It was a bright day, sunshine streaming down on a hillside covered in the reddish brown leaves of fall. The trees on the lawn had dropped their foliage earlier than most. Their barren, skeletal arms reached straight out towards the sun for succor. Then I noticed it, lying in what remained of the shade of the tree: a man with his face planted so firmly into the ground that he might've landed that way from an airplane. His knees rested on the ground with his ass waving high in the air. It looked uncomfortable as hell but I couldn't imagine how he'd managed to fall asleep that way. There were brown-tinted beer cans scattered around the body like leaves. I cut off the burner and stepped outside. Poor Griff; of all the people I grew up with in Boroughtown, he used to be the most responsible, the one most characterized by moderation. Now he was no better than the rest of us. Maybe, just maybe, there was something to Albuquerque's theories after all.

I placed my boot on his ass and gently tipped him over. It made a loud crash when he toppled over into the pile of cans. Griff awoke with a start. He screamed out, flailing his arms and legs. I instantly regretted waking him up this way, "Griff. Griff. It's me. Calm down, pal."

He slowly appeared to regain cognizance. I'll never forget the terror in his eyes when he stared into my own fearful eyes and asked, "Was it only a dream?"

"It was only a dream," I answered reassuringly. I thought that was what he wanted to hear, but tears began streaming from his eyes (What can I say? It was turning into a very emotional day for everyone.).

"No, why did it have to be ripped away from me again? How many times do I have to be *born back* into *this world*?" Ugh, the agony in his voice.

Fuck. I helped him back inside and fixed him a hot plate of scrambled eggs with Cheetos and a strong cup of coffee. He devoured them with renewed enthusiasm. It seemed to bring him back around a bit. "See? It's not all bad." He grunted. It was a positive grunt at least. "Why do you do that to yourself, Griff?"

"Mister Low and Mighty has been sober for a full twenty four hours, eh?" he spat balefully. Ooohh, someone was in quite the mood.

"I don't mean it like that. It just seems like you're punishing yourself unnecessarily."

"No, you've got it backwards. I was relieving myself from the pain of childbirth."

Who knows what he meant by that. "Did the professor knock you up with one of his theorems, lieutenant?"

"In a manner of speaking ... yes, in fact. I am the midwife for his ideas. Trust me, the most powerful concepts are the most painful to conceive."

"I'm pickin' up what you're putting down. The great paradigm shifting geniuses are usually tormented, addicted, filling a hole of some kind ... whatever you want to call it. Freud had cocaine, Hemmingway had absinthe, Phillip K. Dick was on so many amphetamines he couldn't even remember writing his best novels ... Why do you think they end up like that?"

Griff took a smoke out of the pack and lit it. "The thinking is shifted to the right or the left of the norm, man. The same shift of perspective that lets them see things in exciting ways destroys their functional abilities in the "normal" world. But then in some cases maybe it's the other way around. Maybe they're so miserable in society that they retreat from it. Their brain plays on its own loop for so long that it has to start inventing brand new things for the sake of novelty."

I liked Griff's train of thinking here, "I've always thought that you have your deepest insights when you're alone. The outcasts who manage not to go insane create the new paradigms. Sometimes they catch on."

There was a knock at the front door. However this was only a courtesy since the "visitor" had a key to the front door. " 'ey! Can anybody bloody 'ear me? Is this still the domicile 'o Jean Genie Scaputo or 'ave any more resident hoods moved into the premises?"

A woman's voice followed, "Why don't you shut the fuck up for a minute? Always jabbering about this and jabbering about that. Makes me want to drill a hole through my brain."

"Christ, I take ye to merry ole bloody England to meet me ma and pa; first time I been in thirty foogin' years and I can't even get a little appreciation from ya! Oof, hold the door for me will ya love? This might be a priceless work 'o art one day."

It was undoubtedly Bobby-Two Shanks along with

Maybelline, returning from Southwark, England. I rushed to the front door to greet them. Under Two-Shanks right arm was a large framed painting. When he'd come to me for money to take the trip I'd agreed, on the condition that he found me some fine piece of English art. Why'd I do something like that? Well, first because being formerly homeless, I had nothing of my own to decorate my new mansion with and second, because I'd run out of ideas for things to spend my money on. If there was one thing I knew about rich people, they loved spending money on priceless art. Why not kill two birds with one stone?

Two-Shanks and Maybelline dropped their argument, greeting me all smiles in the foyer. "Hey Jean!" they exclaimed in unison. Maybelline leaned down to give me a hug while Two-Shanks set the painting down against the fireplace. I noticed a new ring on her finger.

"How are you, you bloody Brit?" I asked him with a wide smile drawn across my face.

"I tell ya, my soul is rejuvenated. The wonders that it did to me heart," he pounded a fist against his chest, "to see the dirty streets o' the ol' neighborhood." He pulled Maybelline to his side, "The little woman 'ere, never heard no one wit' a fouler mouth than she until she met me ma and pa."

I tried to imagine myself trying to understand their conversations through a storm of fucks, twats, bollocks, shits and all through thick cockney accents, "Ha! Sounds like fun. How are the folks?"

Two-Shanks sighed, "They're older'n dirt, it's true. Ma's had 'er hip replaced, walks with a cane. An' it's sad to see me da sapped of all the strappin' muscle 'e 'ad in the prime o' 'is life ... But da's face still turns the brightest red when 'e drinks too much and he'll still stay up all night tellin' 'is stories. An' ma still gets up fer 'er sermons e'ery Soonday n' cooks the finest stew Loondon's known fer at least two centuries."

Maybelline pulled a bottle of old English brandy from her purse. "We got this for you." My eye twitched. It looked positively heavenly. All my sorrows concerning Marissa could be drowned soundly in that aged brew.

"Thank you so much, Maybelline, from the bottom of my heart ... but I'm actually swearing off the stuff, at least until I can clear a few things up in my head."

"Oh fer fook's sake. I'm sorry mate. We di'n know nothin' about that," Two-Shanks apologized.

"Well, shit. Bobby what are ya waiting for? Show him The Painting!" Maybelline admonished him.

"Oh yeah! I'm excited to see this thing too, Two-Shanks," I added.

"Well," Shanks started, placing a hand on the backwards turned painting, "You know I'm no expert on these things. But I'm no ignoramus about how ta find the right people neither. I hired a *real connoisseur*," he winked with a grin," me uncle once removed, Bradford Simons from South Hampshire. He arranged a showing with some promising young candidates. After a proppa diligence, THIS is the one we selected..." I was positively anxious with anticipation. He flipped over the painting and ... my first reaction was confusion. It took me a little while to wrap my head around what I was seeing. "They call this neo-cubism I think," Shanks explained.

Much of it looked like random splatters of paint, some of it molded into geometric shapes that formed the landscape. In the center was, as near as I could tell, a boxcar with a one-eyed hobo walrus thing. Tufts of translucent smoke billowed out from an extended cigarette hanging from the corner of its mouth, the smoke obfuscating the walrus' one weeping eye. At least I think that is what is happening. I'd probably need to be stoned to know for sure. What the hell? It was weird, just like me and all my friends.

This was the perfect home for it. "It's great, man. Will you hang it over the fireplace for me?" I asked. Honestly, I was shocked that he'd found something so good. I half expected him to return with some pretentious art student's canvas covered in tossed feces and drizzled menstrual blood. Shanks took down the old mantle place portrait of an austere Borough descendant and set the new art in its place. "What's the artist's name?" I asked.

"Uh," Two-Shanks leaned his face in to make out a signature in the lower right hand corner, "Valbrecht. Oh yeah, that's right. I remember the shopkeeper tellin' me 'e's an Austrian git."

"Come here, buddy." I gave Shanks a hug, "I really appreciate it and, most importantly, it's good to have you back."

"Don't mention it, mate. Maybelline n' I are grateful ye sprung for the trip."

Out of the corner of an eye I saw Griff enter the room and lean against the kitchen doorframe. He said nothing to anyone but Two-Shanks noticed him and smiled, " 'allo, Griff." Griff nodded back, his own tempered acknowledgment.

"What do you think of the painting, Griff?" He moved in closer to inspect it, cocking his head to one side. He spent an inordinate amount of time leaned in with an eye on the very finest details.

Finally, he withdrew from the painting and answered, "There's a fine line between the artist and the autist. Both the creative and the insane are coloring outside the lines. The genius of the artist is that sometimes an entirely new picture emerges from his scribblings."

"I'm confused. Does that mean that he likes it?" Maybelline asked.

"I dunno. What ye say, Griff? Yea or Nay on this paintin'?"

"I think it's a good match for our host."

I was so relieved he didn't say something vicious to embarrass us all. I decided to end the affair with a compliment, "It's settled then. We have a hit. Now I hate to bust up the festivities so soon but Griff and I ... we have more pressing matters to discuss."

We all convened in the kitchen to discuss the situation at Kippowaya (Well, Maybelline was flipping between a trash tabloid mag and her smartphone, but she was there.)

"What did you learn?" I asked.

Griff leaned his elbows against the bar with a sigh, "The ghost town you wanna go in to for your girlfriend ... it's got the wrong kind of ghosts. Just to show you how bad it's gotten, the park service and the BLM got run out of that place so often they just folded their cards and went home."

"Who'd they abandon the place to?" I asked.

Before Griff could answer, Two-Shanks interjected, "Jus' wait a damn minute. What girlfriend? Ya can't mean the skank bitch what almost got ye killed before. Does he, Griff?"

The ex-military man's eyes darted between them both. The cross-talk made him anxious. Griff kept his eyes cast down at the table. Words spat from his mouth like bullets from a tommy gun, "Er, Jean: Kippowaya is a haven for the production and distribution of a synthetic drug called 'bath salts'. It's mostly fragmented, disorganized BUT it's also the home base of a small group of neo-Nazis led by a wild dog named Zyklon Ben. Because Kippowaya has become a no-man's land for cops it's where everyone down and out goes to hide: the pushers, killers, pedophiles, rapists, stick up men, the one with sadistic perversions shunned by society and finally, the strung out no-chancers who want to be left alone to die." Griff drew a hoarse gasp of air, then fired off another string of exposition, "Uh, Shanks: While you were gone, Jean purchased a police scanner. Every night since he's listened, obsessively, for any clue to Marissa's whereabouts. This led him to a seemingly disconnected violent crime scene and a secret government research laboratory. Somehow it all worked out because he's found where his ladylove is hiding. Needless to say Jean is still in love with her and thinks she'll love him back when he comes riding his white horse to the rescue. Of course, she'll probably just manipulate him for her own ends like she's done well ... every time before." Red-faced and short-winded Griff had finally finished his diatribe. He planted his face first smack onto the tabletop while he caught his breath.

I was taken aback, "Wow. Is that what you really think? You make me sound like a gullible idiot."

"I'd say that's jus' bout tha start o' it!" Shanks answered for him, "Genie, I 'ate to say it but you're actin' like a man never been round a woman in 'is life. This woman's got her hooks in ya. Marissa, she does not love you, pal. She'd 'ave thrown away yer life for a crack rock. Now it looks like she won't 'ave to because you're willin' to do it for 'er!" Two-Shanks threw his hands up in disgust. He turned to Maybelline, "Love, will ya get me a shot a that brandy?"

But Maybelline barely glanced up from her magazine, "Get it your own damn self."

Shanks became livid, "Woman, you do what I say or you'll be back with the pikeys in the trailer park so fast. I'll let 'em 'ave ya! Think I won't. You'll be out tha door on yer ass so fast yer 'ead'll spin." Maybelline muttered a curse under her breath ... but she got up and poured him the drink. "Thank you, love. Ya know I really love ya." He held up the bottle, "Drink?" he offered. Griff took him up but I abstained. Shanks leaned in, "See that? Tha's how ya 'ave ta 'andle a woman. Ya give an inch, they'll take a mile. Tha man 'as to provide structure, purpose."

I laughed, "I've never met a woman who would take that

from me."

"No offense mate but that's because you were poor and ugly. Now you're a very, very foogin' rich man who's still thinkin' like a poor man. There's nothin' that gets their panties wetter than money … except fer this celebrity shite," he picked up Maybelline's tabloid. There was a ham actor on the cover. "This fucker has women he's never met wantin' to fuck him. Like, in crazy, needful way. That shite is catnip." He slapped the magazine back on the counter, "But my point is that you have the next best thing: money."

"I can see your point, but I'm still ugly."

"That doesn't matter. To some women, I guess it does. But look, they may not love you for your money but they will want you. You have the leverage. If they won't go for it, kick 'em to the curb n' find another who will respect what ye have to offer."

"That seems awful cold. What about love?"

"We're just animals, mate. All the feelings are just biology ya know? Are you goin' to let some chemicals in yer brain drag ya 'round by a leash or are you going to take control for yerself?"

I groaned. Turning back to Griff I asked, "Any idea what Marissa is doing there?"

"Albuquerque thinks she's shacked up with one of the men there."

Marissa, she's beautiful I'll grant ye, but little else. You've put a greedy, selfish woman on a pedestal, Genie. E'ery cent in yer bank account and e'ery romantic gesture in yer 'eart will never, ever be enough to satisfy 'er."

I was flabbergasted, "Suddenly this conversation feels more like an intervention."

"That's cause you're talkin' about a suicide mission, mate. Griff, what would ye say the man's chances are of going in that godforsaken 'ellhole n' comin' out with the girl alive?"

"I'd say that chance is effectively zero. He'll die for sure."

"What?!" I exclaimed, "How come you didn't tell me that earlier?"

But Shanks answered for him, "This is Griff, man. I love 'im loik a brother but are ya really expectin' a man that off his rocker to be yer voice a reason?"

I started to reach for the brandy but caught myself and fumbled for a cigarette instead, "I-I don't know what to say. Maybe you're right. Maybe she did treat me like a chump. But y'all would really just leave her there to die?" I challenged them. The room grew silent.

"Think with yer 'ead, mate. It ain't as sexy maybe but it'll lie ta ya a lot less than that thing ya call yer 'eart."

And this was the guy getting married.

The doorbell rang around 2:22. Roseanna howled to beat the band so she got herself put out. The whore was at the gates. When I saw her standing in the doorway I felt like the wolf in an old Loony Tunes cartoon. Her body was perfect. Knowing that I could have her at my leisure felt like a reprieve from a death sentence. It felt like I'd been locked up on Death Row for ten years yet somehow found himself back out in the streets again.

Evidently it'd grown chilly outside because she had on a tight, black turtleneck sweater. The fabric formed an enticing landscape over her shapely round breasts. It continued pleasingly back out again to her cute little booty draped in purple spandex. *How in awe will the first astronauts to Mars be*, I wondered, *to behold the mountains and valleys of that planetary body for the first time with their own eyes*? If she hadn't been wearing those big hoop earrings that whores wear, I might have guessed she was a model or an actress instead. But I loved those whore earrings on a woman. They signaled to the most primitive part of the male brain, "I didn't come here to play games. Maybe now, or maybe a little later on, but I'm here to fuck you, buddy."

Her face was smooth, symmetrical and innocent-looking. It seemed so perverse: the thought of my cock penetrating her sweet little mouth; those doe eyes forced to gaze upon a dwarf's veiny, ossified manhood. Just the thought gave me powerful wood. I closed my gaping jaw, cleared the frog from my throat and invited her in. Which of course she did; a hefty sum of money had already been transferred into her account. Her words were pleasant, the doe eyes congenial. There was only the slightest tell of disappointment in them when she first saw I was a dwarf; a true professional this one. Surely she'd also noticed my large forehead and thick eyebrows, yet she hadn't dwelled on them either. There'd be time for her to drink it all in, hopefully while I held her captive in the throes of passion.

"Vleased to meet you," she greeted perfunctorily. "Mine name, Sofia."

She was quiet, surprisingly shy. *Was this part of the act?* I wondered. The others had retreated to the pool house with the brandy. Sofia and I had the place all to ourselves. Sofia walked around and did the whole, 'Vow, I cannot velieve how *BIG* it is.' This *had* to be part of the act. No one throws euphemisms like that around on accident do they? She placed her hands against the rear glass and stared out over the picturesque valley. Now it was *her* turn to gape. There were birds chirping outside but all I could hear was how heavy her breathing became. It was rote, almost formulaic, the reaction women had to seeing the place for the first time. But then again, all I knew were whores.

A groggy memory comes to mind: late one night I'd stumbled drunk into the mansion library. I picked a book out at random from the voluminous collection. It turned out to be "Gaad Flycroft's Wonderful World of Ornithology". Inside, there was a fascinating passage on the bowerbird. The interesting thing about the bowerbird is that the males build the most elaborate nests in order to attract females. They're houses really; architectural marvels- and adorning the 'yard' are these marvelously colorful flower petals. Now I wondered if the bowerbird females breathe heavy too.

Sofia' had been wobbling on her high heels a bit, like a novice. I invited Sofia up to my bedroom. No sense wasting time when I could be exploring her young body. I let her know she could take her heels off at the foot of the stairs, let her head up first so I could watch her hips shimmy as she climbed. It was heaven ... or as close as I'd ever know.

I hopped onto the mattress, propping my head up on a down pillow. Sofia stood silently at the door, coyly awaiting instruction. Obediently she asked, "Vut vould you like me to do now, sir?" Strangely, I thought of the arguments Two-Shanks had with Maybelline. For fuck's sake, I thought of my parents. I even thought of how lonely it was to be poor, how it is that those most in need of romantic love are the least likely to get it. *This* was certainly preferable to all those alternatives.

"I want you to undress for me," I instructed. She immediately started lifting the corner of her shirt, with a jerk. "No not like that," I corrected, "Do it as slowly as possible."

"Vut?" she asked.

I didn't answer. She was figuring it out, this wasn't twenty questions. When she got down to her underwear I savored the last glimmer of mystique she held before the great revelation. What a revelation it was. I wish I could show you. She was a living, vivid dream come to life, a living, dick sucking dream. Shortly, I had her lying naked in my bed, that wonder of nature. Biologically speaking, I could never be enraptured by anything more than I was by this whore right now.

"You vant me fuck now?" Sofia offered.

"No ... no. Just relax. I want to know your body better."

It was, in fact, her greatest art. I ran my hands along her skin- the stomach, the breasts, the smooth-shaven legs. Her body was gorgeously pale too. It was warm and soft and gave off a wonderful heat that was like the essence of the beauty in life. She giggled a little bit when I squeezed her nipples.

"Ven you going to fuck me?" she insisted again.

The only part I didn't like was the talking. In her limited

conception of the thing she couldn't understand that I was already fucking her. The fucking doesn't *begin* at penetration. It begins with something mental: anticipation. It begins with something sensory: the touch, the sight, the smell. The penetration is where it ends- with the consummation, the release. Most fucks are uncompleted. I think that's why we're so frustrated as a species. But to be fair, this was my fantasy, not hers.

Mounting Sofia was this grotesquely absurd comedy. Me: the dwarf, badly spaced eyes, bad teeth, overgrown eyebrows, fat. Her: a European beauty, shapely breasts, ass, full lips, thin waist, long, shimmering black hair, green eyes. I was Quasimodo, The Hunchback of Notre Dame. She was Mary, Queen of Scots. It gave me immense pleasure to gaze into her doe eyes, with each stroke searching for some hint behind the façade, that beauty had gotten a measure of pleasure from the beast. I kept at it slowly, patiently, thoroughly.

Finally, after several intense minutes, I heard a genuine moan escape her lips, "Ugghh." The doe eyes glazed. *There* it was. I let myself finish and rolled off. Sofia got up, started putting her pink panties back on.

"No, don't do that. Come here and lay beside me." I instructed.

"Vut? I nut understand you."

I patted the space next to me on the bed. She got the message and crawled beside me onto her back. The panties were still on but I pulled them off again with my forefinger. The scent of our sex was still heavy in the air. "Now we can just lay here, naked and afraid." I rested a hand onto her abdomen so she could understand, "Relax. This is nice." She loosened up into her pillow, waving away my offer of a smoke. "We were both very clear about what we wanted and we both got it. What a novel concept."

"Iz good, yes," she agreed.

"Iz good," I mimicked. It was emboldening, Sofia's inability to understand the English language. I continued, "Better than throwing your life away for 'love'. Fuck love."

Her expression soured. She'd understood that. "No fuck love. Love iz good too."

I lit a cigarette for myself, inhaling it deeply. "I bet love is beautiful ... for people like you."

She nodded, "All the mens in my-my city come for me. I very young; find strong, handsome boy. Many, many man bring gift. But thees boy write beautiful Czech language to me. *Him* I choose."

"Ahhh ... are you still together?"

"No. Was very young theen. Him choose new girl. Also, I vant make monies."

I spoke slowly for her, "Once, I was a poor man. Now, I'm a rich man. Always, I remain a beggar for love."

But she didn't quite seem to understand. "Mmm ... We have leetle onez in my city too. Like youze. Zey play tricks, do magics, have circus. Some beg for ze monies... as you say. Sometime I see two leetle ones together: leetle man and leetle woman."

I often wonder if I'd be attracted to a midget girl. I supposed that I would if I'd ever met one. They looked alright in the pictures. As far as I knew, there'd never been anyone like me in Boroughtown.

"How leetle man like you make so much monies?" Sofia asked, growing more comfortable herself.

She obviously hadn't heard the rumors about my lottery winnings. I had a facetious grin on my face alright, "Don't you know that I'm Jean Scaputo, one of the most successful gamblers in all of America?"

But the jest was lost in translation, "I zee you are very successful man." She reached over and rubbed her hand on my chest as if to congratulate me. But I'd learned a hard lesson these past months. I no longer needed anyone else's validation, ephemeral as it certainly was.

Exhausted from fucking, I rolled over onto my stomach for a nap. "I'm going to sleep now, Sofia. You can do whatever you want: watch TV, swim in the pool. I don't care." But she didn't move except to pull the sheets up over her naked body. *Ah, the selective modesty of whores,* I chuckled to myself.

You know readers, it's not like they say at all. The sleep of the wicked comes easy.

The feeling was fear. I was in Kippowaya, or at least what I imagined it to be (myself having only once glimpsed it from the highway). So the old timey saloon, barracks and other assorted buildings were there as I remembered them but dark as shadows, undefined and shimmering against the dreamscape. I walked up the street, my boots kicking up dust with every anxious step. On the porches, inside the apothecary, the domiciles and other buildings were the shadows of people I'd never met walking upright and independent like sovereign men. As I walked past, they'd stop whatever they were doing and turn to stare cryptically in my direction.

I noticed someone following me, walking on the other side of the buildings. He'd disappear behind those buildings and then reappear in the spaces between them, in the alleys. The figure matched me stride for stride as if I was looking into some perverse funhouse mirror. I was shocked at my vision's failure to notice him immediately. Unlike the others, he was known completely to my mental faculties, existing fully detailed, in vivid color.

His beard of snakes writhed menacingly. Embers of flame burned in his eyes. Although Ulysses moved more deliberately than I, he kept pace with long confident strides. I wanted to scream out, "What do you want from me?" but feared inciting the city of shadows to violence. So instead I repeated the mantra which had banished him once before, "Ahem. Neither the real nor the unreal can harm me..." I could barely hear it in my own head over the ba-rump ba-dump of my heart. In retrospect it was pretty strange to hear my own heartbeat at all within a dream, a dream I'd recognized as such from the start. Ulysses, for his part, wavered in response to the mantra yet did not disappear.

Still, there was no aggression on his part so I turned elsewhere. From the end of the street I could hear a woman crying. This too was dreamlike, swimming through the streets like a muffled echo. I followed it to one of the last buildings on the street, a home or maybe an old post office. Stepping inside the doorway, onto a shadow that felt like wood, I followed the sound to a back room. There, crumpled onto the floor, was my old flame Marissa. She looked up at me with such helpless eyes, sorrowful tears wetting her cheeks.

"Help me, Jean," she begged, "Don't leave me here to die."

Sympathy filled my heart. I approached to comfort her. But when I reached her side she gave up the act. Her tears dried onto a face of anger, a lightning-quick palm struck my flummoxed face and her sorrowful cries transformed to cruel laughter. The force of her strike against me was so great that it jerked my head to one side. There I saw Ulysses, staring back at me through the dust of an old window. He said nothing at all yet I heard his thunderous voice within my mind, louder than trumpets blown by the damned in an orchestra from hell.

"You will die, Jean. You will die and be mine for all time."

~ ~ ~

I was awoken suddenly, mumbling and sweat-drenched by Griff overhead. He quickly explained that here was an unexpected visitor at the front gate; a stranger claiming to be former Mossad, sent by Mitch. Half asleep, I somehow made my way downstairs to the front door in my bathrobe, all brambles and bullywaste. The stranger was tall, thick with sinewy muscle on his arms, legs, chest, everywhere. He wore a light brown camo outfit perfect for hiding both in the desert sands of the Middle East and the badlands of North Dakota. On top of that he wore a black Kevlar vest with a handgun holstered at his hip. He introduced himself as Meshulam Ben-Ezra, "But you can call me Meshy. All my friends call me this."

"An' what 'bout the rest?" Shanks ribbed him.

Meshy looked him straight in the eye and answered, "All of the rest are dead."

Shanks laughed, "I 'ad a feeling you'd say that. Very funny."

But Meshy didn't laugh. He maintained a menacing stare down with Shanks until Shanks flinched (something I'd never seen him do before). Only then did Meshy release the most jocular belly laugh, "I'm only kidding, buddy. Got to maintain the pecking order." Shanks laughed along, but much more nervously this time. It was a strange sight to witness, like two animals jockeying for dominance in the wild.

"Good to meet you, Meshy," I greeted him, "I uh, must say I'm a little bit surprised. We weren't expecting you for a few days."

"This is true," he answered, "I was on holiday with my wife and child in your California. I told Mitch never to disturb me, yet still he do so," he sighed heavily, "Mitch insisted that you were in imminent danger of conducting the extraction yourself and that you would be killed if I did not arrive right away."

Maybelline had been staring lustfully at our macho house guest this whole time. "Oh, it's so generous of you to come all this way to *save us*," she complimented, flirtatiously.

Meshy wasted no time shooting down her implications, both literal and sexual, "I did not come because of generosity or heroism. I came because your lawyer offered me enough money to build my children's children's homes on the ashes of Palestinian dogs."

Knowing Mitch as I did, Meshy's response shocked me. "You do know that Schroderberg's adopted family is Palestinian, right?"

Meshy shrugged, "Eh. It matters not. Money is money." A mercenary's motto if there ever was one.

"Well, to be honest with you, I'm having second thoughts about going through with it. I'm sorry you had to come all this way out..."

"No, no, no," he interrupted, "Contractually, I have to complete the operation to receive the entire payment. It *is* going through tonight, one way ... or another."

I gulped down some spittle held nervously in the back of my throat. Summoning the courage to argue with this mountain of a man, this hardened killer was not easy. But with great effort I made myself object, "I'm very sorry um, Meshy but um, my friends have convinced me it's not worth dying over this woman; your uh, objective."

Meshy laughed his jocular laugh once more, "Ha-ha, ha-ha, ha! You think that I'd want your help on a military mission, little man? The most you can do for me is stand outside the theatre and identify I've not rescued the wrong woman."

Well, when he put it that way it sounded win-win for everybody. Why not save a life? Why not help the man earn all his money? "Alright. You've convinced me," I said throwing up my hands, "Let's make this happen."

"Gusto!" Meshy exclaimed with relish. He had a number of utility pockets on his vest. He pulled out a folded sheet of paper from one and laid it out on the dining room table. It was a finely detailed topographical overview of Kippowaya, composed of thin blue lines. Two of the buildings depicted were highlighted by red squares. There was also a solid green line located on a cliff overlooking the town. "This map I have made special for the mission, based on satellite imagery," Meshy explained. The green line represents our base camp where I will unload my gear and you," he pointed his thumb at me, "will wait until I return with Ms. Stotgard."

"And the red boxes?" I asked.

"This one houses the primary bath salt production laboratory," he point to one of the locations, "It's highlighted as a no-go zone because it's occupied at all times by Zyklon Ben," he snarled the name with contempt, "or one of his two gangster associates. These are, every one of them, very dangerous men." He popped the cap off a black marker from his utility pouch and began tracing a route. "This way I will go along the rear of the buildings, sneak through the alleyway of the domicile housing Ms. Stotgard," he pointed to the other red box, "Then we will retrace my steps back to you at base camp. Now this is the important point for you, Mr. Scaputo. I will be wearing an earpiece. If at a*ny* time you should see danger approaching my location you must radio me immediately with *this*," he pulled out a small walkie radio. "Now tell me straight. Do you think you can handle that?"

I nodded. "Yes, absolutely. I won't let you down."

"Then prepare yourself mentally. We leave at midnight."

Inside I thought, *Goddamn, this is all so fucking abrupt.* But I dared not sound the words.

~ ~ ~

I nervously awaited the appointed time. Even though it was Meshy and not me in harm's way, my mind traced every possible angle from which things could go wrong. And even if things went perfectly well it wasn't so great. I could be committing myself to months or even years of nursing a mentally shattered and physically addicted woman back to health; a woman who frankly didn't give a damn about me when *I* was down and out.

I sat out in the garden sorting these anxious thoughts while Meshy calmly and efficiently cleaned and tested his guns, radios and other equipment for the mission. There was a blazing white full moon proudly hanging overhead. I attempted to drown my focus in its majesty, repeating my mantra, fighting the urge to go running to the comfort of a bottle. But it wasn't until I heard the rhythmic hooting of an errant owl, "Hoot. Hoot. Hoot," in surreal perfect time, that my mind settled onto something approaching calm.

Meshy insisted we leave *precisely* at midnight. I moved without thinking, otherwise I would've failed to move at all. I watched my arms and legs climbing into Meshy's Jeep as if I was watching someone else's dream or a video game. VROOOM! The Jeep's engine roared to life. It carried us down the mountain like that- roaring, roaring as if it were a beast carrying us to the gates of some cruel underworld.

Throughout all this Meshy appeared absurdly calm. He said nary a word the entire drive except once turning to me in my fear and asking dismissively, "Lottery winner, eh?" I answered affirmatively but it was, of course, a rhetorical question. From what little I knew of the man he was much too prepared to harbor any doubts regarding something so basic as his client's character.

When we arrived at the red rock cliff overlooking Kippowaya, Meshy began placing his equipment- sheathing a bowie knife to his side, lodging a tiny radio into his ear canal, mounting night vision goggles atop his head in a state of preparedness. Meanwhile, I took the opportunity to inspect the valley below. It was the first time I'd ever seen the Kippowaya panorama fully, with my own eyes. Kippowaya was antiquated, dilapidated and small: about the size of a football field, only wider perhaps; one dusty thoroughfare with buildings on either side.

First on the right, there was a saloon composed almost

entirely of empty booze bottles held together by mortar. It
even had those old-timey swinging doors you see in all the
westerns movies. The place deserved to be a goddamn
landmark. I suppose it had been once, before the town was
overridden with addicts and thugs. Center left there was a
two-story house marked 'Proprietor' by a wooden sign
swinging from two short lengths of chain below the
veranda. Across from that were the barracks which, at three
stories, made it the largest building in town. This was the
building Meshy had marked as the 'No-Go Zone' occupied
by Zyklon's gang and their synthetics laboratory. And
second to last on the left was an old-style chapel with
pointed roof and a rectangular bell tower jutting out in
front. This was the building where we hoped to find
Marissa. Beyond all that, remained only the skeletons of
derelict oil towers, standing watch over the town like
ancient guardians. *From what I've seen, I think you've
failed to keep the peace old boys.*

Meshy fitted the night vision goggles over his eyes. "Uh-
huh. Ah, yes," he muttered to himself, scanning the
Kippowaya valley below. He retrieved another pair of
goggles along with a Walkie radio from the back of his Jeep.
"Try these on," he ordered, handing me the goggles.

Night vision was disorienting at first. I experienced an
onrush of lightheaded disorientation until my bearings
adjusted. Everything in the natural environment from the
sky to the buttes, from the cliffs to the bramble bushes, were
shaded in green and black light. Meshy himself stood out so
differently it shocked my senses. He was yellow and green
outlines with a bright red center.

"These have heat vision too," I exclaimed with surprise.

"Indeed. This is key to your role in tonight's affair. Look
out over the cliff," he instructed. Down in Kippowaya I
could see some things left undiscovered by my naked eye.
There were about fifteen to twenty faint heat signatures

scattered throughout the buildings. "Right now we have perhaps the most fortunate situation," Meshy continued, "There are three heat signatures inside the barracks. Hopefully this mean that Zyklon and his gang are all clustered in their laboratory rather than roaming the town as unknown variables. Now over here," Meshy pointed out the chapel, "we have a lone female, which we will hope, is your Marissa."

At this point I grew confused, "How can you tell that that's a woman in there?" I asked, "All I can see is a tiny blot of red."

"Press here," Meshy instructed, pointing to a button on the right-hand side of the headgear. "This is how you zoom in. The button behind it zooms out."

"Ahh," I zoomed in until I could make out a human silhouette. "But I still don't get it," I replied.

"Notice the gradient," Meshy answered.

Hmm, the gradient ... the gradient ... "Oh, I think I can make out her tits from here," I finally realized.

"Yes, *the gradient*," he emphasized.

"Well that's fantastic! All you have to do is sneak around the other side of the buildings and scoop her up while no one is looking."

"Exactly. If only one of her two boyfriends doesn't come back looking for her I may get out of this without a fight."

Bobby and Jerome, the true unknown variables, "Oh. Are they down there somewhere?"

"I think it's unlikely. She has a new lover now. With that said, neither of their whereabouts are presently known," Meshy shoveded the Walkie against my chest, "so keep an eye out and alert me immediately if anyone is approaching."

I flicked on my radio power, "Got it."

"Good. Then we are ready to begin at last. When we see each next, I will have your woman." With that, Meshy began climbing carefully down the stone slope rubble towards the ghost town of Kippowaya.

When he'd cleared the last bits of rubble from his boots, leaving the red rock slope for the dirt of the valley floor, Meshy unholstered his Jericho Standard Issue Israeli Police pistol and hustled to cover behind the first wooden building on the left. There were junk food wrappers, condoms and a syringe cluttered in the dirt, modern decay bespoiling historic authenticity.

Meshy's radio came through clear as a bell, without the slightest hint of static or extraneous noise. Damn good tech. "I'm in. How are things looking from up there?" he asked.

"So far, so good; everyone's in the same buildings as before."

Meshy edged to the corner of the building and looked down the alley for any signs of activity. Across the street there were several derelicts inside the saloon. But they were too bombed out to notice anything: one was passed out on the bar and two more were leaned against it, gradually swaying their heads to some silent music. "Dope fiends. What a fucking waste," Meshy whispered. "How's it looking now?"

"There's some spastic movement a couple buildings up, in the proprietor's house."

"But they're still inside?"

"Yeah."

"Then I'm going," Meshy ducked slightly and rushed past the next building, carefully sidestepping aluminum beer and soda cans, plastic wrappers and any other trash that could make noise.

Then, for the first but not last time, something went wrong. I clicked the microphone button, "Meshy we've got trouble. Two spazzes just left the proprietor's building. They're heading for your alleyway right now."

"Oh shit," Meshy lamented. He was right behind the proprietor's at that particular moment, forced to take cover against the wall. The two spazzes were both skinny and wired; one wore a tattered plaid shirt, the other was shirtless. For the record, it was about 45 degrees out, brutal winds blowing down from The Great White North, not that either man seemed to notice. The plaid-shirted one crouched down to his knees, "I'm telling you man, I've got the primo stash right here. I'm only sharing with you cause we're best buds ... but you gotta keep this a secret between us."

The shirtless one had a violent tic, his shoulder kept jerking to one side. When he answered his friend it was in rapid fits and starts, "It's ... just between ... us, Golden; our ... s-secret."

"Ok then," Golden answered, prying loose a board from the bottom of the wall. Collected inside was a veritable mountain of cigarette butts. He scooped a handful into his shirt pocket, "This should settle us for the rest of the night."

By this time, Meshy had edged himself to the corner of the building. But when he stepped forward to get a look at the men, he made a misstep onto an old glass bottle buried, obscured within the sand. I could hear it shatter through his microphone. The spastic men had too. Golden turned towards the noise and asked, "What the fuck was that?" Meshy hurriedly fastened a silencer onto his Jericho and waited behind cover with bated breath. He obviously hadn't wanted it to come to this and certainly not so early.

But just when Golden was about to head his way, the shirtless man took his spazzing to another level, "The spirits! I already told you, Golden. The spirits haunt this place."

"Oh shit. R-r-really?" Golden asked. Now he was

spooked too.

"Fuck yes. Don't you see him? He's walking towards us right now. Fuuuuck!" the shirtless man cried out in anguish, flailing his arms and legs at an invisible attacker. He'd got a taste of the salts and it'd drove him crazy. Some invisible foe appeared tackled him straight to the ground.

"Fuck this. I'm getting out of here." No sooner had his friend's feet left solid earth, than Golden was running in panic onto street.

"Are we clear?" Meshy asked.

"Yeah. Zyklon, or one his men, came out to check on the commotion. But he's focused on catching up with the dude who ran off. Now's your chance."

"Great," Meshy sighed. He opened up into a sprint. There was no way he'd be caught in that area if Zyklon decided to check things out for himself. But that didn't happen anyway. The gangster snatched Golden by the shoulders. Upon interrogation, Golden started twitching and yammering about ghosts.

"Shut the hell up you goddamn crazy," Zyklon commanded. He hauled back with a hammer fist and punched Golden out right on the spot; stone cold onto the ground. Then Zyklon strutted back into the laboratory, wiping the blood from his knuckles; danger averted.

Meshy halted his sprint beside the chapel. His nose involuntarily crinkled, neck turned, muscles themselves revolting against a foul miasmic wafting through the alley. "Close call, eh? By the way, I've found some old friends of yours." Stacked one on top of the other were the rotting corpses of Bobby and Jerome, bullet holes riddled through their chests. "Looks like an execution by firing squad," Meshy observed, crouching down, noting the state of the bodies, "Not too smart, a black and white thug partnership cutting deals with Nazi skinheads? Not a brain cells wasted between the two of the two 'em."

"Nothing in the world is more dangerous than sincere ignorance and conscious stupidity," I replied, paraphrasing a famous man.

"There's your eulogy gentlemen, Amen." Meshy bowed to their Final Remains, shirt sleeve covering nose from stench. "Alright," Meshy returned to his feet, "I'm headed inside now. Wish me luck." I needed to gasp for air. I'd been holding breath without even a conscious notice. *Oh no*, I thought, *He shouldn't have asked that of me.* Maybe he didn't know me so well after all. Of all the men I ever knew, I had the most mercurial fortune with luck. Meshy may very well have sealed his death sentence.

Meshy rounded the side of the chapel, nudging open the bullet-shaped door, checking both sides of the vestibule for foes before entering. Nothing remained of what the chapel once was; the stained glass windows were long since shattered, the pews sold at auction and the minister's lectern splintered for kindling. Meshy checked the stairwell to the little bell tower. It too was devoid of humankind, a kingdom reclaimed by dust and cobwebs. All that remained for him to check were two small ancillary rooms in the back. "I'm detecting someone's heat signature. Here goes," he whispered, hustling cautiously into the rightmost chamber.

There, lying on soiled mattress under dust-covered blankets was Marissa, shivering in her sleep below a shattered window. *At last.* "I've got eyes on the target. Just gotta wake her up and we'll get the hell out of here." Meshy placed a hand on her shoulder and shook it so gently as if he feared he might accidentally break her in two. Her frame was so thin now that it felt downright skeletal within his grasp. Gradually awoken from slumber she rolled over and opened her eyes, instantly confused by the strange figure before her. Marissa was in the most deplorable condition. Her face like Famine; gaunt and bloodless riding her pale horse beside Mr. Death himself.

"Wh-who are you? Zyklon is that you, baby?" She was in a daze, whether from drugs or slumber not immediately clear. "Get into bed beside me. I'm so *cold*," she pleaded. Meshy lifted Marissa to her feet. Draping her arm around his shoulder for support, he walked her out of the room. The simple effect of walking awoke her nervous system Bringing her around to consciousness and it agitating the confused woman, "Wait, I don't know you. Where are you taking me?" she demanded.

Meshy tried reassuring her, "I'm taking you somewhere safe."

"I don't want to go," she rasped. The vitriol in her growl surprised me. This wasn't exactly the woman I'd remembered. That woman had died, resurrected as this living corpse before me.

Against a junkie's weakened resistance, Meshy brought them both to the chapel door. But just before he struggled Marissa through the threshold she became possessed with a renewed vigor, feral and strong; shoving her would-be savior, caught off completely guard. It was just enough to create the separation she needed to bolt away into the bell tower. Marissa sprung up through the short spiral staircase of the bell tower, tearing apart the sticky spider webs netting her face, with Meshy in now desperate pursuit. He caught up, reached out for her, clenched his strong fist on her ankle but it was too late. She'd wrapped her fingers tight around the iron bell's braided rope. Meshy yanked at her ankle but she clung on for dear life. This had the effect of lifting half her body into the air suspended between Meshy and the rope. The bell jerked hard to one side. GONG! Marissa got her other fist around the rope. She was completely in the air now, shaking the damn rope violently back and forth while Meshy tried to reel her into his arms. GONG! GONG! GONG! GONG!

My heart pounded wildly within my chest, my brain

struggling to acknowledge just how thoroughly shot to hell this whole operation was. "Meshy, look out! All three of the guys in the barracks are running in your direction!"

Meshy finally planted both arms firmly around Marissa's waist, pulling her from the awful rope into a fireman's carry. His powerful leg muscles sailing them both down the staircase, pumping with strength and speed like well-oiled steel pistons. "I'm only going to have one more slim chance to get out of here alive," Meshy told me, "If I don't make it, I want you to promise me that my family will still get all the money." For the first time since we'd met there was a subtle hint of fear in Meshy's voice.

"Of course. I promise you that, no matter what," I answered.

He ran through the door at breakneck speed, immediately catching sight of the three men bolting in his direction. They wore biker gear: black jeans and leather jackets with patches of skulls, swastikas, American flags, eagles, pin-up girls and gang paraphernalia. Zyklon was immediately distinctive from the buzz cut henchmen by his cleanly shaven head, manicured goatee and muscular physique. Like Meshy, Zyklon was an alpha predator.

Meshy darted into the alleyway, hoping to avoid detection, sprinting behind the buildings to safety. But before he could Zyklon, the deft general split his men in different directions. One moved quickly through the next alley over. It was only a matter of seconds before Meshy would be cut off. "The jig is up," Meshy whispered anxiously, "I'm aborting the mission." It was down to survival now. He released Marissa from the fireman's carry and she went running into Zyklon's arms.

Zyklon would surely know where he was now that he had her; but it was too late for the gangster currently combing through the alley. The best move was to take him out by surprise, dwindle their numbers. Meshy rushed behind the building to the alley, gun at the ready. As he popped around the corner, the skinhead had his weapon at shoulder level too, but Meshy held the element of surprise. Thoop. Trigger finger pulled, the Mossad's silenced Jericho fired a lucky bullet through the skinhead's temple, blowing out the back of his head. His body dropped fast and hard into the dirt. Lucky, lucky lucky; it'd been a split-second shot that *just* managed to hit its fatal mark.

After Zyklon conversed with Marissa, the Nazi appeared to be rethinking his tactics. "Zyklon's reconvened with the third man. Something's up, Meshy." But what exactly he had in mind I couldn't discern.

"Okay. I'm taking cover in the building; try to take them out from there."

Meshy rushed around to the front. The skinheads saw him and opened fire. He got a bullet in the back of his Kevlar vest and another in his shooting arm before he even made it through the door. The wooden plank walls of the building were ancient, rotten and ineffective at stopping bullets fired with the explosive power of modern guns. A bullet pierced through the wall striking Meshy again, this time drilling into one of his calves. He had to have better cover or it would be over quick. Looking around, it was apparent that he'd entered an old bank. A medium height standing safe still remained in back. Meshy positioned himself between the safe and the wall, pushing it against his back with the strength of his legs. But those steel pistons were leaking oil now. His blood streamed out from his wooden into the floorboards.

I could hear his anguished grunts and the cries he tried to stifle out of masculine pride. The safe started to move, screeching across the floor. The pain, the effort involved I cannot even begin to imagine yet he managed to move it all the way across the room to the front wall. Now their bullets ricocheted safely off the steel bulwark. Meshy collapsed, seated behind the safe, trying to catch his breath.

The firing stopped. The skinheads could hear that their bullets were hitting solid steel. "Meshy, they're right outside now, sneaking up on the front door from your left."

Meshy popped up from behind the safe and fired through the wall. Zyklon screamed out in agony. Two bullets had lodged into his right shoulder. But that didn't dwindle the gangster's courage. Zyklon ducked down and hollered furiously at his henchman, "Fuck it. Bum rush the sumbitch." They both charged into the bank, Zyklon pushing the henchman out front. Thoop. Thoop. Thoop. Thoop. Bullets riddled the henchman's body like a colander. Zyklon pushed his body forward like a shield, slamming the corpse into Meshy, driving him hard against the wall. They struggled for the gun. It went to ground.

Meshy regained his stance, tried to grapple Zyklon's leg out from under him. He didn't quite succeed; perhaps the skinhead had had some judo training himself. However Meshy ended up charging them both right through the door and body slamming Zyklon onto the thoroughfare.

I threw my goggles to the ground. You could see them from the cliffs plain as day. There was a flurry of punches thrown between them. They rolled around like savages. With Meshy on top, Zyklon unsheathed a knife, driving it upwards into his adversary's chest. Mortally wounded, Meshy extracted his own knife, dragging it across Zyklon's neck until it split open end to end. Meshy collapsed on top of him. Their blood pooled all around them soaking into the sand.

I just stood there in shock, unbelieving. All that was left was Marissa, all alone once more. She'd been hiding somewhere down the street. I could see her coming out now, walking towards the dead men with both hands over her face in terror. Golden came out to gawk at the carnage as well. He and Marissa just stood over the bodies for a moment. Then Golden walked over and wrapped his arm around her, offering his pipe as consolation. They walked away together into the saloon. *You bitch*, I though. Look what you've caused. Everywhere you go lives turn to ruin. I'd loved you once. No more. Ever again. Standing on that dirty cliff I realized something I swore to myself I'd never forget. Love is a fog; a fog that burns with the first daylight of reality.

I woke up the next morning to wet kisses. Roseanna was standing over me on the bed, lapping her tongue against my stubbled cheek. I stroked her newly soft and full coat. "Breakfast time, eh girl?" Something felt different that morning as if I'd shed the skin of my past. The fear of leaving Boroughtown behind was gone, replaced by a fear of stubbornly remaining the same, refusing to grow and adapt in a life where I only had so much time to get things right.

I lurched down the steps in my dirty bathrobe with Roseanna close at my side. "Good girl. You love daddy now don't you?" As I poured the kibble into her bowl I thought long and hard about who *really* loved me and not who I *wanted* to love me. Standing there, half awake, it was all so clear. I picked up the phone and gave Barbara a call. She was happy to hear my voice, as always.

Anju arrived shortly thereafter to whisk me over to the Gambini détente. I let my window down so I could feel the cold air on my face. I was still in my moment of total spiritual awakeness, the kind you stumble upon by accident once every few years. "Meditation is the key, sir," Anju told me, "I experience this feeling almost every day."

When we arrived at the law office, a pedestrian recognized me through the open window, "Hey! Screw you, freak. I'd make you choke on those millions." Anju parked at the curb in front of Schroderberg's. The hostile man was still lurking around.

"I think we're going to have a problem, sir," Anju warned.

"I think you're right," I concurred, "Let's just rush into the building before there's any trouble."

But the man headed us off as soon as we stepped onto

the sidewalk. Anju tried to put himself between us, "You really must calm down, my friend. Things are not as you think. If you..." but the man shoved him aside.

He lifted me up and slammed my body against the glass window. He got so close that I could smell his last meal, "My sister lost her house because of you, you monster. She and her kids had to move in with me. My wife HATES my sister. Now I have a sister in my house and not a wife! You fucked my life!" He pulled something out of his pocket. There was a flash of steel. Then, suddenly, the office door swung open and the man was muscled off by three large Italian bodyguards. I thanked my lucky stars for that. There'd been way too many close calls lately.

The meeting itself went smoothly. Mitch had everything pre-arranged and the Gambinis were all business. Bing bang bada-boom. We bought out their controlling interest in the town and, of what remained in their stake, they agreed not to foreclose. Afterwards, I gave Mitch the bad news about Meshulam Ben-Ezra. Mitch agreed to send Meshy's family everything he would've been due if he'd been able to complete the mission.

Next, I went to Savoy's to enjoy one final bagel and coffee. I didn't recognize the new owner's but sweet, fat Dolores gave me a smile and a warm hug. Of course, there was more harassment from the public. But I patiently explained to each heckler what I'd done to save them from their predicament. Eventually they all left me in peace.

With the last of my Boroughtown responsibilities completed, I was ready to sever ties forever. I picked up Roseanna from the house and met Barbara at the rail yard, just like we'd discussed that morning.

"What will we do for money?" she asked with concern.

"Don't worry about that. We'll pick it up somewhere down the line." I told her.

The trained rolled out of Boroughtown just like I'd seen it do a thousand times since I was a child. Only this last time, I was finally on it.

EPILOGUE

My name is Ramon Rodriguez. I'm an old school reporter (older than dirt actually) working the beat in San Miguel de Allende, Mexico. I'm set up in this sweltering office downtown without air conditioning. In the summer I'm desperately plugging one of several fans into the outlets, switching the breakers ... whatever it takes to get the faulty electricity flowing in this hijo de puta. I need relief from the heat. I need relief from the debts: bar tabs, alimony, loans, car payments ... the list goes on and on I'm afraid.

I need to write another book. That's right. Maybe it'll be a hit & I can afford some air conditioning or avoid having to fight the repo men off with a crowbar. My interest has always been in telling stories about hard luck people thrust into extraordinary circumstances. I just needed some inspiration. Fuck's sake I had nada for so long.

I was sitting in my swivel chair one sleepy afternoon with my feet kicked up on the desk. My broken office window was propped open with a telephone book though the air was too still to do me any good. I'd just written an awful fluff piece on the philanthropic efforts of a vicious cartel boss who'd been pressuring the local press for some good PR. I felt disgusted with myself for writing blatant propaganda but when my editor says, "Just write the damn thing" by God I'm just desperate enough to do it. It was about that time that a refreshingly cool breeze blew into the office for the first time all week. It felt good against my old pock-scarred cheek.

The phone rang. It was mi hermana, Julietta calling with an idea for a book. She'd immigrated to the Northern

United States some years ago, settling down in an obscure town called Boroughtown, North Dakota. Julietta was in a fit of excitement about what she called "the story of the century". *Sure, I'm thinking, we're only sixteen years into the century so maybe she's right.* Anyway she rattled off a yarn about recent happenings in her eccentric little town. It was a story of exotic drugs, prostitution and a multi-million dollar heist. In the middle of it all, was a notorious dwarf named Jean Scaputo. I sat rapt by the phone, listening for hours, until Julietta had told me all she knew.

The kicker was that the guy had left town one day, never to be seen nor heard from again. Feeling a golden angle deep in my journalistic marrow I decided I'd write Jean's story. I envisioned a climactic ending where I found the lost man and figured out once and for all what had become of him. I put out feelers with my contacts across North America but nothing much happened for a while. I spent the next months researching and writing the book, eventually conceding that I might not have that ending I'd promised myself.

But towards the end of my project something turned up. I was in my office at the San Miguel Tribunal once again, this time staring in the bathroom mirror lamenting the bags under my eyes. The phone rang and I sighed, thinking it was another bill collector. Fortunately it was Martine Roya, a private investigator I'd hired to find Jean Scaputo. He was churly, fat and a liar but damned if he wasn't one of the best investigators I've ever known. "I've got him," were the first, wonderful words out of his mouth. He'd been waiting a long time to say that.

I pulled out a pad of paper and a pen, "Where?"

"You won't believe me. He's been living right under your nose this whole time. There's a hacienda in Southern Baja California. The address is..."

I scribbled it down onto my note pad. "Excellent!

You've really outdone yourself this time amigo."

"Thanks. You know I had some extra... business expenses following his trail through Tijuana."

I rolled my eyes."Oh, is that so? The booze and hookers kind of *business expenses* again Pedro?"

"Hey, it was part of the gig this time. You should see the kinds of places this little man has been to! Most of it would either twist your stomach or give you a hard on. My informant is a bartender in a Tijuana titty bar the little man frequented. My informant's seen it all, takes a lot to turn his screws, and you wouldn't believe the kind of sordid shit we had to get into together, on *my* tab, before he gave up the goods."

"I see. Well, take it up with my editor. He might cut you another check if you ask *real nice* and tell him those expenses were for hotels and airfare. Just don't tell him the truth."

"You're the best Ramon. Talk to you later amigo."

There it was. Finally. I'd been on Jean Scaputo's trail for six months. I knew everything there was to know about his time in Boroughtown but I needed more. If I was to write the story of that idiosyncratic town in the Badlands of North Dakota, filled with eccentric tycoons and criminal conspiracies, I'd need the epilogue to the story of its famous prodigal son.

I dressed sharp, for me anyway, in light brown suit and black tie. I decided to bring a small film crew along for posterity and I wanted to look good doing the job I love. But as soon as we arrived to the hacienda, out there in the desert, I realized how hot it was going to be and left the jacket in the van. The damn heat, always the damn heat: the bane of my existence. I briefly considered moving to Canada.

Approaching the front stairs I saw him. *There* sat the famous man, in a wicker chair on the shaded deck of the hacienda, drinking a margarita: 4' 1" tall, bearded, his hair now grown out shoulder length, wearing a red & green Hawaiian shirt unbuttoned to expose his tanned pot belly.

"Hi Ramon! Good to see you," he hollered, "Have a seat."

I shook his hand and sat down in one of the wicker chairs on the other side of the table. The camera crew introduced themselves as well before setting up their equipment.

"Señor Scaputo, it's a pleasure to speak with you. Mi hermana lives in Boroughtown and she speaks of you like a local legend. It was her stories that got me interested in this project."

"You mentioned her name on the phone. I don't think I've had the pleasure."

"No, you wouldn't have, señor. She moved there some years after you'd left. But the memory is still strong there. The legend is strong."

"You're too kind. I'm nothing but your typical lazy American pervert slash alcoholic. Only difference is I lucked into some money is all."

"I'd say, judging by your history, you've done a lot more than you give yourself credit. As you know my friend, I hope we can be friends, I am writing a history of Boroughtown around the time of your lottery winning. You had the instrumental role in a great social upheaval there. Although vilified as a heel at the time, in retrospect the town would have been destroyed without your intervention."

Jean didn't seem to care very much one way or the other. "I suppose so. Can I get you something to drink?"

"That would be fine thank you."

"Manuela! Mojitos for our guests please!" he yelled through the open door into the kitchen.

"Sí, Mister Jean," a plump Mexican woman answered from inside the house.

I continued, "There are many who are curious to learn what became of the little man who went from reviled outcast to erstwhile savior. I would take much joy in learning about your time since leaving Boroughtown."

"I don't suppose it would hurt anything to tell you."

"Excellent! You do me a great honor, señor." I motioned for the camera crew to begin rolling. It was about then that Manuela walked onto the deck with our drinks. She set them on drink coasters around the table. We all thanked her graciously. They were ice cold and just what we needed there in the sweltering heat of the desert.

The little man looked a little lost."I'm sorry. Like most drunks I've developed a terrible memory. Remind me who you are."

"The name is Ramon Rodriguez. I've written a number of periodicals in the Spanish language press. I've written a book on the Chicanos working the oil patches of Texas during the 1894 boom. I can leave you a copy if you'd like"

"Great! It sounds fascinating Señor Rodriguez. Encantado, by the way"

"Ha ha! Muy bien, muy bien." My laughter was a little too strong. I didn't care to mention it but his Northwestern Americano accent created the most atrocious butchering of the Spanish language I'd ever heard. But he looked so confident slinging the words that I couldn't help but be patient with him. "You look like a man totally at peace with himself out here in the desert. Some might find it odd to say a man who has wandered so far from his home has actually found himself in the process. Tell me first what happened after you found your way out of the badlands of North America."

"I got lost in a different kind of wilderness, Ramon."

Jean was clearly enjoying the attention. His words were practically dripping with theatric melodrama. *Pulitzer here I come.* "You say you were lost. What kind of accident caused you to lose your way?"

"I'm not sure I'd say my life took the turns it did because of accident. Sometimes you get lost on accident and sometimes lost is exactly where you want to be."

I started writing, overjoyed that I would at last capture the mysterious second half of this enigmatic legend's story for my loyal and beloved readers. Jean Scaputo told me all about the years since he'd last been seen in Boroughtown. With Barbara and Roseanna by his side he traveled all over the globe: from the sexual decadence of Bangkok, to the misery of the Calcutta slums (where he spent a million dollars building subsidized housing incidentally). He'd hiked the rainforests of Brazil and swam over the Great Coral Reef in Australia. Roseanna would often stay behind in the hotel, especially as she got on in years, but they were posh hotels and she lived a life of comfort.

Three years into the adventure Jean picked up drinking again in Mexico and Barbara left him. She moved into a condo near her parents in St. Bart's. She and Jean still keep in touch to this day but the drinking had made cohabitation impossible. A few years after that Roseanna passed away. She died peacefully in her sleep while she and Jean were on a beach off the coast of Spain.

Jean's tale went on and on with one adventure after another. He'd loved many other women, some for years at a time, but in the end they all left him. He'd made peace with the ephemera of love, learning to enjoy while it lasted but letting go when the time came as well. Finally when his tale ended I was ready to ask the question I'd been dying to know.

"Mr. Scaputo, at one point in your journal entries you asked what at the time must have seemed a rhetorical question. It was something like, and I'm not quoting exactly here, 'I wonder if it is better somewhere out in the world or if every city in the world was just a different version of the same fucked up town I've grown up in. It's something I've often asked myself in San Miguel."

He laughed. "Yes. I remember feeling that way like it was yesterday."

"So now that you've been around the world, maybe you can answer that question for your younger self and me: Was there a better place out there somewhere?"

Jean took a sip of his drink and thought this over for a moment. "Well, I'd have to say..."

Suddenly the camera boy interrupted, "I'm sorry, sir but the camera has run out of tape."

I smashed my cigarette angrily into the ash tray. The boys stood still, afraid to upset me any further. "Well what are you telling me for? Didn't anyone bring another tape?" This was rank incompetence of the highest order. Whatever happened to professionalism? The boy holding the boom mic snapped out of his fear trance. He dug into a little black case by his feet. Inside was another tape. I breathed a sigh of relief. He handed it off to the other boy and it was loaded inside the camera.

"Ok. We're ready to go now, sir."

"Are we rolling?"

"Rolling, sir."

I turned back to Jean, "So is there somewhere better out there for us to find, Mr. Scaputo?"

Jean laughed, "For a time it always seems so but... not really, I'm sorry to say. Everywhere it's about the same three things: money, power and sex. You either have them or life stinks."

"What about love?" I asked him, perplexed that he'd forgotten such a primal human motivation.

Something tugged him away from our conversation, a memory perhaps. His expression turned grave. He finished his drink and pushed his chair back from the table. Waddling over to an old record player he kept in the sun room by the patio Jean lifted the needle and set a record down inside. "That's the thing that makes a sad song great. Would you like to hear a song like the last gasp of a dying planet?" The needle dropped.

About the Author

Jason Kessler is a fiction author & poet from Charlottesville, Va. Writing has been Jason's labor of love since he was a child punching out short stories on his mother's antique typewriter. Lately, he's written the screenplay *Oasis*, a book of poetry *Midnight Road* and his first novel *Badland Blues*. He's currently at work on his second novel.

www.newpulppress.com